A Distant Path

A Civil War Story of the Southwest

By Pamela Burns

****

This is a work of fiction. Names, characters, places, and events are either the product of the author's imagination or used as fiction.

****

****

ISBN-13: 978-1508680482
ISBN-10: 1508680485

****

Printed in the United States of America

Acknowledgements:

New Mexico and the Civil War, by Dr. Walter Earl Pittman, published by The History Press, Charleston, South Carolina, second printing 2011.

The Ghosts of Fort Garland A Tribute to the Veterans Who Served Here, by Jack Rudder, publisher Jack Rudder, Alamosa, Colorado, 2010.

****

I want to thank my husband for helping me edit this story, and for helping me keep my facts straight and my imaginings real. And I want like to thank my sister Janice, who tried to keep my commas and grammar correct, but who forgives me (I hope) for my imperfection.

****

Special thanks to the National Park Rangers and Volunteers of Pecos National Historical Park Glorieta Pass Battlefield, and the National Park Rangers of Fort Union National Monument Santa Fe National Historic Trail for their knowledge of Civil War history and their enthusiasm to share it.

Thank you Fort Garland Museum and Friends of Fort Garland for your dedication to the preservation of the fort and its history, to my friend Theresa, President of the Friends of Fort Garland, and her husband Jack, also a writer, who has been heard to repeat that he "values the truth so much that he uses it sparingly," and that he tries "not to let the truth interfere too much in a good story".

History is not made only by kings and parliaments, presidents, wars and generals. It is the story of people, of their love, honor, faith, hope and suffering; of birth and death, of hunger, thirst and cold, of loneliness and sorrow.

From Sackett's Land
By Louis L'Amour

****

A Distant Path

May 10, 1861
Temporary State House of the Confederacy
Richmond, Virginia

The naval officer posted at the door gave a discreet knock. Jefferson Davis stood and then walked to greet his old acquaintance Colonel George Seagram.

"Jeff, I congratulate you on your Presidency," Seagram said as the men shook hands.

"Thank you, George. With your presence here, am I correct in assuming that you have decided to serve the Confederacy?"

"That is correct, sir. I have resigned my post at Fort Union in the New Mexico Territory. There is an opportunity that I would like to discuss with you, Mr. President," the colonel said.

"I'm listening, George, please sit down."

When they were seated, Colonel Seagram said, "I left Fort Union as did several others loyal to the new Confederacy, and I believe that the remaining Federal cavalry and infantry troops are undermanned, demoralized, and undersupplied for their tasks at hand. Soldiers are being called to serve at Union forts in the East to fight *The Big War*, as they are calling it out West. Union forts in the New Mexico Territory are being abandoned and burned as men and horses march north and east. Mr. President, my estimates are that altogether there are less than three thousand regular army soldiers in the forts along the Rio Grande River, and including Fort Union. Astute Native Indians have observed this shift in the balance of power and their attacks on settlers and travelers are increasing in frequency and severity."

Davis nodded. "What is it that you would like to discuss, George?"

"I believe that the Federal hold on the New Mexico Territory is weakened, and my recent command post, Fort Union, is a military key. If you will support me in this, I believe that a force of volunteers can march from Texas up the Rio Grande River to Santa Fe, relying upon confiscated supplies from the abandoned forts along the way, and foraging from the countryside, and then move northeast and take Fort Union," Seagram said.

Davis leaned back in his chair. "Then from Fort Union north and west," he said. "This would be consistent with our strategy to take the gold from the mines in Colorado and California to fund our efforts to expand the Confederacy from coast to coast."

"Yes, sir," Seagram said. "With your permission, I will take command of Confederate forces in Texas and Arizona. I believe there will be a substantial number of volunteers in the New Mexico Territory who will be glad to take up arms to defend our cause. Though there are only a handful of black slaves, the New Mexicans have made slaves of Native Indians, or placed them in servitude in such a way as they may never overcome it. Local laws support slavery."

Davis stood, and then with respect, Seagram did as well. They shook hands again.

"I approve of your plan, Colonel, that is, General Seagram," Davis said, and Seagram smiled. "You can begin to recruit here in Virginia for your Army of New Mexico in the time before you leave. You may need more than a few able men to serve as officers in your new endeavor. And good luck to you, George. It's a daring plan, but it's good that you won't be needing resources from here. We need to keep those close, you understand."

"Indeed I do, sir, and thank you. Your confidence is well placed in me. You won't be disappointed," General Seagram said, and departed.

Jefferson Davis walked the few steps to the second floor hotel window and stared unseeing at the bustling street below. The modest two-story Richmond hotel had been converted to the State House while the new White House of the Confederacy was being readied. In this building, his office was small and isolated, a parallel he felt at times reminiscent of himself and his position. The heavy weight of his commitment to his Presidency settled upon his shoulders as the war with the Northern States, the War of Northern Aggression, was beginning to escalate.

He returned to his desk to review his agenda for this morning's meeting with his Cabinet. The agenda included, among other things, military organization, the new treasury and currency, the postal service, and the diplomatic failure with Washington over Federal properties on Confederate soil.

The Confederacy was much less industrialized than the Northern States, with far fewer factories, railroads, and munitions facilities, and possessed less than half the population of the North.

Open harbors and international commerce were critical to the success of the Confederacy. Southern prosperity was dependent upon the export of crops such as cotton, rice, sugar, and tobacco supplied by a multitude of farming communities and rural estates. For this, Davis believed, slavery was indispensable. If violent confrontation was necessary, the people of this new nation must be prepared to die to secure it.

May 10, 1861
Overland Stage Line
St. Louis, Missouri

As she handed her carpet bags to the driver, Mersey Lockwood read the words *St. Louis to Santa Fe* printed above the door of the Overland Stage. The two hundred fifty dollar fare sent to her by her father allowed forty pounds of baggage for the fifteen day trip. The trunk had cost extra, but the books and school supplies locked inside were more valuable to her than all of her other possessions combined.

The driver handled her belongings with ease, including the heavy trunk, lifting them to the baggage area on top of the coach. He wasn't a big man, but he was sturdy and capable-looking, and good-natured as he bantered with drivers of nearby coaches while passengers arrived and baggage was loaded. His face was square and tanned and weathered. He had a ready smile, a trimmed handle-bar mustache, a crooked flat nose, and clear hazel eyes under dark bushy brows.

"You can get aboard, Miss," the driver said to her after loading her belongings. "We'll be leaving just as soon as I get the other five travelers aboard. They just made a last minute trip to the relief station. I reckon they'll be back soon."

He tipped his hat with a leather-gloved hand, opened the door for her, and held her elbow as she stepped up into the coach. She glanced at a lantern clamped to the outside of the coach near the driver's seat. It reminded her that they would be traveling day and night.

Mersey took the seat just inside the door facing the rear, though there would be nowhere safe from the trail dust. Inside the coach, brown leather upholstery covered the benches, brushed and wiped clean, but not new. The wooden floor had been swept clean of mud or debris. The coach smelled a little of tobacco and stale sweat, and dust tickled her nose.

There were five windows on each side of the coach, a rectangular one in the door, two smaller ones on either side of the door, and two adjacent to the benches, these with leather drop-down curtains. There looked to be room for six people to sit in comfort, three people on each of the two bench seats, though she expected there would be eight or nine passengers at any given time. Maybe the expression was ancient, but *misery loves company* could, without a doubt, be the motto of any stage line.

Mersey stared out the window at the hustling scene around her, and rather than dwell on the grueling journey ahead, she let her mind drift in thought. Two years ago her stage ride with her Aunt Andrea had transported her from Fort Leavenworth, Kansas, where her father had been stationed, to this same city, St. Louis, Missouri. From St. Louis, they rode the train to Newton, Massachusetts where Aunt Andrea taught rhetoric at Auburndale Female Seminary, and Andrea had arranged for Mersey to attend.

Mersey's memories drifted to Randall's earnest face as he asked her to marry him, to stay with him in Boston and teach primary school while he finished his law degree at Harvard College. If she had said yes to Randall, she would not be taking this distant path.

She had met Randall at one of the social events arranged between Auburndale and Harvard. Though she cared for Randall a great deal, she didn't believe she loved him enough, not as he deserved to be loved, because she had chosen without hesitation to follow her dreams, not his.

Auburndale was a finishing school, and for two years Mersey had studied the liberal arts of grammar, rhetoric and logic, as well as arithmetic, geometry, music and astronomy. She was eager to share her knowledge with her future students. She believed ignorance could be an insurmountable disadvantage.

Mersey shifted in her seat and tucked her full skirt closer to her body to make sure she wasn't taking up more than her share of the space, and to keep the fabric from being caught underneath someone, or trampled and torn by spurred boots. In moments, five people would join her in here, side by side for hours, days, maybe even for weeks. Others would come and go, joining her and then departing down the trail, veritable strangers traveling together in this cramped space for fifteen days. She stifled a groan. She sighed, then smiled. She was going to Colorado.

Mersey thought about her parents. Her father was an officer and surveyor for the Army. Her mother had been the daughter of a successful architect. Her parents had met while her father attended West Point. According to Aunt Andrea, Mersey's mother had been an accomplished pianist, but had given up a promising future to marry Mersey's father. And after her parents' marriage, her mother struggled with her husband's long absences and the frequent relocations. A soldier's family was required to accept uncertainty, which was worse in times of war. When Mersey was six, while her father was away on duty, her mother had died of influenza. Mersey remembered the sadness and loneliness she had felt after her mother's death until Aunt Andrea had come to stay with them.

Andrea was young then, only seventeen, but she had added stability to Mersey's childhood that she may never have had otherwise as her father advanced in rank. Aunt Andrea always said that Mersey had her mother's sweet nature and gentle ways, but she had a good slice of her father's backbone too. Andrea had shared her love of teaching with Mersey, and had been essential in helping Mersey begin to shape her own dream of educating children in the West.

This War Between the States was an unknown and destructive force with the potential of altering so many lives, so many hopes and dreams, including hers, for in her dreams, there was always peace.

I am convinced that you should stay with me until this war is over, Aunt Andrea had said shaking her head. *It won't take long, I'm sure, for these war-headed men to come to their senses, though the Southern States' newly elected President, Mr. Davis, should have requested an army of diplomats seeking compromise instead of appointing a Secretary of War, and commissioning a gaggle of new generals who are in the business of war.*

But after the Union soldiers had surrendered Fort Sumter, and then Virginia, Arkansas and Tennessee had joined the first seven States to secede from the Union, even Aunt Andrea was beginning to doubt that diplomacy could prevail and that the war would be short-lived.

The door opened then, and a tall, lean man wearing a black Stetson hat and a hip-length tan leather coat helped a slender, pretty, strawberry blond woman into the seat across from Mersey. The woman carried a little girl, a miniature of her mother and about three years of age. Two boys climbed in after her, crowded onto the woman's lap, and stared at Mersey. The man followed, seated himself beside the woman, and tipped his hat to Mersey. He then retrieved both boys from the woman's lap. He shifted and his unbuttoned coat fell open, exposing a navy blue cloth shirt and black leather vest. Mersey saw a gold badge pinned to the vest. She could see now that he wore a gun belt and holstered gun on his hip. The gold badge said United States Marshal in the circle around a gold star.

The woman wore a pearl gray traveling dress similar in style to the lavender one Mersey wore, with long sleeves, a little lace trim at the collar, a small bustle, and with a minimum of petticoats so as to satisfy fashion but not make travel even more uncomfortable. The little girl wore a pink dress with white lace ruffles, white pantaloons and stockings, and sturdy shoes. The boys wore red cotton shirts, belted dark brown wool pants and black boots.

They had just settled in when the coach rocked a little sideways as the driver and the messenger climbed up onto the driver's seat. The driver whistled through his teeth, gave a snap of the reins, and the coach bumped and swayed forward into the rushing traffic on the streets of St. Louis.

"We're the Townsends," the woman said with a smile. "This is my husband, Thomas. I'm Bevin, and these are our children."

Mersey detected a lilting Irish accent.

"I'm Bartholomew," the older boy said, hiking his thumb toward his chest. "But everyone calls me Bat, on account of my baby brother Eddie here use'ta couldn't say his r's right."

The younger boy's ears turned red and he jutted his small chin forward. "I'm not a baby anymore."

Bat smiled. "Pert' near," he said, "And that's Susie." The boy indicated the little girl who was now peering at Mersey from her mother's shoulder.

"Hush now," his father said, then leaned his head out the coach's passenger window and raised his voice to ask, "What's happening ahead, Driver? Why are we stopping?"

The driver called down, "A lot of Missourians are sittin' on the fence about whose side to take in this new war, and most just deal with both sides, but Governor Claiborne F. Jackson called out the Missouri State Militia when the Union Army seized the arsenal at Camp Jackson. The Union soldiers didn't take too kindly to that and attacked the Militia. Now they're parading the Militia as captives through the streets of St. Louis."

Townsend started to shift the boys and open the coach door, intending to join the driver, but his wife stayed him, putting her hand on his arm. He looked at her and nodded. "Are you expecting any kind of trouble, Driver?" Townsend asked out the window.

"None, sir," the driver responded. "We'll just wait 'till they pass by and then be on our way."

The marshal kept his eyes focused on the street outside the coach, alert and ready for any necessary action, Mersey thought. There were hostile voices outside, jeers and taunts, directed at both the Union soldiers and the Missouri Militia. The Union soldiers' voices could be heard telling those observing to stay back, or telling the Militia soldiers to move along.

Bevin said, "This war will tear families apart."

"Why, mama?" Eddie asked. "Why will families get torn t'pieces?"

"Fathers will be fighting sons, and brothers will fight against each other," she explained.

"Like me and Bat?" he asked.

"Much worse, sweetheart," Bevin said.

Bat sat watching Mersey. "What's your name?"

"My name is Mersey Lockwood."

"Mersey, I ain't ever heard a name like Mersey," Bat said.

"Bartholomew, that wasn't polite," Bevin said.

Mersey smiled. "It's alright. My mother named me after a river in England near where she was born, a place that held happy childhood memories for her. I've never met anyone else with my name."

Bat was staring at her now. "You're real pretty when you smile," the boy said. "And you look right pretty in that dress that's kind of the same color as your eyes."

Mersey smiled again.

"That was a very nice compliment," Mersey said.

Bat must be seven or eight years old, Mersey thought, and a little charmer. The boy had thick dark hair and deep blue eyes like his father's. Eddie had his mother's strawberry blond hair, and from the two missing teeth in Eddie's grin, she figured him to be five or six. Eddie started to say something but Bat spoke first.

"The stage coach driver said that where we're goin', there ain't many women, so if I find a good one, I better marry her before somebody else snatches her up," he said, and Eddie frowned at him.

Bevin caught her breath, and though Thomas didn't take his attention from the street, his lips twitched into a smile.

"Are you already marrying somebody?" Bat said.

Mersey hesitated, amazed by what he seemed to be asking her. "Are you asking me to marry you?"

Bat nodded. "Yes, ma'am, I am."

"Hey, wait a minute," Eddie said crossing his small arms over his thin chest. "I was gonna ask her."

"You're too little," Bat told him, shifting his eyes to Eddie and then back to Mersey.

Bevin gave her a sympathetic look, and Thomas turned his head a little to hide his wide smile.

"Well then," Mersey sighed, noting the boy's determined expression. "I appreciate the offer, and you are quite a handsome gentleman indeed, but I'm just not quite ready to get married." She smiled at the boy. "Maybe you can ask me again in a few years."

Bat nodded. "I can wait, for a while, I reckon."

The driver cracked his whip like a gunshot and shouted, "Gid'yup!" The coach lurched and rolled forward, and they were on their way.

The Santa Fe Trail

Fellow passengers came and went, business men, doctors, lawyers, judges, and wives joining their husbands further west. In Independence, Missouri, Mersey met a mail-order bride named Dinah Douglas.

"I'm going to marry a rancher in Santa Fe," Dinah said. "I started west with my folks in a covered wagon on a wagon train, but they died of cholera, and I had no way to go on and no money to go back. I sold our wagon and my folk's belongings, but that didn't last, and soon I had no way to keep paying my room and board. The woman who ran the boarding house found an advertisement in the newspaper and helped me answer it. The rancher is a widower and has two small children, and he needs a wife. Everything will be fine, I know it. I'm stronger than I look and I'm a hard worker, and he sounded so kind in his letter."

Mersey looked at the young woman's pretty face, the pale blond hair, and the cornflower blue eyes. Dinah was a slender girl, maybe sixteen years of age. Mersey said a prayer that everything would be what the girl expected when she arrived in Santa Fe.

In Council Grove, Kansas, a distinguished woman with a confident bearing and about fifty years of age boarded the coach. The woman was sturdy, attractive, and expensively dressed. Mersey introduced herself and the woman's face glowed with surprise and pleasure.

"What a marvelous thing!" she said. "I knew your mother. She was a wonderful woman. I was so distressed when I heard of her illness and death. I'm Louisa Canfield, and I am delighted to meet you."

"It's so nice to meet someone who knew my mother," Mersey said. "I hardly remember her."

"All you have to do is look in the mirror, child." Louisa patted Mersey's hand. "Your mother and I were great friends, both married to officers, and. . . . " Louisa laughed, a cheerful tinkling laugh, "partners in self-pity in this awful Army life out West. I miss her."

****

For a long stretch of prairie after Council Grove, they followed a mail coach headed for San Francisco, California. The mail coach carried eight passengers and was accompanied by eight armed guards and a supply wagon.

The hours of daylight increased with springtime. The miles stretched out. The passengers in the coach watched the seemingly endless plains of grass, and the children stared through the windows as wildlife crossed their path. Antelope and deer scampered away when the coach approached, and herds of buffalo still shedding their winter coats grazed the prairie. Eagles soared in search of prey in the blue sky above, and wild horses nickered and pranced, watching the stagecoach from a distance, as did wolves and coyotes.

Native Plains Indians were seldom seen as the coach passed through their hunting grounds, but if they let their presence be known, the passengers became silent and watchful.

"Papa, who are those Indians out there?" Bat asked. "Are they going to shoot arrows at us?"

"No, son," Townsend answered. "Those people may be the Osage, the Kansa, or the Pawnee. They have treaties with our government, and as long as we honor their treaties, they will not attack us."

****

The twenty four hour days along the well-worn trail were grueling. The roads were bumpy and jarring, or muddy and slippery, or just plain dusty, with dust in quantities that would torment them, depending on the direction of the wind. They stopped for meals, or to relieve and refresh themselves from the tight quarters. They stopped to change drivers and horses every fifty or sixty miles.

The drivers were a rough and ready bunch between the ages of twenty five and forty years, loud and strong and able-bodied, charming, attentive and helpful to the passengers. Mersey learned that each driver drove the same route for both directions, supporting her belief that they knew every rock and pothole on the trail, even in the dark. They cracked their custom-made silver-inlaid handled whips with every arrival and departure at the stations, announcing their presence, and causing the four or six horse teams to prance with the whip-crack sound.

When the coach was overly full, Marshal Townsend would ride shotgun with the driver. The drivers seemed grateful for the marshal's presence. They would at times slow the coach and call out, "Strange riders are approaching," and Townsend would open the door and climb up beside the driver.

For whatever fortune they drew, whether bad fortune was deterred by Townsend's presence, or that they met no one who intended them harm, their trip was uneventful.

Mersey sometimes held a sleeping Townsend child by night, and once upon a sunrise, while she held little Susie, the coach topped a hill, and Mersey saw the dew sparkling like diamonds on the grasses below them. They left the flat prairie behind and entered the foothills of Colorado Territory. Mersey felt a contentment and peace, a sense of belonging, of oneness with the land that she never felt in the East.

Mersey was uncertain if her mother would have wanted to live at a fort as remote and harsh as Fort Garland where her father was now commander. But Mersey was certain that she herself would thrive there, thrive in the rugged Colorado wilderness. She loved the vastness of the land, the infinite potential. When she turned back, Bevin Townsend watched her, a look of understanding on her face.

"My family left Ireland when I was ten," Bevin said. "These rolling hills remind me of our home."

"Ireland must be very beautiful," Mersey said.

Bevin nodded, and then looked at her sleeping children. "Beauty is in many things, but love is the thing that endures."

****

The drivers retrieved Mersey's trunk containing her school supplies each day and Mersey did her best to entertain the restless Townsend children, and any other children on the stage, with slate tablets and chalk, or counting boards. Eddie would sit on her lap and ask, "What shall we do today, Mersey?"

In the course of their travel, Mersey learned that Marshal Townsend was assigned to the newly formed Colorado Territory. He would be based in Denver where he would guard the court justices and transport prisoners. Bevin was in an early pregnancy with their fourth child. They planned to purchase a large home, and Bevin would manage it as a boarding house.

When they reached the station at Bent's Old Fort, the Townsend children explored the former fort.

Bat asked the driver, "Why is this fort all torn down and burnt up?"

The driver, a man in his late thirties, explained that the Bent brothers had built the fort for trade, and it had been a small town unto itself with supply stores and a blacksmith shop, where trappers and traders, and all kinds of travelers, including the Indian tribes, came together to trade buffalo robes in peace. Explorers, adventurers, and even the U.S. Army had used the fort for wagon repairs, food, water, company, rest and protection. Then in 1849, it had been abandoned because of a cholera outbreak. Lots of people west of the Missouri and in other parts of the country were sick with cholera that year. After that, the Bent brothers had burned and destroyed most of the fort, and now it was used only as a station by two Stage Coach Companies.

The Townsends left the Santa Fe Trail coach at Bent's Old Fort to take another coach and another trail, the Cherokee Trail, northwest to Denver. After many hugs and goodbyes, well wishes and promises to visit the Townsends in Denver, and a few tears, Mersey re-boarded the coach to continue southwest to Iron Springs.

The day was clear, and the Rocky Mountains rose in a blue haze to the west, increasing in grandeur with every mile. When she stepped off the coach at Iron Springs, the driver approached her and tipped his hat.

"I hope you had a good trip and will travel with us again, Miss Lockwood." Then the driver cocked his head toward a group of men. "Those soldiers are waiting for you, Miss."

Mersey turned and a short, wiry, grizzled man of about fifty approached her, his warm dark eyes questioning. His tanned face wore the creases of years of squinting into the sun, and his dark hair and beard were touched with gray. He was dressed in a dusty blue uniform with sergeant's stripes on his sleeves.

"Miss Lockwood?" he asked, hat in hand.

"Yes, Sergeant, I'm Mersey Lockwood."

"A pleasure t'meet ya, Miss. I'm Sergeant Isandro Valencia Sandoval, cavalryman and head wrangler for the cavalry mounts and transport animals at Fort Garland. My friends call me Sandy."

"I hope you will count me as a friend then. I'm happy to meet you, Sandy," Mersey said, extending her hand.

Sergeant Sandoval pulled off a worn leather glove and gently shook her hand. His western style speech rolled with the inflection of his native Spanish.

"We have four days of slow uphill climbin' an' then 'bout four more days of mules pullin' that wagon over the Sangre de Cristo Pass, one of the most twisted, narrow, rocky, steep ol' Indian trails back through those mountains yonder to get to Fort Garland. Do you need a bit of time to rest up, Miss?" he asked.

"Only a few minutes, Sandy, thank you," Mersey said. "I'm anxious to get to the fort."

"And the Colonel is mighty anxious too, Miss. He's plannin' a big celebration'. He had a dozen men workin' on buildin' the school house hopin' to be ready in the fall. All a bunch a' young uns' need now is the teacher."

"I am so happy that he could manage to get the school house built," she said.

"Well, the framin's been done, and the walls are up. It's all the finishin' that needs doin'. The Colonel thought you might want some say in the finishin' of it," he said, walking with her toward the stage coach. "We'll get yer gear loaded if ya show me which of those belongin's are yours."

"Of course, thank you," she said.

Sergeant Sandoval observed the other soldiers as they fed and watered the mules, refilled the water barrels, and checked the soundness of the wagons.

"We can stay for an hour. Those soldier boys have been whinin' for a cold drink and a hot meal. Then we'll be gettin' on up the trail. I brought a gentle little mare, sure-footed and sound, if you want to ride a spell instead of bouncin' along on a wagon."

"I would love to ride the mare," she said. "I have sorely missed riding."

He grinned. "Then ya better ease back into it, Miss, or sorely is what you'll be," he warned with a wink of his eye.

Before the coach departed, Louisa Canfield approached Mersey and gave her a fierce hug.

"I am going to be with my husband in our home in Santa Fe. He has been put in charge of the Union forces in the New Mexico Territory, and he is now serving at Fort Craig. If you need anything, child, don't hesitate to contact me at this address," Louisa said and handed Mersey a card.

"Thank you, Louisa," Mersey said. "It was a great pleasure to spend this time traveling with you."

July 27, 1861
Fort Bliss, Texas-New Mexico border

General Seagram sat at a long, polished dining table in the Commander's quarters at Fort Bliss. A feast was laid out before him. At a knock on the door, Seagram looked up from his meal to see Major Hector Franklin of the Arizona Rangers.

"Come in, Major Franklin. Please, join me for dinner while you give me your report," Seagram said. "I trust it is good news."

"Thank you sir, indeed there is good news. The San Elizario spy company is quite an asset for obtaining timely and accurate information," Franklin said as he seated himself near the general.

"Try the roast beef, Major, it is excellent, as is the wine," Seagram said.

"We are fortunate, sir, that the Union Army didn't have time to destroy everything in their haste to abandon Fort Bliss," Franklin said.

"Please, proceed, Major," Seagram said. "I am not a patient man."

As I have noticed when your pleasures are interrupted, Franklin thought. He cleared his throat and proceeded.

"On July 24, our Texas Mounted Volunteers, the TMV as they call themselves, made an unsuccessful attempt to take Fort Fillmore, forty miles north of us on the Rio Grande River. They attempted this against a superior force, twice their number of experienced cavalry. Because they were unsuccessful, they moved another ten miles north to the town of Mesilla where they were welcomed by southern sympathizers."

"How are we doing on disrupting Fort Fillmore's supply trains?" Seagram asked.

Franklin bit his tongue. They could have been doing much better if Seagram would place his scouts at strategic locations ahead of the northern forts, make communication a priority, and have men positioned, ready to strike when any opportunity presented itself. Their forces needed those supply wagons as much as they needed to keep them out of Union hands. Things needed to be done now, this summer, before winter set in.

"Sir, forty men of the San Elizario Spy Company have been successful in capturing horses and mules from Fort Fillmore. Coupled with Apache raids, the fort's ability to fight or run has been hindered."

"Go on," Seagram said, and took a drink of wine.

Franklin said, "Two days ago, 380 well equipped, well trained infantry, supported by two mountain howitzers and mounted rifleman left Fort Fillmore to engage our TMV in Mesilla. Our TMV fired on them from behind adobe walls and from rooftops. The TMV wounded the leader of the cavalry and two of the men firing the artillery. The Union soldiers abandoned the field."

Seagram said, "Well, it is a giant feather in our caps, is it not, for our two hundred fifty six men, just six small companies of Texas Mounted Volunteers to seize this victory. Our amateur soldiers were able to accomplish this, riding horses brought from home, armed with old shotguns, and supplying their own ammunition."

"Yes sir," Franklin said, then he smiled. "Though the Union soldiers outnumber our Confederate forces almost two to one, the Regiment of Fort Fillmore is abandoning the fort and retreating ninety miles further north to Fort Stanton, after the commander decided that Fort Fillmore is indefensible against artillery."

Seagram chuckled. "That's rich," he said.

"Yes sir," Major Franklin said, "since we have no artillery."

November 5, 1861
New Mexico Territory

Major John Steele rode through the drifted snow over the rock-strewn trail, his shoulders hunched, cavalry hat pulled low and greatcoat billowing. He felt chilled to the bone, the coldest he'd ever remembered being. He turned his mount in a half circle left and looked behind him, squinting through stinging eyes, attempting to see the progress of the small caravan he led.

Through the wind-driven sleet, Steele's view of the mounted cavalry and the mules pulling the wagons behind him faded in and out again. At times, powdered snow blinded him as it was picked up from the ground by the wind and hurled, pitched and swirled at him. They had made good time until this storm had descended without warning, the low visibility slowing them down, even halting their progress at times. The weather in these mountains was unpredictable and unforgiving.

With visibility of twenty feet, if they encountered any hostile force, man or beast, the confrontation would be accidental, and either hand to hand, or hand to paw fighting must ensue, because he was sure his fingers were too numb to draw and fire his pistol. The advantage would go to the one most guarded, most vigilant who could react first. But then who would be out in this storm besides this caravan, if not by necessity, poor planning, or by misfortune.

With gloved fingers, Steele pulled the collar of his wool coat closer to his chin, moved back along the trail to signal his sergeant to call a halt for a much needed break, and then dismounted. Steele's warm exhaled breath clouded the air. The puffs of moist air from the horse's nostrils clung and froze to his bridle. Steele moved to the horse's flank and pulled a handful of oats from his saddlebag.

"Almost there, boy," Steele said.

As The Black ate from his hand, Steele gave him a gentle rub on the neck. The Black was a magnificent thoroughbred, three years old, black as midnight, wide in the chest, built and born to run. The stallion was Steele's only link to what he had left behind, his only link to his dreams of the future.

After an hour of rest, the snow lessened. The north wind remained relentless and cold as it transformed the storm gray sky into blue. Snow-capped mountains loomed across the landscape in all directions with forests of tall pines and leaf-bare aspen, and other shrubs and trees native to this rocky, majestic desert that he couldn't yet name. Tall yellowish and white grasses breeched the snow-covered ground, waving in the chill breeze, the living green of their stems gone after succumbing to freezing winter temperatures.

In the valley just west of their position, Steele found that he was able to observe what had to be Fort Union. The eight points of the earthen star-shaped fort sprung from a dormant meadow, and sat near the curving foothills of a mountain range. Cannons sat mounted on parapets on the four inner angles of the star, each aimed southward. The defensive position indicated an expectation that a threat would come from the south, from New Mexico Territory, not the east. The bronze cannons sitting on the parapets of Fort Union were nicknamed *Napoleons* because they had been used by Napoleon the Third. They were safe, reliable, and effective at close range, with a maximum range advancing to sixteen hundred yards. Effective range could be less when firing uphill, as these would be, and the air was thinner at altitude. The cannons' load could be affected as well. Less air friction would increase speed and distance. Steele felt the altitude effects as well. His breathing was harder with exertion, and his endurance had decreased.

Though the main part of his military service was in the cavalry, and though not an expert, Steele had a good working knowledge of artillery. He had trained on artillery at another star-shaped fort on the coast of Maryland, Fort McHenry, famous for its defense of Baltimore Harbor from the British Navy in 1814. On the battlefield, artillerymen were lucky to have dry powder to use in their guns while bullets whizzed around them, and as an enemy cavalry charged down on them, and as enemy artillery with superior range to their own, bombarded them. Having men with enough grit not to panic under those conditions was the most an officer could expect, and it would be unrealistic to expect mindfulness to calculate air friction and wind direction as it effected velocity and trajectory. It was training and repetition that aided accuracy.

Another look at the hills above the fort to the south made him frown. An enemy force firing down on the fort using light twelve-pounders would no doubt hit the interior of the fort, and the cannons on the parapet would fail to reach the enemy artillery to take them out. He felt an eager anticipation to participate in the planning of the fort's defenses.

Steele signaled for his men to remount and continue on. They had traveled for fifty one days over far-reaching prairies to these mountains, a gradual climb of more than five thousand feet in elevation over seven hundred miles. The craggy grandeur of the Rocky Mountains was like no mountain range he had ever seen. For the last four days they had approached the mountains, watched them rise in the west until now, they were surrounded by them.

Fifty one days was near record time to travel with mounted soldiers and supply wagons pulled by oxen, from Fort Leavenworth, Kansas to Fort Union in New Mexico Territory. Instead of taking the Mountain Branch of the Santa Fe Trail northwest through Bent's New Fort and Fort Lyon, and then south over the treacherous Raton Pass, Steele had used the Cimarron Cutoff that took them southwest at the Cimarron river in Kansas, saving his company over a hundred miles. The Cimarron Cutoff held a greater risk of hostile Indian attacks, and shortage of water.

They had started this journey in late autumn instead of the safer time of early spring. There was no way of knowing how many men over time had lost their way and gotten trapped at high altitude in the winter without enough provisions. As autumn had turned to winter, natural grasses no longer provided extra feed for the oxen and horses. Rivers and streams for drinking water were frozen, or worse, dry.

Steele had been careful in his restocking of rations at Fort Larned in central Kansas, the last provision resource for the final four hundred miles. He had streamlined their rations and wagons for speed and pushed his men and animals hard, traveling twelve hour days instead of ten. Steele understood the nature of this rugged mountainous terrain, where death could come in a flash with the leap of a mountain lion, or the charge of a thousand pound grizzly bear. This wild country held no mercy for anyone injured or sick. A man could be surrounded by a sudden forest fire, or swept away in a flood, or buried alive in the crush of an avalanche.

The Plains Indians had returned from their summer hunting grounds to their winter camps along the Santa Fe Trail. An ambush was still a mortal threat by those Native bands refusing to accept treaties and withdraw from their homeland. An encampment of Jicarilla Apache had been close to their route near Wagon Mound, a pilot point on the Trail. But a fast moving train of wagons with twenty mounted cavalry carrying rifles, pistols and sabers must not have interested the warriors of the camp, maybe because their winter stores were well supplied. And though Steele was certain he had seen only the warriors the Apache had let him see, he had felt their watchful regard as they followed his procession until it moved away from their camp.

This had been the most arduous journey that he had attempted in his military career, the most daring. As he considered the mountains in the distance, he knew it would be no easy feat to continue through them on horseback as the winter settled in. He felt relief that they had reached their destination without mishap, and didn't need to go further west.

He stared at the isolated fort and felt the familiar feelings of dread and loneliness. He had requested to be here, needed to be here. Regret gripped him. His beloved State of Virginia, the home of three generations of Steeles, had seceded from the Union. To avoid the most heart-rending consequences, he'd made the only choice he could, a choice to seek this distant path.

Fort Union

The sun broke through the clouds high overhead, warming the wool of his coat. Steele rode past the trenches, the two hundred foot angled walls of the four outer points of the star, and through the gate into the earthen structure that was Fort Union. The square inner structure consisted of seven hundred fifty foot long walls at a height of seven feet with their foundations partially underground. Looking up, he saw firing platforms and artillery placements. The four large angular parapets formed the corners of the inner star, and in these angles, he saw storehouses, including the powder house for munitions. He frowned. The cannon above the munitions storage would draw enemy fire, creating a potential for explosive destruction that could leave them without ammunition.

The Commander's headquarters, officers' quarters, and company barracks were framed against the inside walls, enough to provide housing for close to five hundred troops, Steele estimated. He led his men and wagons to the whitewashed stables that formed a long line in the center of the parade ground.

The fort was a fascinating combination of structure and activity. Steele was surprised to see that tents were erected on the parade grounds, tents that could not provide climate-worthy protection for winter lodging. It was possible that additional troops arrived before barracks could be built to accommodate them. Now he and his twenty cavalrymen were here as well.

****

Colonel William Anderson looked up from his desk, stood, and extended his hand in greeting.

"Major Steele, welcome to Fort Union."

Steele stepped forward and grasped the Colonel's hand. He responded with a respectful dip of his chin, his Virginia gentleman's drawl barely discernable.

"Thank you, sir. It's a pleasure to meet you, Colonel, and a pleasure to be here."

"A pleasure?" the Colonel asked

A speculative gleam entered the Colonel's dark eyes. A single shake of his head and a pursing of his lips conveyed his doubt of the polite response.

"It would be acceptable, make that expected, to change that opinion once you've become familiar with this unforgiving landscape and the hardy souls who inhabit it, though I can presume the reason behind your request to be assigned here."

Steele said nothing, for his reasons for asking to be posted here were his own, and personal.

Anderson studied Steele who stood military straight, and impeccable in his blue wool uniform. The Major was in his late twenties, tall, hard muscled and dignified. His intelligent, watchful eyes revealed no insight into his emotions other than polite attention. He was young for his rank of major, and young to have earned the service medals on his chest, but then war tended to expedite promotion. The major was regular army. Had he been leading volunteers, promotion often happened even sooner. One man was made a brigadier general at the age of twenty three by leading volunteers instead of regular army.

"It's not too late to change your mind, Major. You distinguished yourself at the Battle of Bull Run, though that battle ended with a retreat of Union forces to Washington." Anderson paused. "Sorry for that. I know you know how it ended, but I'm sure you would have General Grant's ear, should you request a different post."

Steele met Anderson's eyes. "It is my honor to serve the cavalry here, sir."

Anderson nodded. "Then let me get you caught up on what is going on here. Have a seat, Major."

Steele lifted the saber in the scabbard at his side out of the way as he sat in the sturdy wooden chair facing the Colonel's desk.

"We have what we call a three-sided war, Major," Anderson said. "The soldiers of this fort need to be prepared to confront hostile forces from two separate and distinct factions, the Confederates, and the Native Indians. The Confederate Texas Mounted Volunteers, according to the best information we have, are preparing to take New Mexico Territory by storm in the next few months, and of course the nomadic Indian tribes who roam this territory would be happy to dispense with all of us. Though a few local tribes are peaceful, for most of them, war is their way of life, and having constant enemies has made them strong. Between the Kiowa, Comanche, Ute, and the greater threat, the Apache, the raids and skirmishes with the settlers and settlements here are becoming more frequent, almost constant. The raids are for livestock generally, but our soldiers are often called upon to provide pursuit for recovery of whatever was stolen. And maintaining patrols because of these raids is a continuous drain on this fort's resources. The Native Indians are alert for any sign of weakness, and no doubt have observed the return of many of our men to the warfront in the East."

Anderson met Steele's eyes as he continued. "This fort is the greatest supplier for the Union forces on the Santa Fe Trail, and for forts in the Colorado Territory, including Fort Garland, where I'm sending you."

Steele's dark brows lifted. "You are sending me to Fort Garland, sir?"

Anderson shifted in his chair. "We have it on good authority from a captain serving at Fort Garland that the commander there, Commander Lockwood, is not making adequate preparation for defense against Confederate forces, or in defense of Indian threats against the settlements in the surrounding area."

Steele nodded, but said nothing.

Anderson said, "Fort Garland is located in a high mountain valley referred to as the San Luis Valley, one hundred fifty miles north of Santa Fe along the Spanish Trail. The valley has an average elevation of seven thousand five hundred feet, and covers eight thousand square miles. If you think you've been cold, wait until you get there. The valley is an ice box."

Steele nodded again, listening, remembering the journey over the mountains in the blizzard.

"The fort is there for the protection of the small town of San Luis, and several smaller settlements, and with the recent influx of prospectors into the mountains, to try to keep the peace with the nomadic Indian tribes there," Anderson said.

The Colonel tapped a stack of papers on his desk.

"Captain Charles Kendrick has given several written accountings of the chaos and lack of direction that he has observed at the fort. Colonel Graylon

Lockwood is commander, but my nephew, that is, uh, Captain Kendrick, has indicated that there is no one truly in charge there, though he does what he can to fill the gap."

Anderson grimaced, thinking of his nephew's dramatic reports. He had facilitated getting Charles, his sister's only child, admitted to West Point. Charles' promotion to Captain and assignment to Fort Garland had come on his recommendation, following his sister's frantic pleas to get her son far away from the war. The young pup needed to be far away from his mother's apron strings regardless, and though the boy lacked the ruthless ambition that was often considered a commendable trait in a military man, he had shown promise. His hope that Lockwood would provide the military guidance the boy needed had not materialized.

"Lockwood is a good man. As a captain, he was part of the original expedition with Colonel J. J. Albert who was sent to survey the Colorado and Zuni Rivers a decade ago. He's a topographical engineer and architect by training." Anderson shook his head. "According to Kendrick, Lockwood sits in his office all day and draws sketches of bridges across the Rio Grande River Gorge, an impossible dream I assure you. According to these reports, requests to improve the fort's defenses fall on deaf, disinterested, ears."

"Is there any corroborating evidence that these reports are accurate, sir?" Steele asked.

"I have no evidence other than these accusations, and that's another reason why I'm sending you," Anderson said. "I need for you to assess the situation and determine how bad it has become. Captain

Kendrick lacks the experience to command the fort. I need a more mature and experienced officer there."

Anderson cleared his throat. "I want you to know that I am not throwing away the key. This is temporary, I promise you, not more than a year at most. Fort Garland is, how shall I put it, not a prize location, or even a desirable one for a young officer with your potential for advancement. As I said before, you would have Washington's ear for any post you might seek."

"I appreciate your explaining all this to me sir, but at this time I have no desire to be posted anywhere but where I am needed. What of the Confederate forces? Do we know their numbers and location?"

"I just sent a seventy-one page report to Washington summarizing events of the past six months. I've had a copy prepared for you. There are companies called the Texas Mounted Volunteers, and the combined Confederate forces include the Texas Mounted Rifles and the Arizona Rangers, so there may be some former Federal regular army along with the volunteers," the Colonel said picking up a large envelope and handing it to Steele. "Our intelligence reports," he paused, "rumors would be a more correct term, are late, exaggerated, and too often incorrect regarding the Texas Mounted Volunteers. Based on these reports about the strength and advance of their forces, we are abandoning forts and destroying supplies in anticipation of their movement. Our tactics are often laughable, depending on your point of view," Anderson said, a wry smile touching the corners of his lips.

Steele accepted the envelope filled with papers.

"Reliable intelligence and reconnaissance are critical in battle strategy," Steele said.

Anderson nodded. "Have you heard the German word zugzwang, Major?"

"I believe it is a term used in the game of chess," Steele answered.

"Yes," Anderson said. "Meaning that in the game, though compelled, it would be safer not to make a move. I would have to presuppose that this is the current endgame strategy that our Union leaders have adopted to use against the Confederates in the New Mexico Territory. Better safe than sorry, I suppose. Regardless, you can look forward to several hours of entertaining reading, Major."

Steele glanced at the thick envelope in his hand, then looked up as Anderson spoke again.

"I know the Confederate General in charge of the Texas forces," Anderson said. "His name is George Seagram. He was in my class at West Point, and his knowledge of this territory is enough to make him a considerable threat. He once commanded this fort."

"Your knowledge of his abilities could be a decisive advantage as well, sir," Steele said.

"It is something to consider in the broader scheme of things, yes, thank you, Major," Anderson said, then added, "this is a rather unexpected turn of events, is it not, Major?"

"I'm used to the Army, sir. I will serve wherever duty dictates."

Anderson said. "The unofficial intent of sending you to Fort Garland will be to have you, sooner rather than later, assume command. Understand that Lockwood hasn't been notified of his replacement, but he's not a stupid man. I'm sure, as soon as he sees you, he will know what is coming in his next orders from Washington. He will be asked to retire, Major, and your papers as new commander will be enclosed in the same satchel."

When Steele nodded, Andersen smiled. "So, let me be the first to congratulate you, and warn you, that as commander, you will no doubt have your work cut out for you. The volunteers and irregulars that help make up the Colorado Territory cavalry and infantry have been described as a raucous bunch of thieving, drinking, brawling, tough and undisciplined men. Among them are former miners, trappers and others who never found the fortune they came west looking for. They serve, not out of love for the Union, but to keep from starving and freezing to death." He reached to shake Steele's hand. "I wish you good luck, Major. Right now Lieutenant Corbin is waiting for you just outside in the hall. He will brief you about the men and supply wagons going with you, and about the man who will guide you and the route you will take. I'm sending an extra fifty regulars with you in addition to the twenty who accompanied you here from Fort Leavenworth. These are experienced men, some of whom fought in the Mexican-American War, and others are experienced with Native Indian warfare. From my nephew's reports, they'll probably have to build their own barracks when you get to Fort Garland, so I'm sending as many supplies as you will need. You are scheduled to leave at first light."

"Thank you, sir," Steele said shaking Anderson's hand. "I look forward to it, sir." With a moment's afterthought, Steele reached into his inner shirt pocket and produced a small paperback manual. "I brought something for you, sir. It's a copy of Cooke's Cavalry Tactics just approved in Washington."

"I've heard of it, Major. It uses single-rank formation to simplify the instructions for volunteers," Anderson said.

"Yes, sir," Steele said. "It was used with success by the British against Portugal in '34."

"Keep it, Major, you're going to need it with the volunteers at Fort Garland. We have more regular army here, only a few volunteers, and I'll have my orderly send to Washington for a copy for me."

"Yes sir, thank you, sir," Steele said, and then he saluted and left the room.

****

A slender dark haired man snapped to attention as Steele exited the colonel's office. Steele returned the salute and the man said, "Lieutenant Corbin at your service, sir. I am here to take you to the men and supply wagons for your inspection, sir, and then to direct you to your quarters."

"Thank you, Lieutenant. I would like to meet our guide and review our route to Fort Garland."

"Certainly sir, our guide is a half-Ute, half-Apache man named Pou Nachay. He is very familiar with this area, sir," Corbin said.

"Good, let's get started, Lieutenant," Steele said, and they stepped out into the crisp mountain air.

As they walked along, Steele asked, "How do you like this earthen fort, Lieutenant?"

Lieutenant Corbin cast him a wary glance. "Well sir, to tell the honest truth, I don't like it much. Her defenses may be sound, but there is no comfort here. The pine posts that support the corners are rotten with termites. The rooms are partially underground, and they are damp and the air is poorly vented, and some men have gotten sick from it. Most of us moved into the tents, but, well, it's getting too cold, so we'll have to move back indoors. There's talk of abandoning this fort and building a new one, but with the war and all, it's hard to tell when that will be for sure, a couple of years, I reckon."

Corbin looked around him. "The walls are made from earthen bricks over wood frame, as you can see. The mixture must not have been right with some of the bricks." He pointed out where the walls had separated from the frame. "Some bricks have eroded into the ditches, including parts of the parapets that support the cannons. Portions of the fort though, including the part that houses the powder house and munitions store, were built to be bomb proof."

That explains the location, Steele thought. He waited and Corbin continued.

"One of the officers thinks we're sitting ducks here if the Confederates make it this far north, and they might. If they're smart enough, and I suspect they are, putting light twelve-pound cannons on those ridges to the south of us would be out of our reach to defend against. They could fire into the heart of us."

Steele looked at the ridges above and south of them, and agreed. He had seen the flaw in the location from where he stood this morning, looking down into the valley.

"But we're here," Corbin said. "And it's our duty to lessen the danger to the folks coming up the Santa

Fe Trail, and to supply all of the forts south, north and west of us, so," he shrugged, "our being here is important."

Steele smiled at the younger man. "You're a good soldier, Corbin," he said.

"Thank you, sir, I strive to be," Corbin said.

****

They found their scout in the stables. The scout's long blue-black hair hung straight and loose over his shoulders and down his back, secured with a leather band tied around the crown of his head. A woven red wool blanket was draped over his shoulders in lieu of a coat. He was quiet and still as he leaned against the wooden railing of a horse's stall, though his dark eyes tracked every movement around him, watching Steele and the lieutenant as they approached.

The lieutenant introduced them and Pou Nachay kept his eyes lowered after shaking Steele's hand. Pou Nachay was a man near Steele's age, lean and broad shouldered, and just shy of Steele's six feet one inch in height. He wore a tan buckskin pullover shirt, laced at the neck, with beadwork on the fringe, and buckskin trousers tucked into knee-high moccasins.

"Do you have a map of our route to Fort Garland?" Steele asked.

Pou Nachay was thoughtful for a moment, then picked up a buggy whip, and used the handle to draw a map in the soft dirt. He drew two points about eighteen inches apart. Then he drew a jagged line between the two, and looked back at Steele.

Steele tipped his hat back, grinned and squatted beside the dirt lines.

"Where is water?" Steele asked.

Pou Nachay grinned back, and squatted beside him. He drew four circles at points on either side of, and close to the line.

"How many days between the water holes?" Steele asked.

Pou Nachay made lines indicating either one or two days between.

"So, with the wagons, over this terrain, it will take about seven or eight days?" he asked.

Pou Nachay nodded.

"Any known Native Indian camps?" Steele asked.

The scout studied the route for a moment, then drew what looked like arrowheads at two points of distance away from the line. One arrowhead looked to be in a more direct route between the forts.

"Comanche?" Steele asked.

Pou Nachay shook his head. "Apache," he said.

"So, we're avoiding those routes?" Steele asked.

The scout nodded again, and then drew a small group of box shapes close to the route.

"This is the Taos Pueblo. They have been peaceful for many years. We will camp near there," Pou Nachay said.

November 9, 1861
Taos Pueblo

Heavy gray clouds filled the sky and concealed the tips of the mountains as far as the eye could see, and snow was falling, adding to the snow already covering the ground, covering the trail, though Pou Nachay appeared to find the trail easily.

Steele was able to discern thin strands of darker gray wafting from the valley ahead. Smoke, he thought. From fires, cooking fires, or just for warmth. The temperature stayed below freezing. The frozen snow on the ground cracked when The Black stepped through it. The weather would add many more hours, perhaps days, to their journey.

Pou Nachay was returning from his forward surveillance, and Steele could tell by the set of the scout's jaw that he had something to report. He had come to appreciate the scout's no-nonsense methods, only reporting if there was something unexpected that needed attention.

Steele knew the plan was to camp by the Taos Pueblo where there could be shelter for the men and horses in earthen structures instead of braving the elements in tents near the questionable protection of rock faces. There was also the possibility of a warm meal. Pou Nachay had told him of the Indian fry bread. Steele planned to trade with the Pueblo Indians, hoping to try some along with their repetitive meal of beans and salt-pork.

"Major Steele," Pou Nachay said as he joined Steele and the two sergeants who rode at the front of the train.

Pou Nachay glanced at the sergeants before he continued. "We should not camp here, but should move further beyond this Pueblo," he pointed with his rifle toward a point some miles ahead.

"Now wait just a minute here, Scout," Sergeant Booker said, then turned to Steele. "We been pushin' these men and animals almost to the breaking point, and the weather is makin' it rougher on them, sure as shootin', sir. We won't make it to the point this scout is directin' us to before nightfall. There's just no *hurry up* left in this train today. Besides, we been lookin' forward to a warm bed," he stated grinning.

Steele wondered at the man's mention of 'warm bed', but he addressed Pou Nachay instead.

"What did you see with your forward surveillance that you need to report, Pou Nachay?" Steele asked.

"The Pueblo has sickness, Major. An old woman shouted at me when I started to approach and told me to stay away, that many of the people have fever, caught from a trapper who traded with the people, and most of those with fever are covered with small red spots." Then in one of the rare moments when Pou Nachay met Steele's eyes and held them, he said, "The men can't hunt. For those few who are well enough to cook, they have no meat to cook. Of those who get sick, many die."

Sergeant Booker spoke again. "Well, now, most likely they got measles. That's a horse of a different color then, ain't it, sir."

As The Black shifted under Steele, impatient to be moving again, Pou Nachay was still holding Steele's gaze, sending a silent message. The people of the pueblo, the Native People of this land, people like

Pou Nachay, were sick, and they were at risk of starving. Steele stretched in the saddle and looked back over the lumbering train of wagons.

"Sergeant Booker, if the animals need a little break to keep going, let's lighten their load, say, three weeks' worth of dried apples, corn meal, flour, lard, and salt-beef, enough for fifty men." Steele waited for Pou Nachay to agree, but he remained still. "Make that sixty men," Steele amended, and then Pou Nachay gave one nod of his head.

"And those two milk cows that calved on the trail, they're slowing us down, too," Steele said. "Leave them here." Then he turned back to Pou Nachay. "Go with Sergeant Booker and show him the best place to leave those things."

The relief in Pou Nachay's eyes was evident as the two men rode to obey Steele's order. Then Steele turned The Black into the wind, and signaled the wagons and men to keep moving forward.

November 14, 1861
Fort Garland

Fort Garland was a sprawling group of single story wood and earthen buildings surrounded by a fence of tall wooden posts. It was situated on a flat plain near where two rivers converged and near the base of the Sangre de Cristo mountain range.

Steele and his men and wagons rode up to the large wooden gates where they were greeted by two sentries who stepped forward with salutes. Steele introduced their company, and the sentries directed them to the stables where the horses and oxen could be taken care of, and the supplies unloaded.

****

"Sir," the second lieutenant said and saluted Steele. When he returned the salute, the lieutenant opened the door and invited him into the hallway of the Commander's quarters.

"I'm here to see Commander Lockwood," Steele said. "I'm…." and before he could continue, the lieutenant stated, "He's expecting you, Major Steele."

Steele raised his eyebrows at the statement, a little surprised and impressed at how the news of his arrival had been relayed to the Commander, as he had come directly from the stables to introduce himself. He nodded and then he walked to the Commander's office door, which stood open.

A serviceable wooden desk with a gleaming unmarred surface had been placed at the ideal position in the room for the natural light from the window to illuminate the workspace, and a well-groomed gray-haired man of medium build sat at the desk pondering the papers before him, pen in hand.

Steele rapped his knuckles on the open door.

"Enter," the commander said.

Steele saluted. "Major John Steele reporting for duty, Commander Lockwood."

Commander Lockwood stood and returned the salute. "At ease, Major," Lockwood said, extending his hand in welcome.

"Thank you, sir," Steele said removing his hat and gloves before shaking Lockwood's hand.

Steele glanced around the room. The furnishings, a long table, chairs, and bookshelves, were sturdy, though worn. The walls were decorated with intricate sketches of bridges, attesting that at least part of what Captain Kendrick had reported was true, though in what context remained to be seen. His attention returned to the desk. Official-looking papers were sitting next to photographs of an impossibly deep and wide gorge.

When Steele and his men had ridden into the fort, none of the rampant chaos the captain had reported to be ongoing was apparent. The fort activities appeared orderly and purposeful, the walls and buildings were in good repair, the livestock were healthy, and the horses were well-cared for in the stables.

Lockwood looked Steele over, his expression curious. "I wasn't expecting you, Major," he said, "but I welcome you nevertheless."

"I believe my arrival has pre-dated my official orders, sir. I have a letter from Colonel Anderson explaining his assessment of current events," Steele said handing the letter to Lockwood, unsure of how his arrival would be interpreted by the Commander.

"I was expecting my service to be at Fort Union, but Colonel Anderson sent me here without delay."

"Yes, understandable with winter about to lock us into this valley," Lockwood said opening the envelope. "You said *reporting for duty* Major. You're staying then." It was more a statement than a question as he scanned the contents of the letter.

At Steele's affirmation, Lockwood continued, "And you brought my best scout back to me, and seventy regular cavalry, I see."

"Pou Nachay is your scout, sir?" Steele asked.

"Yes, his family is here, well, his half-sister and her two children. She is a milkmaid and laundress. She is a competent seamstress, and skilled at leatherwork and beadwork I'm told by my daughter. Please sit down, Major Steele," Lockwood invited, gesturing toward a chair facing his desk before walking behind it. "And tell me what Colonel Anderson sent us in those many wagons. Any chance there might be a payroll chest? It's been a few months since our men got paid. Our last payroll detail was attacked by an Apache war party and one of the payroll guards stashed the pay chest in his favorite fishing hole somewhere between here and Fort Union. It's anyone's guess where that is. The guard died soon after he was found on the trail by our patrol, and the rest of the guards died of their wounds as well, so it's never been found."

Steele sat in the chair across from Lockwood.

"There is a payroll chest," he said, and with the Colonel's relieved look, he continued. "As well as flour, corn meal, dried beans, dried apples, salt-beef, salt pork, seeds for planting, and several cases of brandy for you, sir, with Colonel Anderson's complements," he added with a smile. "There is also ammunition and new rifles, and he sent a man skilled with making and laying adobe bricks. The Colonel thought that the man could help with building any new barracks and fortifications you might need."

"That was all very thoughtful of him, though our food stores are in good shape, but since we now have a few more mouths to feed, it will be useful indeed," Lockwood said. "Colonel Anderson is an old and good friend."

Steele cleared his throat. "Sir, I requested and brought four mountain howitzers with us," he said.

The Commander looked surprised, but recovered quickly. "A smart choice of field guns for this terrain, Major Steele," Lockwood said, his face grim. "You must have some updates on the Confederate movement. They're not so far away now, I gather."

Then abruptly, the colonel stood. Steele stood as well, figuring that his meet and greet time was ended when Lockwood added, "Lieutenant Hawkins, the young officer at the door, will show you to the Officers' quarters and to a private apartment. Our Sutler's store is well supplied for any additional things you may need. The lieutenant can arrange a time this afternoon for us to meet again and discuss those updates, as well as your duties and interests."

"Yes, Commander," Steele said.

Lockwood checked his pocket watch. "We have a parade inspection scheduled for our troops in one hour, so you can see our men and formations."

'Perhaps you and your men would like to join us."

Steele realized that it wasn't a suggestion and he would have to step lively to get his men mounted and into formation. His opinion of the man's command ability was rapidly forming a picture opposite the one Captain Kendrick had painted.

"Oh, and another thing, I will arrange a get-together for you, Major, to meet the other officers of this post and their families on Saturday. Your arrival deserves a celebration," Lockwood said clapping a gentle hand to Steele's shoulder, and then he turned his focus back to the papers on his desk.

"That's very kind of you, sir. I'll look forward to it," Steele said.

The Commander looked up again. "And I'm sure you will meet my daughter Mersey before that," Lockwood said. "She is the only family I have here and I'm a little surprised that you didn't already encounter her when you entered the hall. She must have left early for the schoolhouse. It's their first day and she's been so excited it's nearly intolerable."

Lockwood smiled and his hazel eyes twinkled, and he shook his head. "For such a gentle woman, she can be a bull in a china closet if she wants something, turns everything upside down and inside out, and no one is safe. And I'll warn you beforehand, she's a crier, just like her mother was. She has abundant tears for any occasion, joy, sadness, hurt, anger, and sometimes her motive is a mystery even to her, so don't take it personally. But if she's upset enough, the tears just evaporate and turn to steam that comes out her ears."

The Commander laughed, but Steele felt a twinge of alarm, imagining a giant bull with red watery glowing eyes, and hooves for appendages, steam wafting from its nostrils and ears, and he felt an overwhelming urge to run away, an unknown sensation for him.

A stuttered, "Y-yes, sir," was all he managed.

Mersey

Mersey stood beside the yet-to-be-rung school bell hanging from the awning above the stoop of the school house. She secured a wayward curl freed from its pin by the chill wind, gathered her wool shawl more closely to her, smoothed her long buff-colored skirt, and looked around the parade ground. Boys and girls of varying ages were playing, cheeks rosy from the cold, little clouds of white misted with their breaths as they laughed, and shouted, and ran chasing each other, waiting for their first day of school to begin, and she was filled with a sense of joy and anticipation. Living at Fort Garland with her father and teaching school were the culmination of her dreams.

She looked at the large, flat-roofed, square and rectangular adobe buildings within the fort, their twenty inch walls insulating those inside from the extreme cold or intense sun of this high altitude desert, or if needed, insulating those inside from the penetration of bullets or arrows.

Mersey looked beyond the wooden perimeter fences at the rugged sandy terrain where grass, trees, and shrubs fought for survival in the foothills of mountain ranges surrounding the valley in every direction. To the west lay the perilous San Juan Mountains. And just to the east, the snow-covered peaks of Little Bear Mountain and Mount Blanca towered fourteen thousand feet into the blue sky. The two mountains were part of the Sangre de Cristo Mountains, named the *Blood of Christ* by early Spanish explorers for their reddish hews when the mineral-rich granite reflected the light from the rising or setting sun. The high, rugged Sangre de Cristo mountains extended nearly two hundred miles from northeast of Fort Garland to Glorieta Pass in the New Mexico Territory.

Mersey shivered, feeling the frigid air settle a little deeper into her bones. But when she stepped from the shadow of the school house steeple into the sunshine, she was grateful for the power of the sun to warm her just a little, even on the coldest day. She had hoped to start this school year two months ago, but finishing the school's inside walls, the desks, the supply shelves and cupboards, and installing the stoves had taken much longer than anticipated. Delay after delay had plagued them.

First, a significant number of regular army soldiers had been reassigned and relocated to forts back East. The remaining soldiers, in addition to the normal duties of protection of settlers and livestock, had also helped with flash flood evacuations when snow had melted too rapidly in the mountains. Next there were wild horses to break to saddle, grass fires to put out or divert, and so on. Her father had not had the man-power to spare. But it was ready now. Mersey checked the watch pinned to the embroidered pocket on her blouse, reached up after what had seemed an eternity of waiting, and pulled the bell cord.

At the glorious sound of the bell, all of the children stopped playing and began walking or running toward the school house. Mersey smiled as she watched an older boy stop one of the smaller boys, extract a kitten from the boy's pocket, and order him to take it back to the milk-house and be quick about it. There was a family resemblance between the boys. Brothers, she thought.

It was then that she saw the Ute Indian scout leaning against the front post of the barracks with his arms crossed over his chest, and he was staring at the front of the Sutler's store. She looked in the direction of his stare and then she stepped forward. She saw two children with their backs pressed to the display of the Sutler's Store window. The children were looking up with wide eyes at a large man, dressed in a blue uniform coat, who was glaring down at them. Mersey couldn't hear what the soldier was saying, but he was frightening the children.

As the other children began to greet her and file into the school room, Mersey said, "School will be starting in a few moments, please go in and take your places."

Then Mersey walked across the well-manicured winter-yellow buffalo grass that covered the parade ground, her long skirt snapping with the light breeze and her determined stride. She calmly but deliberately stepped between Master Sergeant Jennings and the two Indian children.

"Hello Cochetopa and Antera," she said.

Mersey smiled at the children, noticing that their buckskin clothing had been brushed and cleaned of dust. Their long dark hair, pulled back with leather ties, was shining and well combed. The boy Cochetopa was about ten years of age, and his sister Antera was six. Mersey knew that these children lived with their single mother, a Ute Indian woman who made her living at the fort, sewing and taking in laundry. The children were niece and nephew to the scout watching so intently. She believed his name was Pou Nachay, and Mersey glanced toward him, then back at the children as she asked, "Are you on your way to school?"

Both children nodded. "Yes'm," Cochetopa said.

Mersey turned then to face Master Sergeant Jennings, and she lifted her eyes from the level of the middle of his chest to his face. The man's cool blue eyes raked her from head to toe. She lifted her chin.

"Master Sergeant, I'm sure you didn't mean to delay these children. They are nearly late for school."

He shifted his stance and cocked his head, studying her challenging expression. "I saw them admiring the dolls and marbles in the Sutler's window there. I was just reminding them what the punishment would be for thieving."

Jennings was in his mid-thirties, a big man with broad shoulders, a barrel chest, and legs like tree trunks. His stomach was flat and solid. He was rough and hardened, and in the few months that she had been here, she had seen him threaten to use his fists on more than one hapless soldier who had somehow drawn his displeasure. He had been at Fort Garland since it was built, had helped build it three years ago, and her father had informed her that the master sergeant had much experience as an Indian fighter in his years as a cavalry man.

Jennings smiled at her, more a flash of strong white teeth, and leaned a little closer to her.

"And you're wasting your time trying to teach these savages to think like whites. They'd rather slit your throat as soon as your back is turned," he said, taking a step toward her then, so that she had to look up at him.

Mersey had been at the fort only since early summer so she was still learning the culture and politics of the fort. Her insistence on including the Indian children in the school room had been met with distracted endorsement by her father and quiet resentment by many of the families of the soldiers at the fort. Jennings had no children who attended the school, she was sure, but he clearly had an opinion regarding her decision to provide education for all children of the fort who wished to attend.

Mersey refused to be intimidated by the man and gathered her courage. Her father was, after all, the commander of this fort, and therefore the superior officer for all the men, officers, enlisted, and volunteers, including this burly master sergeant. She squared her shoulders.

"May I remind you that my father has approved their attendance. These are impressionable children, Master Sergeant. An education will help them make responsible choices as adults," she said.

Jennings stepped closer again and now Mersey could read the tiny print *U.S. Calvary* on the top button of his coat. She fought the urge to step back.

Jennings shifted his eyes and his position, and Mersey saw that Pou Nachay had joined them on the boardwalk in front of the store. The man didn't speak, and his face showed no emotion, but his dark eyes were sharp and alert as he watched Jennings.

"This is no concern of yours, Scout, so stand down," Jennings barked at the man, then turning back to Mersey he continued in a forceful authoritative voice. "And we'll see, Miss, what the new major has to say about it when he gets here. Captain Kendrick says the major's going to take over this fort, and even if he doesn't, I'm sure your daddy will turn many lesser duties over to him, and he may just agree that havin' Indian children learnin' white ways is a waste of time. They don't want to live like us. They want to live in their old ways, and they've started wars to prove it," Jennings said as his voice escalated to the level of the drill-sergeant that he was. "Lots of good soldiers and other good folks have died by Indian hands and...."

"Atten-hut!" a voice commanded, and Jennings looked startled before he recovered himself, turned an about-face, and snapped a salute.

Mersey looked to her right and recognized Lieutenant Hawkins standing next to a tall man that she had never seen before, a man who wore an immaculate uniform, and gold oak leaves gleamed on the shoulders of a major.

The major returned Jennings' salute and then stated "At ease," before his clear gray eyes settled on Mersey in an assessing way. When he looked at Jennings again, his look pinned the master sergeant to the boardwalk.

The men facing each other were the same inch or so over six foot in height, the major slightly taller, and though Jennings carried heavier, bulkier muscle, there was unleased power in the major that was just as formidable. Neither of the men spoke.

Lieutenant Hawkins cleared his throat.

"Miss Lockwood, Master Sergeant Jennings, may I introduce Major Steele, our second-in-command."

Still unnerved by the sudden appearance of the major and being overheard in what would be interpreted as ungentlemanly behavior no matter the provocation, Jennings stammered, "Sir, Major Steele, I wasn't expecting…."

A quizzical black brow arched over one gray eye, and Jennings corrected, "Uh, I mean to say, it's an honor to meet you, sir, and if there is anything…."

The major's deep refined voice interrupted him. "Commander Lockwood has ordered parade formation if you would please assemble your men and horses right away, Master Sergeant."

"Yes, sir, right away, sir," Jennings said, relieved to be dismissed. "Ma'am," he said to Mersey, then he turned and hastened away, shouting for Sergeant Sandoval to prepare the horses and for Corporal Smith to assemble the men.

Major Steele's eyes were again considering Mersey as she reached behind her to gather the children to her side, and she was surprised at how his focused interest unsettled her. She had lived among the officers and gentleman of the Army her entire life, many of them as handsome and dashing as the major, but this man was different. There was an intensity of self and purpose in him that she had rarely, if ever, encountered before in anyone as young as this man. And she was sure his speech had an element of southern influence, an unexpected quality in a Federal fort since the onset of the Civil War, a war that divided men's loyalties, forced them to choose sides, a war that was rapidly approaching the newly formed Colorado Territory, and this fort, from the East. Jennings had said that a new major was coming to take over. If her father were ordered to leave, what of her dream for the school, the school with its hand-carved miniature desks and sunlit windows, new chalk boards, and little pot-bellied stoves in two corners? She frowned, forcing herself to view this potential shattered dream without resentment. This was normal, expected, the standard. She had accepted Army life, had accepted what was required of men like her father who made soldiering their life's work. Soldiers followed orders. Soldiers moved their homes and families to serve where ever their orders sent them, often at the drop of a hat. This man, too, who stood before her so self-assured and imposing had come to serve this post in this extreme country when he may very well have longed to be somewhere else.

If her father had to move on, if this new schoolhouse couldn't be for her, then there would have to be a new teacher to take her place, and she would ask to build another school, at a new fort, with a new community's support. She straightened her shoulders and bolstered her resolve. Maybe she was destined to be the John *Johnny Appleseed* Chapman of school houses in the West. She would do her best to bloom where she was planted, as Aunt Andrea would say. She forced a smile.

The lieutenant broke the silence then and spoke to Mersey in a gentlemanly manner. "It's a pleasure to see you again, Miss Lockwood."

Mersey turned her attention from the major to Lieutenant Hawkins, who was smiling at her. As a single officer at the fort, he had been especially attentive to her whenever they had met over the past few months.

"Thank you, Lieutenant, it is nice to see you again as well." She turned to Steele and extended her hand.

"I'm pleased to make your acquaintance, Major. I'm sure my father will welcome your assistance here." Then she glanced at Jennings' broad retreating back. "And your arrival was most fortunate, thank you."

Steele observed Miss Mersey Lockwood as she studied him, and he had watched a waterfall of emotion cascade over her very appealing face, from surprise and suspicion to reckoning and resolution. He wasn't confident that he had passed inspection. He wanted, in an almost adolescent way, to have made a favorable first impression on this remarkable creature. Steele removed his right glove and captured her hand in a warm, firm grip.

"Thank you for the gracious welcome. I will endeav'ah' to exceed all expectations of duty for you and your fath'ah," he said with a polite bow.

Steele winced inwardly. His drawl had escaped him before he could rein it in. He didn't want to examine it too closely, but he realized that his lapse into his drawl had to be due to his disarming response, his instinctual awareness of the woman whose hand he was still holding. Her hand in his was small, and soft, and cool, and she gripped his fingers with a feminine strength and confidence that he couldn't help but approve.

So this lavender-eyed beauty was the dread bull in a china closet, destined to turn every world, including his, upside down and inside out. Her hair was a rich sable color, long, but pulled back into what she must have intended as a replica of a prim, strict, schoolmistress' bun, though curls escaped every pin, and if the glowing smile she had given those two children was any indication, she could by no means be strict. Her skin was golden from the sun, smooth and flawless. Though she dressed in a simple, practical style, his eyes were drawn to her slender curves. She was just tall enough to fit perfectly in his arms, and he felt a sudden longing for the opportunity to prove his theory correct.

Steele reined in his thoughts and straightened then, glanced behind him at the men being assembled, and at Master Sergeant Jennings. He had overheard the man threatening that a new major was coming who would take over, maybe change things, and though the look in her eyes was warm, she was nevertheless, he realized, regarding him in a cautious way.

"Forgive me, Miss Lockwood, I couldn't help but overhear what the master sergeant was shouting," Steele said with a polite dip of his head. He looked again at the two Indian children at her side, then to Hawkins he said, "Would you mind escorting these children to the school, Lieutenant? I would like a word with Miss Lockwood."

"Of course, sir," Hawkins replied.

"Please excuse me, ma'am," Hawkins said to Mersey, and he escorted the children away.

Mersey noted that Pou Nachay had moved away as well. He must trust that the children were safe now with this stranger who had taken command of the situation, and she turned to Major Steele, who hadn't released her hand.

He spoke again in that low drawl. "Though I don't agree with Master Sergeant Jennings tactics, I agree with him in principal. Educating the Indians in our ways has no foreseeable benefit to them, or for us. They have no desire to give up their way of life and embrace ours, and their way of life will only clash with the progress of this country."

She snatched her hand back as if burnt, shocked by his statements. "What are you saying, Major? Are you saying that the Indian people should be excluded from learning how to help make the rules that they will be compelled to live by? Are you saying, too, that these people will be excluded from the progress of our country, a country whose allegiances are already torn apart by questions of human rights and dignity?"

Mersey watched his face become a mask. Something like sadness flashed in his eyes and she couldn't look away as his eyes captured hers in a blazing regard.

"I'm stating reality as I see it, not as I wish it to be," he said, then touched his fingers to his hat brim. "Good day to you, Miss Lockwood. I will seek your fath'ah's approval to ensure that your students are not detained in any mann'ah in the future."

Feeling a mix of irritation and determination, Mersey stared at his broad shoulders and straight back as his smooth purposeful strides carried him toward the parade ground. He did not look back at her as he approached a spirited black stallion and climbed into the saddle with the ease and confidence of long practice.

Mersey calmed herself. Though he didn't agree, he had given his assurance that he wouldn't allow interference if the Native Indian children wanted to attend school. Though he communicated his doubt of any benefit, he had also made it clear that he wouldn't impede her efforts to allow all children the opportunity of an education if they desired it. Major Steele just did what her father had already done for the school, made a decision to stand aside and let it be what it could be.

Mersey had met few men like her father, men who listened, and even rarer were men who listened to a woman. To Mersey's knowledge, her father had never made a decision based upon a biased consensus, or influenced by some orator's supposed common sense, or another's perceived fairness, or even to make right anyone's self-serving goals. Men who made difficult decisions based upon accountability were rare indeed. Her father intended that his decisions would stand the test of time. And just now, she found that she held a little bit of hope that Major Steele might also be made of this same metal.

As Mersey turned toward the school, she was bumped off-balance, but then caught by firm gloved hands. She grabbed strong forearms for support.

"Many pardons, Miss Lockwood," Kendrick said recovering from his surprise, and he smiled down into her eyes, his hurry all but forgotten as he grasped her shoulders. "Had I not been in such a rush to join my men, I could not have missed seeing you step into my path. I beg forgiveness and hope that I have caused you no distress," he said.

"None at all, Charles," Mersey said, looking at the handsome, fair-skinned, brown-eyed man, his lean strength holding her steady. "I can assure you that I am quite unharmed."

Just then Sergeant Sandoval approached. "Captain, yer men are mounted an' waitin', sir."

Sergeant Sandoval winked at Mersey. She smiled.

Captain Kendrick frowned at the sergeant. "Thank you, Sergeant, that will be all," Kendrick said, then glanced at the parade ground.

Mersey followed Kendrick's frowning look and met Major Steele's intense gray eyes.

Kendrick's regard returned to Mersey. "Miss Lockwood, please allow me to make it up to you with a dance, or several, this Saturday night in welcome of our new second-in-command," he said as he released her shoulders, tipped his hat, and hurried away to join his cavalry company.

So the dance on Saturday night must be what the card was about from the Ladies of the Regiment. She had all but ignored it in her focused effort to make the first day of school the best it could be.

Mersey took a moment to observe the men gathered on the parade ground. The rough edges on the volunteer soldiers were obvious compared to the men like her father, Major Steele and Captain Kendrick, who were regular Army. Even Master Sergeant Jennings looked the gentleman compared to the callused men of the volunteer companies. Captain Roberts was the officer who led the volunteer infantry, but he seemed to fit in well with his men, both in near-contempt and borderline disrespect of authority, and in audacity. His leadership had been rumored to include participation with his men in several drunken brawls.

Kendrick, unlike Roberts and his infantry, seemed to set himself apart from any camaraderie with the volunteer cavalry, but Kendrick appeared too often to take the easy path with the men, and let them seek their own level of discipline, as was Jennings' example to the men under him as well.

Mersey felt that her father delegated too much to Captain Kendrick. Kendrick was a young officer, and her father, in an attempt to teach responsibility, gave him authority over the cavalry volunteers, but then her father did not seem aware that the declining discipline was affecting the fort's more vulnerable residents. Mersey feared for the safety of the single women and the Native Indians, as the volunteer companies did not respect them.

Would Major Steele change that? Would he even see? Would he even care? She had heard it said that an officer should have a gentleman's manners, a scholar's head, and a lion's heart. Would Major Steele be such an officer? Dare she hope?

Her eyes went again to the major, his appearance almost noble as he sat his great black horse, his gray eyes striking right and left in assessment of the men facing him. She heard the command to *Present arms!* as she entered the schoolroom.

First Day of School

When Mersey entered the schoolroom, she was startled to see that none of the children sat at the desks. Instead, Cochetopa and Antera stood against the wall on the right side of the room, and all of the other students stood on the left. No one talked. They stood looking at each other, and then they all turned to look at her.

Mersey knew that whatever she did next might have a lasting effect on the relationships of her students. She didn't think that the atmosphere was hostile, at least she hoped not. She hoped there were just cultural differences and a lack of comfort with someone unfamiliar. Mersey walked to the front of the room, and wrote her name on the blackboard. Then she turned and met the eyes of every child. She smiled, trying to hide her apprehension as to what she would do if this failed.

"Good morning, boys and girls. My name is Miss Lockwood. I am your teacher. It's very nice to see all of you here today. I'm glad that you are standing, because I need you to stand for a game I want us to play before we begin our class. I am going to ask you some questions, and you will answer by moving to different parts of the room. I will give you directions about where to move after each question. Alright, here we go," she said. "If you were born at this fort or any other Army fort like this, please move to the front of the room." Mersey gestured to the front of the room to the right of her desk. "And for everyone who was not born at a fort, please move to the back of the room."

Several children moved to the front. Cochetopa and Antera and the rest moved to stand at the back, but stayed separate on each side of the room.

"Good," Mersey said. "If you are an only child, that means you have no brothers and sisters, please move to the center of the room."

A few children moved from the front and the back to the center of the room between a row of desks, and Mersey joined them. Most stayed where they were.

Mersey watched the children's faces as they payed close attention to her instructions, losing their wary expressions and engaging in the game.

"If you like kittens, I want you to move to the front of the room on this side of the desk." Mersey pointed.

Some of the children giggled. The older boy she had seen in the yard earlier with the younger boy, nudged him with his elbow, and the younger boy moved to the front of the room. This time it was a larger group of children. They were crowded together in a small space, their faces lit with smiles, and Antera was with them.

"If you know how to ride a horse, please move to the back of the room on the left," Mersey said.

There was a moment's hesitation, but then all of the older boys and a few of the girls moved to the back of the room. Cochetopa, still keeping a distance between them, joined them. Mersey watched them eyeing each other now with curiosity.

Mersey spoke her next question without hesitation. "If your mother or your father works at Fort Garland, please move to the front of the room on the right side of the desk."

All of the children moved forward then, and crowded into the small space, and then Mersey squeezed in to join them.

"Let's take a look at the people around us," she said, and they did. "Each of us has a mother or father who works at this fort. This is something that we have in common with each other. It is something that is the same for each of us. In this schoolroom, we are all alike, no matter what happens outside these walls."

Some nodded their heads, others just looked at her, seeming to understand.

"Very good," Mersey said. "Now for my last question, if you came to this school to learn things like reading, and numbers, or writing and history, please go to a desk and sit down."

When they did, Mersey breathed a sigh of relief.

Ladies' Choice

Steele stood surrounded by the officers of Fort Garland in a room everyone called The Theater. The room had a stage for performances as well as a large dance floor. His smile was polite as he responded to the teasing and personal questions thrown at him, and for the most part, he evaded answering them.

"Have you heard that having to serve at Fort Garland is a penance for military sins, Major Steele?" Lieutenant Hawkins asked wearing a wide grin.

"And why would that be, Lieutenant Hawkins?" Steele asked.

Lieutenant Noland, who worked with the artillery company, answered with a chuckle "Because of the extreme cold temperatures in the winter that try to nip off your favorite parts, and the gigantic mosquitos the size of crows that try to carry you away in the summer, of which you will soon learn."

Steele maintained his smile as his gaze swept the room and his eyes came to rest on Mersey Lockwood. She was wearing a velvet amethyst-colored gown, a matching ribbon held up her glorious sable curls, and she looked beautiful, and happy. He had been stealing glances at her as she moved about the room, and admitted to himself that he was searching for her each time he looked up from his conversation with the officers.

When she wasn't being interrupted by children coming to her to untie a knotted shoe lace, retie a hair ribbon, straighten a bow tie, or any other imagined excuse by those children to be on the receiving end of her glowing smile, she was assisting the other ladies to set up a refreshment table. He watched her sigh, brush her hands down her skirt, and turn in his direction. When her twinkling lavender eyes met his, his foolish heart skipped a beat, and he fought an urge to ignore the men speaking to him and go to her side.

The sound of silverware tapping against glass drew all eyes to the front of the room where Commander Lockwood stood.

"Ladies and Gentlemen, may I have your attention, please. The gracious Ladies of the Regiment are providing a delightful array of treats for us, and we will begin with a toast. Ladies, if you would be so kind, as to serve the brandy."

Several trays containing small round glasses full of clear brown liquid were taken up by the ladies in the room, and offered to all but the children, who were given glasses of punch. Steele moved to accept a glass from Mersey's tray, thanked her, and then stood near the wall until everyone was served.

"Tonight we have the pleasant duty of welcoming a new officer to our fort, Major John Steele," Lockwood announced, and a round of applause followed. "I offer this toast in your honor, Major Steele. May your experiences here at Fort Garland prove to be most advantageous to your career, and your service most fulfilling in your advancement."

There was a brief pause as the possible meaning of Lockwood's words settled on those attending. Mersey searched her father's face, finding nothing but a sincere smile without resentment or regret.

"Here, here!" echoed in the room as glasses clinked together and brandy was sipped.

"Speech, speech!" followed the applause.

With everyone looking at him in expectation, Steele moved away from the wall and walked to stand beside Commander Lockwood.

Steele spoke. "Thank you, Commander Lockwood, and I would like to thank everyone present for this welcome, for I do indeed feel welcome," he said, knowing that he had not hidden his drawl very well, as always happened when he felt nervous.

He looked at Mersey and she gave him an impish smile, as if she somehow understood that he wasn't comfortable with this kind of recognition. He felt a little more at ease then, being on the receiving end of that smile, and he thought she must have bewitched him. He cleared his throat and continued.

"I am proud and honored to serve with you, and will do my utmost to serve you well."

The applause began again, with more enthusiasm this time. Commander Lockwood reached out to shake Steele's hand and then clapped him on the back.

Turning to the people in the room again, the commander said, "If you will all forgive a small delay, the ladies will get the children to bed, and the musicians will set up for a dance. I hope you will all join us here again in half an hour."

****

When the officers and their wives reassembled, Commander Lockwood informed them that the first dance was traditionally ladies' choice. Wives sought their husbands, and Mersey remained where she was. She faced her father from across the room. He was her first partner for this dance, but she hesitated.

Colonel Lockwood winked at Mersey, and tipped his chin ever so slightly to his right. Noting his gesture with curiosity, she turned then to her left, and regarded John Steele, who was watching her with intense, clear gray eyes. She gave Major Steele a tentative smile, and he bowed his head. In his polite regard, he never took his eyes from hers. She told herself that it was the right thing to do to ask the guest of honor to be her partner. She was the only single woman present. It could be considered her duty as a hostess, could it not?

When she reached him, he offered her his hand, and she took it, his large warm callused fingers surrounding hers, and he escorted her to the dance floor as the melody began. She rested the palm of her hand on his shoulder, and his hand splayed on her back, and when he moved, he led her into the waltz in steps so skillful that she thought her feet no longer touched the floor.

As they danced, Mersey felt the stares of the other officers in the room, and she began to doubt the correctness of her actions in asking the major to dance. He wore no wedding ring, but she knew nothing about him. She fixed her eyes on a gold button on his chest, wishing for an excuse to escape the room, a Mersey-sized opening in the floor perhaps, to avoid the scrutiny for whatever careless blunder she had made.

Steele felt an acute awareness of the enchanting woman in his arms. The warm scent of vanilla clung to her fingers, and he wondered which of the culinary delights arranged upon the refreshment table had been prepared by these competent, feminine hands.

Moments ago when her father had announced a ladies' choice dance, he'd felt a tightness in his chest, hoping that she would choose him. And then her eyes had met his and she crossed the room to him, and his heart had leaped in anticipation of holding her this way, the way he had longed to from the moment he met her on the board walk. She had captivated him. He couldn't remember the last time he had reacted this way to a woman he had just met, if he had ever reacted this way before, and now he couldn't stop staring at her expressive face.

She had just glanced around the room, and he felt her stiffen in his arms, and then she focused those lavender eyes on a button on his chest. Wanting to understand her sudden discomfort and wanting to put her at ease, Steele leaned his head close to her ear and said, "You are a delightful partner, Miss Lockwood, and forgive me my curiosity, but I can't imagine what is so fascinating about that particular button on my uniform."

Mersey looked up at Steele and felt her cheeks flush with embarrassment. She glanced around the room again before meeting his eyes.

"I fear that I put you on the spot by approaching you in such a way," she said. "For this dance, I mean. We have only just met, after all. If you have a wife or a betrothed, I may have offended you in my ignorance."

Steele smiled and dipped his head closer to her again, his eyes gentle on her face. "On the contrary, Miss Lockwood, I am supremely honored that you chose me for this dance," he said. "And there is no one to take offense, I assure you most sincerely."

Mersey relaxed a little then, and enjoyed being led in the dance by Major Steele's flowing, confident steps. All too soon, the music stopped and Mersey stepped out of his arms.

Steele thanked her for the dance, smiled and bowed, and felt an almost overwhelming desire to keep her close, a powerful reluctance to let her get away. He had been right. She fit him perfectly.

As the next waltz began, Steele watched as Captain Kendrick approached them to claim Mersey. When the man smiled down at her, pulled her close to execute a fast turn, and kept her there in the circle of his arms, Steele had the unexpected urge to throttle the man. As soon as the music ended, and another tune began, Lieutenant Hawkins was there to take Kendrick's place.

Kendrick waited then, not far from where Hawkins and Mersey were dancing, for his chance to reclaim her. The captain couldn't keep his eyes off of Mersey, frowned as she laughed at something Hawkins said, and Steele realized as he observed the man that he was infatuated with the lovely school teacher. Kendrick was young, maybe twenty three or four, a little above average height, and had the lean muscled build of a cavalryman.

Kendrick was a mystery, as were his questionable accusations against the commander. Steele could detect no malice in Kendrick, what little he knew of him. Was it ambition alone, or was there some other motive for disgracing the commander? Steele was determined to find out.

The dancing went on, with Mersey the target for whoever could reach her first after each tune, and

Steele watched and brooded, hesitant to behave as all the other gentleman vying to please her, not knowing how to distinguish himself as more interesting, more memorable, more…something than the rest of the pack. He didn't examine his feelings for wanting her to notice him above all others. He was sure now that she had chosen him for the ladies' choice dance out of politeness, or out of obligation. Officers behaved in essentially the same ways, were charming and polite and attentive at the same levels, and looked roughly the same in uniform, though Steele felt confident that he had tread less upon Mersey's small feet than most. That should be memorable to her, he hoped.

Recalling the commander's toast, he hoped he was not memorable to her as a threat to her father's position, and that thought made him frown. The threat, to his regret, was well founded.

Steele patted his shirt pocket, where he had placed the letter he had received today. He'd intended to leave it in his quarters before he left for the dance, but he'd forgotten. He reached to touch the battered envelope with his fingers before registering that someone was speaking to him. He looked down to see Lieutenant Noland's wife smiling at him, and with a knowing look, she told him that a quadrille would be beginning soon. If he wanted to claim Mersey for the dance, he should step forward now. His eyes searched the room. He saw Mersey slip over to the refreshment table. To his surprise and relief she was unattended by her roomful of suitors. Steele thanked Mrs. Noland, not even disconcerted at that moment that she had read him so easily, and he advanced toward Mersey.

Mersey looked up at him as Steele approached her.

"Miss Lockwood, I'm surprised that a lady of your popularity has to retrieve her own punch," he said. "Allow me." He handed her a glass of punch from the table, and took another for himself.

She grinned and ducked behind his shoulder, attempting to conceal herself from the room behind his broad chest. "I consider this a strategic retreat. It's quite exhausting being the only unmarried lady in a room with an unfair number of unmarried men. And what of you, Major? Other than when you were compelled to accept, I've yet to see you dance."

"That is precisely why I am here, ma'am. One of the other kind ladies warned me that if I didn't pay attention, that I might miss the opportunity to accompany you in the quadrille."

The music started. He offered her his hand, and when she took it, they joined the other couples on the dance floor.

****

Mersey grabbed her cloak and escaped the merriment of the Theater. She strode to the railing of the boardwalk and looked up at the stars. She breathed in the fresh air that was so cold she could feel it as it moved inch by inch through her nose to her lungs. A movement to her right startled her. She clutched her cloak tighter around her, but then the movement was followed by the distinctive sound of the iron heel plates of cavalry boots across a boardwalk, and Major Steele walked into the light reflected through the window.

"I'm sorry if I frightened you, Miss Lockwood," he said. "I simply meant to alert you to my presence."

She found his deep, soft-spoken drawl soothing.

"It's quite all right, Major. And I didn't mean to disturb you. If you wish to be alone, I can…."

"No please, Miss Lockwood, don't leave, I…." he paused. "I am grateful for your company."

Mersey watched him reach to his coat pocket, a pocket that appeared to contain a small rectangle of paper, a letter perhaps. She studied his face in the reflected light. He had a good face, strong, masculine, handsome, with intelligent eyes, eyes with laugh lines at the corners that seemed to contradict his serious and composed expression.

"For the guest of honor, Major, you seem to be avoiding the honor due you," she said.

"John," he said to her. "Please call me John, Miss Lockwood."

"Then you must call me Mersey," she said.

"Are you making another strategic retreat from your many admirers, Mersey?" he asked, watching the light from the window sparkle in her eyes.

"It was the tobacco smoke. My eyes were starting to water, and I knew that I was about to succumb to very unladylike coughing. I would open a window, but you can depend on the windows being frozen shut around here from October until March, I'm told."

She threw him a conspiratorial look and added, "Please don't tell on me, but I left the door open to allow some of the smoke to escape and…."

A man's voice interrupted, "Good Lord, someone left the door open, and we'll all soon have frostbite on our…." and the door clicked shut.

She laughed, and John chuckled, a deep, warm rumble that she felt to her toes.

"And you, John, what are you escaping?"

He glanced away. "I don't feel much like dancing, I'm afraid," he said, and his fingertips reached to touch the paper in his pocket.

She was helpless to hold her curiosity at bay at the nature of the document, and why it might upset him.

She said, "That's the second time I've seen you reach for that letter, Major Steele."

"John," he corrected, and he thought she might have smiled up at him, though it was hard to be sure in the low flickering light.

"John, that's the second time I've seen you reach for that letter in your pocket. Are you expecting bad news?"

"No, I, uh, I already know the contents of this letter," he said, glancing at her face.

He leaned forward and placed his elbows on the railing, his hands clasped in front of him. The position brought his face more to the level of hers, and he could see the questions in her eyes.

When he didn't say more, Mersey said, "I'm sorry, it's private I'm sure, and I didn't mean to be…."

"It's alright," he assured her. "I know the contents of the letter because I wrote it, and it was returned to me today unopened," he said.

Mersey didn't speak, letting him choose to tell her more if he wished.

He took a breath, and his words came out in a soft rush. "You might have guessed that my home was in the South. My home was in Virginia. And as you might also guess, my family was angry and displeased with my decision to stay at my post in the Union Army."

He looked at her to gage her reaction, but, if anything, her expression had softened. He felt encouraged to go on.

"My family doesn't have slaves, has never had slaves in the three generations that we have been in Virginia, but still my family is entrenched in the Southern way of life. They are close to other land owners who do own slaves. My fiancé….no, let me correct that, my *ex*-fiancé lives the life of a southern belle with all the trappings." he said.

"She renounced you, when you stayed with the Union," Mersey offered.

He nodded, and he became quiet once more, and from the look in his eyes, his thoughts were very far away. Mersey felt like he might have forgotten that she was there, so he surprised her a little when he spoke again.

"My father owns a horse ranch. We breed the finest, most spirited thoroughbred horses in the State of Virginia, maybe in the whole country."

The bitterness in his voice had been replaced with an unmistakable pride.

"Including your beautiful black stallion I saw you riding the day you arrived. He's a grand animal."

"Thank you," he said.

And he was quiet again.

Mersey spoke into the silence.

"You gave up everything, everything except your soul, and a dream or two, to serve the Union."

He went still for a moment, then stood and turned to face her. They stared at each other.

She thought she had intruded too much into his privacy.

He thought she had hit the nail on the head.

Gazing into her lavender eyes, he felt as though he were falling into their depths, and he didn't know how to break the fall.

Then the music began again.

"Shall we go back inside, Mersey? I find that I am feeling more like dancing."

November 20, 1861
New Drill Officer

The Monday following the dance, Commander Lockwood called his officers together for their daily briefing.

"Gentlemen," the commander said. "Major Steele brings us some riding expertise that we have not had before. From this day onward, Major Steele will direct all drills and training for the cavalry. He will also oversee the artillerymen as they become proficient with the new mountain howitzers. So now, I'll turn this briefing over to the major."

****

Steele sat upon The Black with Kendrick to his right, and Sergeant Sandoval to his left, facing ninety mounted men in three rows of thirty. The M1841 twelve-pound mountain howitzers, manned by the artillerymen, were eleven hundred yards behind him, facing forward toward the cavalry. Flags spaced one hundred yards apart and lining both sides of the training field snapped in the wind.

Steele shouted into the cold wind. "This drill will show you that there are very few ways to maneuver against cannon fire. The number of cannons, the terrain, and the steadiness and speed of your mount are most of the elements, except for one important one, the human element. Speed is your ally. The soldiers manning the artillery aimed at you may estimate inaccurately in their haste to stop you from reaching them, because I guarantee that they will be trying to stop you."

The men waited in silence for Steele to continue.

"Though the larger twenty four and twelve pounders have longer range, these mountain howitzers have a maximum range of about a thousand yards, and at that range, solid shot will be fired at you," Steele said. "The cannon shot coming at you will change the closer you get to the cannons. At about four hundred yards from enemy artillery, the solid shot will be changed to canisters which contain one hundred forty eight .69 caliber lead balls that have a similar effect to a huge shot-gun. When we begin the drill, remember your formations and listen to Captain Kendrick for maneuvers."

Steele thought again of Anderson's definition of zugzwang. Sending men and horses against cannons made no sense. The only sense was to take out enemy artillery with your own artillery, and that would be his strategy. Keep his men under cover until that could be accomplished. He wouldn't lose any man if a better strategy could be brought to bear.

He nodded at Kendrick, "On my signal, Captain."

"Yes sir," Kendrick replied.

Sandy said, "Major, those men sittin' there are scared spitless 'cause while they was practicin' fighting with their sabers, they saw and heard those guns firin' all mornin'. Those twelve pound cannon shells have been hittin' the targets purty reg'ler. Should ya tell 'em there ain't any live ammunition for this drill"?

Steele grinned a wolfish smile. "They'll figure it out before long, Sandy,"

Steele turned and rode back the eleven hundred yards to the howitzers and dismounted.

The short barrel cannons were mounted on wheeled axels that could be unpinned to come apart and be transported on mules or horses with special pack saddles. The cannon barrel weighed about two hundred twenty pounds, and with the carriage, a total of five hundred pounds. The four cannons were lined up in a row, spaced twenty feet apart.

Each cannon was set in place on four inch by four inch wooden posts with the tail support resting on the ground. The gunners stood ready by the gunner's quadrants to set the angles of the cannons by degrees.

Steele called out to the artillerymen. "From this morning's exercise, remember that with four men per cannon, the best time any team had to get the howitzer back into position and reload and recalibrate after firing was one minute. Three men required more time, and then even more time was needed with two men manning the cannon."

The men were listening with full attention.

Steele continued. "Our desired kill zone is between nine hundred yards distance from our position in increments down to two hundred yards, and then closing from two hundred yards in front of us is point blank range. We will mock fire one cannon to determine range, and with the signal from Captain Kendrick, we will adjust long or short, firing all cannons at once with this wide terrain using one minute timed intervals between each mock firing. The gunner will watch the flags at each one- hundred yard interval as the cavalry advance in order to estimate the next distance to fire, and set the angle. The cavalry will be at full gallop at one thousand yards out and will continue riding at us at full charge."

"Lieutenant Noland, are your gunners ready?" Steele asked.

"Yes sir," the man answered.

"This drill is to help you get a feel for the time it takes for a cavalry charge to reach your position from one thousand yards," Steele said.

Steele glanced to the man standing at his left.

"Our timekeeper, Lieutenant Hawkins, will shout the intervals," he said. "Keep in mind that at roughly two hundred yards out, their Kentucky rifle fire can reach you with reasonable accuracy. And also keep in mind that if I see any of you step anywhere within thirty feet behind the cannons in the recoil area, you will be on latrine duty for a month."

The men chuckled.

Steele looked down the field, lifted a green flag from the ground, raised it and waved it in a wide arc.

Kendrick saw the flag wave, then shouted, "Do not draw your rifles until my signal! Bugler, sound the charge!"

Hawkins signaled at each one minute interval as the artillerymen watched the advance, and called out yardage. Steele waved a red flag simulating when the cannons would fire. Kendrick shouted orders to expand ranks, to spread out.

At five hundred yards Kendrick called out, "Present rifles!" and at two hundred yards, he called the cavalry to a halt, explaining that this would be the point in their charge on a battlefield that they would aim and fire their rifles into the enemy artillerymen. In closing the last two hundred yards, there would be no time to reload, therefore after firing, they would use their sabers or bayonets.

The artillerymen and officers discussed their observations of the cavalry charge as Kendrick had his men insert the flags closer to the center of the field while they moved back into position.

Steele said, "On the next cavalry charge, we will narrow the field and simulate alternating two cannons at thirty second intervals with the same procedure as before."

They repeated the exercises again and again, until Steele shouted, "Well done! Dismissed!"

When the men returned to the fort, spirits were high. Today's exercise had relieved some of their uncertainty, and boosted their confidence, and they were starting to like their officers a little bit more.

Falling for You

It was a very brisk Saturday morning as Steele walked with Lieutenant Hawkins on the boardwalk from the officers' quarters toward the Commander's office. They had been requested, along with Kendrick and Roberts to meet with Lockwood to discuss a change in patrol routes. Both men's eyes were drawn to the schoolhouse where a slim young woman was perched on the top of a rickety wooden ladder as she attempted to secure a sturdy rope to a bell pull on the school bell.

Mersey was six feet up the ladder, and counting the height of the boardwalk, almost seven feet off the ground. In order to reach the bell pull to replace the rope, she had leaned the ladder against a single square post that helped support the awning over the door, and in that precarious position, the boardwalk did not provide a wide enough foundation for the base of the ladder. Because this was so, one ladder leg was only partially supported, leaving an inch or so on solid wood, and the rest on thin air.

"Sir," Hawkins said a little alarmed. "That right leg of the ladder is about to slide off of the boardwalk. She's bound to fall."

"I was just noticing the same thing, Lieutenant," Steele said as they changed direction to approach the schoolhouse. "If she will just stay still until we reach her…."

"I'll wager she's a wiggler, sir," Hawkins said.

"No wager there, Lieutenant," Steele said breaking into a run. From the corners of his eyes, he saw

Hawkins on his left and Kendrick on his right, do the same.

Mersey shifted to thread the rope through the pull when she heard a grinding scrape, felt the ladder tilt and list, and she gasped as she sensed the ladder begin to fall. She tossed away the rope and too late made a grab for the post.

What her fingers gripped instead of rough wood was the warm wool of a coat, and she landed against the hard chest underneath. The unmistakable sound of fabric tearing accompanied the breath whooshing out of that same hard chest, and she looked up into the amused gray eyes of Major Steele as he fell flat to his back on the parade ground, cushioning her fall. Sprawled on top of him, and crushed flat against him somehow, she stared with wide amazed eyes into his.

"I am so sorry, John," she said as she moved to get off of him, but realized that the firm wrap of his arms pinned her to him. .

Kendrick, though relieved that Mersey didn't seem injured, was half-angry that he hadn't been the one to save her from the fall, was more than half-resentful that Steele had gotten there first, and fully, bitterly jealous that Steele was holding Mersey as Kendrick wished to hold her, like he intended to keep her right where she was.

"Miss Lockwood!" Kendrick said in a concerned voice. "Are your hurt? For heaven's sake, let me assist you up!"

As Kendrick reached for her, Steele loosened his hold, but as Mersey shifted she saw that the lace of her shawl was caught tight by one of the buttons on his coat, and she shifted to disentangle it, managing to plant an elbow on Steele's rib.

When he grunted, she looked at him.

"I seem to be quite attached to you, sir, but forgive me, I am forgetting my manners, and bludgeoning you in my attempts to gain my freedom, it appears."

His lips twitched at her proper tone under the circumstances. This was most undignified for an officer to be in such a predicament with half the fort watching, but, since no one seemed to be hurt, he couldn't help but appreciate the humor in it, and found he liked the idea that she was *quite attached to him*, whatever she had meant by that.

"Thank you for your chivalry, sir," she said. "Are you terribly injured?"

"Terribly, horribly, embarrassingly injured, I'm afraid," he answered, his eyes twinkling.

She smiled at him then. "It was your pocket that ripped, nothing more revealing, I believe. I grabbed for something in a futile attempt to save myself, and it was your poor pocket that bore the brunt."

"In that case," he said. "I am only terribly, horribly injured."

"Mersey," Commander Lockwood said, as he had now joined the others who surrounded the couple on the ground. "May I assist you up, my dear?"

"Father, my lace shawl has caught on one of Major Steele's buttons," she explained.

Steele thought, buttons again. He was beginning to have an odd fondness for buttons.

Mersey continued, "This shawl was a parting gift from Aunt Andrea, and I am trying not to ruin it by tearing the lace."

To Steele she said, "If you could just hold still for a moment, I just need a little leverage…."

And she elbowed him in the ribs again as she reached to free the button.

Masculine hands from three directions reached for her shawl which was a little too close to the bodice of her dress, and she batted them away.

"Please don't try to assist me," she said, and, "What an impossible mess," she added, and then she began to laugh until tears fell from her eyes and she laid her head on Steele's chest, unable to control her mirth.

"Mersey," her father scolded. "This is ridiculous. I will buy you another shawl."

"No, please allow me the privilege," Kendrick said. "Miss Lockwood, you must stand up!"

Steele spoke then, fighting his own laughter. "I believe I have an acceptable solution," he said in a reasonable tone. "If you will permit me, Miss Lockwood, I will hold you secure, and the men may lift me, righting us both. Then you may be better able to save your shawl."

She could only nod her response as his arms tightened around her again.

At his signal he was lifted, and as he set her on her feet, the shawl slipped free of the button.

"That was perfect," she told him. "Thank you."

"My pleasure, ma'am," Steele drawled, and with reluctance, he let her go.

Mersey glanced at her father, remembered he had informed her of an officers' meeting this morning, and looked back at Steele.

"Please allow me to mend your pocket during the officers' meeting, Major Steele," she offered.

"Miss Lockwood, that would be most kind," he said, but his eyes were oddly serious, as though he appreciated that she would care about something as silly and personal as a torn coat pocket.

As she walked away, and Kendrick joined her on the boardwalk, Steele heard Kendrick say, "Miss Lockwood, I shall hope that in the future when you attempt to do something so….."

Steele could help Kendrick fill in the blanks with things such as foolhardy, or careless, or hair-brained, knuckle-headed, reckless….

But with Mersey's challenging expression, Kendrick saved himself by saying, "With an endeavor such as this one…." But he lost himself again when he added, "You must always ask for help."

Mersey's eyes narrowed when she replied, "But I didn't need help…."

Kendrick said, "The evidence establishes that you most obviously did need help…." The curious crowd lost the rest of Kendrick's gentleman's reprimand when the pair entered the Commander's quarters.

Steele shook his head. He would, without a doubt, have attempted the same lecture and be of the same mind as Kendrick, that is if his mind hadn't been so beguiled and befuddled by having that same reckless woman in his arms. He would have made the same mistake with Mersey as Kendrick had just now.

Steele was beginning to realize how much Mersey valued her independence, and her right to make her own decisions. He had to rethink his strategy, and when he dropped off his coat for her to mend, he would ask her permission to order two infantry privates to see to the threading of the bell pull. But if she refused….he would see to it that she would never come to harm, not on his watch, no matter how many times he needed to save her from her own decisions.

Cabin Town

In the fading sunlight, Mersey walked outside the gates of the fort to the small Cabin Town where many of the civilian workers lived who provided essential services for the fort. The sunset hues of the sky disguised the make-shift condition of the cabins somewhat, but Mersey knew that the cabins were made of poor materials, were in poor repair, and were less than adequate shelter from the elements.

She had often spoken to her father of needed improvements. Most of the inhabitants of the cabins were single women who possessed neither the know-how, nor the time, nor the resources to improve things. Fresh clean water from Ute Creek was one of very few basic provisions for their comfort. Changes were taking place over time, but winter was upon them again, and winters here were harsh and bitter, and her first concern was the welfare of the children.

The Cabin Town dwellers provided services such as making soap, doing laundry, tending the milk cows, milking, churning butter, mending and sewing clothing, repairing boots, and there were a few women living here who were happy to take care of the carnal needs of the soldiers for cash.

One of the better small cabins belonged to the new adobe brick maker, and another to the family of Pou Nachay, the scout. Those two men worked to make their cabins sturdier and more weather-proof.

It was Pou Nachay's home that Mersey sought. She was looking for Cochetopa and Antera's mother, Alameda. The children hadn't attended school for the last two days. Mersey wanted to know why. If the children were ill, was there something she could do, or was there something else that prevented them from attending school?

Women and children huddled around cooking fires near their cabins, eating and staying warm, and lamps were being lit all over the little community as the sun fell lower in the sky. A few soldiers milled about, collecting laundry or mended clothing, but most of the soldiers were still in the Mess Hall eating their evening meal.

Mersey found Pou Nachay's cabin only because she recognized Cochetopa outside it tending a fire. The cabin was located about half way between the gates of the fort and Ute creek.

Cochetopa greeted her as she approached. "Hello, Miss Lockwood," he said.

The boy looked well enough, she thought. "Hello Cochetopa, it's nice to see you. Is your mother here?"

The door to the cabin opened then, and Antera came outside, followed by Alameda. Mersey hadn't seen Alameda for a several weeks, and hadn't realized that Alameda was pregnant. Now she was very pregnant. Mersey hoped she hadn't shown her surprise, but Alameda's smile seemed shy, or maybe embarrassed. Mersey held out her hand and Alameda took it.

"It's nice to see you again, Alameda."

"You too, Miss Lockwood. Please come inside."

"Thank you, and please call me Mersey," she said.

Mersey and Alameda sat on hand-made wooden chairs, with hand-made cushions, and the children sat on a small bench near a wooden table. The cabin had wood floors and log walls sealed with plaster. There were two bedrooms off of a small hall. A small pot-bellied stove stood against the wall at the end of the hall. The chimney pipe was blackened, but appeared sound, and a small pile of wood lay next to it, as did a blanket roll.

Mersey thought that Pou Nachay might have used one of the bedrooms, but it was also possible that he slept on the floor on the blanket roll. He wasn't with the family just now, so he must be on patrol.

"May I offer you some fresh milk, or something to eat?" Alameda asked, her hand resting on her pregnant belly.

"No, thank you," Mersey said. "I won't stay long. I just wanted to know…."

"Why the children haven't been in school," Alameda finished for her.

"Yes," Mersey said, "That is why I came, and to ask if I could do something to help them attend?"

"I've needed the children to help with my duties. I am able to keep up with the mending, but the milking and butter churning are difficult for me. It is for a short time. My baby comes soon. When I am able again, I will send Cochetopa and Antera to school."

Mersey looked at the children who looked at her.

"I will bring them school work every few days and help them with it, if you think they may have time in the evening."

Now the children were looking at their mother, and she smiled at them.

"I would not wish for them to be behind in their school work. I accept your offer," Alameda said.

Mersey stood then. "Thank you. Tomorrow is Saturday. I will come after the evening meal,"

Alameda and the children stood and accompanied Mersey to the door.

"You should come early, before dark. It is not safe for you to be here when it is dark and Pou Nachay is not here," Alameda said.

Alameda's words were proven true as Mersey stepped outside.

****

Steele was returning to his apartment after a brief meeting with the munitions sergeant when he saw Commander Lockwood step out onto the boardwalk in front of the Commander's Quarters. Lockwood looked to his right and then to his left.

"Good evening, Major," he greeted when he recognized Steele, but he looked around him as if trying to decide in which direction to proceed.

"Good evening, Commander, is there something amiss?" Steele asked.

Lockwood said, "I'm sure it's nothing, and any moment now, I will feel foolish for worrying...."

Steele heard the concern in Lockwood's voice. "May I be of any assistance to you, sir?" Steele asked.

Lockwood looked at him, his expression a little sheepish. "It's Mersey," he said.

Steele felt himself go on alert.

"She's one of two places, I'm certain," Lockwood said. "She makes unreasonable amounts of dessert for us, and then takes the remainder to the infirmary, not wanting it to go to waste, she says. Most times, she tells me when she's going, but I was in a meeting with Captain Kendrick after dinner. She must not have wanted to disturb us."

John waited.

"I assigned Captain Kendrick to look into a pet project of hers, you see, to throw them together, I admit. I know Kendrick's family well, and they are good people." Lockwood shook his head. "Kendrick has yet to meet her expectations on the project, but it wasn't until after I invited him to dinner that I knew that dog wouldn't hunt."

At Steele's curious look, Lockwood explained. "Mersey has this *test*, Major. If a man comes to our table, and let me tell you, Mersey watches him like a hawk, if he shows any notice that the china doesn't match, it's curtains for him. She could care less if the china doesn't match, and that's what makes it a test. Kendrick failed with flying colors. Not only did he notice, but he offered to have his mother choose an appropriate lady's pattern, and ship it to her. It was a sad moment. The man was delighted with himself for solving her *problem*. And the icing on the cake, so to speak, was when Kendrick asked Mersey why she was worrying her 'pretty little head' about her pet project anyway."

Steele smiled and tucked the information away.

"Well then, Major, it's growing quite dark now. If you'll excuse me, I'll walk on down to the infirmary, and escort my daughter home," Lockwood said.

"Commander," Steele said, a feeling of unease prickling the back of his neck. "You mentioned that Mersey would go one of two places. If I may be of assistance in your search, and I assure you that it is no trouble," Steele stated to deflect any objection from the commander. "What is the other place?"

"Lockwood said, Oh, I didn't mention which project, no, that's right I didn't. I hope she would not go there with the sun setting so early in this winter sky." Then he looked at Steele. "Sometimes she goes to Cabin Town."

****

Mersey stepped out of Alameda's cabin as the last rays of sunset faded to dark, and in the firelight she saw two rough-looking men wearing sheepskin coats over army shirts and trousers. They stood together in Alameda's small yard. They were volunteers, Mersey thought, and they weaved somewhat in their stance. She suspected the men had been drinking hard liquor, though it was banned at the fort.

"Well now, Jocko," one of the men said. "Looks like there be one for each of us tonight."

The one named Jocko leered at Mersey. The man was tall and thin. In the flickering light and shadow, his face looked grotesque, unshaven and covered in scars and puckers in the skin that marked him a survivor of small pox. His teeth were stained from tobacco use and he reeked from lack of hygiene. His clothing was soiled as if he wiped greasy hands down the front of him.

"Who gets who, Curly, or do we share 'em both?" Jocko slurred.

Mersey tensed.

"Come back inside, hurry," Alameda whispered.

But it was too late.

The one named Curly moved with an animal quickness, much quicker than Mersey would have imagined that he could move in his condition, and he grabbed her arm. He wasn't a big man, but Mersey could feel his wiry strength in his grip as she tried to pull away. His skin was swarthy, his dark hair overlong and wavy, his features even. Some might have called him handsome if not for the feral gleam in his eyes, and the vicious twist of his mouth.

"Yes, sugar," he said. "Let's all go back inside."

"You will let go of me and leave us alone, now!" Mersey ordered.

The men snickered.

"Captain Kendrick, your protector, ain't here right now, is he, and it's after dark, so we figure you must be looking for it. It's your lucky day, sugar," Curly said, tightening his grip and Mersey cried out.

"And don't worry none, little Indian princess," he said to Alameda, "'bout that belly bein' all swolled up, 'cause Jocko and me, we know how to work it."

A cold terror gripped Mersey, and when she glanced at Alameda, she could see that Alameda was just as terrified, as were the children. Mersey hadn't told her father where she was going, never considering that the trip back to her house would be made in the dark. He wouldn't know where to look for her. She was on her own.

Even if she screamed, she doubted her screams would be heard at the fort. It was dark now and much colder. Mersey could see that very few people were still outside, just four women and an older child, but maybe someone would go for help.

Curly spoke loud enough for the women to hear.

"Ah now, sugar, I can see in your eyes that you're considerin' callin' out for help. But no one's gonna bother us, for their own sakes. They know better'n to interfere with Jocko and me.

Curly looked around them at the women who stood by their cooking fires, and as each person met Curly's eyes, they glanced away, their reaction letting Mersey know that there could be no help from the Cabin Town inhabitants. Curly smiled at her, a very unpleasant triumphant smile, knowing he had made his point.

Mersey reached deep through her panic, grasping at her last hope.

"My father is Commander Lockwood," she said, and knew her voice trembled, and she was fighting tears. "You will be court-martialed and thrown into prison, if not hanged, if you harm any of us."

"Well now, ya see, it don't matter none to me and Jocko who your father is or isn't. This is our territory, not his, and whatever happens here, Master Sergeant Jennings has our backs, so let's get on with this. You're just wastin' our time, sugar, and we ain't had our fun yet."

Curly sneered and jerked Mersey toward the cabin door. She knew it was now or never, so she gave a yell a Confederate would have been proud of, and slammed her knee into Curly's crotch with all her might.

Curly released her, bellowing his rage and pain as he bent double, and as she turned to push Alameda and the children away from the men, Jocko rushed forward, grabbed her hair in his fist and jerked her head back.

Mersey screamed, reached back and scratched his hand, kicking and struggling against his hold, trying to scratch his eyes, and then he let go so suddenly that she almost fell backwards.

****

Steele reached the gates of the fort, and the sentry greeted him.

"Evenin', Major Steele," he said.

"What is your name, Private?" Steele asked.

"Duran, sir," the man answered.

"Private Duran, did Miss Lockwood pass this way this evening?" Steele asked.

"We just changed the guard sir, but yes, sir, I believe so, sir. When I relieved Private Wilson, he went to notify Captain Kendrick that she had gone to Cabin Town. Captain Kendrick has ordered that he be notified if ever Miss Lockwood goes to Cabin Town, and then Captain Kendrick came by here a couple of minutes ago in a rush, sir."

****

Mersey heard the sound of a fist connecting with flesh and bone, and a grunt, and when she turned around, she saw Captain Kendrick in a fist fight with Jocko. He knocked Jocko to the ground, and then reached for his sidearm.

"Stand down, soldiers! By order of a superior officer, you are under arrest...." Kendrick began, unsnapping his leather holster, but Curly had recovered, and hit Kendrick from behind, striking him hard at the base of his neck with both fists clenched together. Kendrick fell to his knees.

Then both men were on him, hitting and kicking Kendrick with such viciousness that he struggled to defend himself from the blows.

Mersey curled her hands into fists and started to go to them when a fierce voice growled, "Stay back, Mersey!" and she froze.

Steele was a blur of movement as he threw Jocko and Curly off of Kendrick. The men rolled to their feet and turned on Steele, coming at him with murder in their eyes.

Steele's head snapped around at the merest hint of movement beside him, and then he faced forward again as Pou Nachay stepped out of the darkness to stand at his side.

Jocko's and Curly's eyes widened in shock at Pou Nachay's appearance, and both had a moment of pause before they attacked, launching themselves at the two men standing ready.

Steele caught Jocko in mid-air, and slammed him to the ground.

Pou Nachay shifted and caught Curly with a swift kick, spinning him in the air before he hit the ground. Side by side, Steele and Pou Nachay landed blow after blow to the faces and bodies of their attackers until both Jocko and Curly were writhing on the ground, bloody and groaning.

Master Sergeant Jennings came running to them then. "What's going on here?" he yelled. Then he looked at the faces of the men on the ground. "Jocko and Curly," he said, and swore.

"Master Sergeant Jennings, arrest these men for…." Steele ordered, but Jennings interrupted him.

"Now just a minute, sir," Jennings said, standing to face Steele, narrowing his eyes, throwing his thick shoulders back and lifting his massive chest.

Jennings stance was intended to intimidate, but it was wasted on Steele as he stared back at the master sergeant.

"These are two of my best fighters," Jennings said. "We can't go arrestin' them without hearing their side of the story, now can we. Just leave these two to me. Let me take care of this. You don't understand. Things are done different here in Cabin Town."

Jennings glanced over his shoulder at Mersey. He glowered at her before turning to glare at Steele. "She should have known better than to come here alone after dark."

Steele took a purposeful step toward the master sergeant, on some level acknowledging that the man was an experienced fighter and outweighed him by forty pounds of muscle, but not caring one bit.

"Their side of the story doesn't matter, Master Sergeant. No explanation can justify their actions. They assaulted a lady, and they attacked superior officers when ordered to stand down. That's a court-martial offense. You will arrest these men, Master Sergeant, or join them in the guardhouse," Steele said, his hand moving to his pistol.

Jennings tensed, and hesitated, as if indecision gripped him. He saw Steele's eyes flicker with something dangerous, and he said, "Yes, sir." He turned and stepped forward, reaching Jocko and Curly in one stride. To them he ordered, "Get up and get moving," and he followed them as they staggered, leaning on each other for balance, back toward the fort.

Pou Nachay moved to stand with Alameda and the children.

Mersey moved to help Kendrick, who was trying to get to his feet. She slipped her shoulder under his arm and her arm around his waist, steadying him.

"Thank you for helping us, Charles. I'm so sorry you are hurt," Mersey said.

"Mersey, I'm so glad that you're safe now. I was terrified that you would be harmed," Kendrick said. "I should have warned you not to…."

Steele strode to Kendrick, anger visible in every stride.

"Captain Kendrick," Steele barked. "I will make an appointment for us with Commander Lockwood as early as possible in the morning, and let you know exactly what time you are to arrive. A thorough written report as well as an oral report will be expected from you then regarding the lack of discipline among the volunteers."

Mersey felt Kendrick tense at Steele's command.

"Do you need assistance to return to the fort, Captain?" Steele asked, his eyes cutting to Mersey's arm still held firm around the captain's waist.

Kendrick straightened away from Mersey's support.

"I can make it, sir, and thank you. I am not eager to consider what may have occurred had you not arrived when you did," Kendrick said, and then he left the yard to return to the fort.

Steele watched Kendrick walk away, and when he cut his gaze to Mersey again, his face had turned to stone. All of his good intentions to respect her decisions had dissolved beneath his fear and outrage at what had almost happened to her. He wished he could pound his fists into those two animals all over again, and he found himself lashing out, but now she was his target. His eyes blazed as he stalked toward her, his words were commands, low and clipped, and dripping with his drawl.

"And you, Miss Lockwood, you are nev'ah, am I clear, nev'ah to set foot outside this fort again without an escort, day or night. And you are nev'ah to be without an escort after dark inside the fort."

Mersey stiffened at his *do NOT challenge me on this* tone.

Lifting her chin, she said, "My father…."

"Will hear of this near catastrophe, if not by you tonight, by me tomorrow," he growled.

He was standing close to Mersey now, and he was leaning toward her, nose to nose. His hands were on his hips, and his eyes were shooting flame.

"Your fath'ah will agree with me," he ground out through his teeth.

Mersey had lost the surge of terror and anger and protectiveness that, moments ago, had filled her with the courage to fight, leaving her shaking with relief. She knew what happened next, what always happened next, though she fought it.

Steele watched Mersey's eyes well with tears, and his rage vanished in a heartbeat. His arms ached to gather her to his chest and hold her close, to protect her from any threat and from all harm. He had been terrified for her when, in the firelight, he had seen her fighting against her assailant.

Kendrick had arrived moments before him, and Steele had the awful advantage of hearing Mersey's scream. Kendrick's intervention with the attackers had given Steele the time he needed to cover the distance to reach her.

Mersey turned her face toward Alameda and the children. All that had happened, the desperate helplessness of what would have occurred settled on her like a shroud. Her behavior had been naïve and unaware, unprepared for the menacing threat.

She looked back at Steele.

"What of them? This was a near catastrophe for them, too," she said, her voice breaking. "I am so grateful to you for what you did just now, but I am not the only one at risk here, John."

Mersey had an overwhelming need to touch him, to feel the solid strength of him. He was safety, their protector, their guardian. She lifted her hand and placed it over his heart as her tears began to fall.

"They need protection, too," she said.

Steele turned then and looked at Pou Nachay as he stood beside a very pregnant woman. He had placed his hands on the shoulders of two young children who clung to him, the same two Native Indian children that Mersey was with the first time he met her.

Tonight he had been so intent on getting to Mersey and keeping her from harm that he hadn't seen the others who were threatened.

Mersey watched John as he stared at Alameda and the children, and as he began to understand the enormity of the situation, the look on his face tugged at her heart.

Steele looked back at Mersey, and placed his hand over hers, and he was struck by another realization. No other woman of his acquaintance would have behaved in the way that Mersey had, would have risked her wellbeing for the sake of this family so different from her own. The women he knew, even the women in his family, would have considered these people beneath their notice. He stared into Mersey's eyes, her beautiful eyes, and he felt humble, and thankful.

"Thank you for making me see, for helping me understand," Steele said, and he very gently wiped Mersey's tears from her cheeks with the pads of this thumbs, and when he felt her trembling, he tucked his hand under her elbow for support, and brought her with him as he walked to Pou Nachay and his family.

"Ma'am," Steele said, tipping his hat to Alameda. He glanced at the children. "I am sorry about this violence tonight. These men will be jailed, and await trial. Are you and the children unharmed?"

When Alameda nodded, Steele turned to the scout that he had been more than glad to see step out of the dark to stand beside him.

"Pou Nachay, thank you for coming to our aid. You're a skilled fighter and a good man to have on our side in a fight," he said, extending his hand.

"I thank you for what you did to protect my sister and her children, Major," Pou Nachay said, grasping Steele's hand. Pou Nachay's eyes shifted to Mersey. "And you, Miss Lockwood, I thank you also."

Mersey wiped away the last of her tears and nodded to him. His handsome face was chiseled in sharp relief in the light from the campfire, his deep-set dark eyes shadowed under heavy brows. He stood ready to make any sacrifice, devoted to the protection of his family.

Mersey stepped forward and embraced Alameda, and then the children.

"I will see you tomorrow evening," she promised, and she felt Steele tense beside her, still holding her elbow in his warm grip, and then he led her away.

"Goodnight," Mersey called out, looking back at the family standing so still outside their cabin.

Mersey thought she heard Pou Nachay ask, "Alameda, were they the ones?"

Mersey heard no reply as she and Steele walked in silence to the fort, both lost in their own thoughts.

Steele greeted the sentries as they passed through the gate.

"Private Duran, did Master Sergeant Jennings bring two men through here to the guardhouse?" Steele asked.

"Yes sir," Duran answered.

"And did Captain Kendrick enter this way?" Steele asked.

"Yes sir," Duran replied again.

"Good," Steele said. "Have a good night, Private."

"Yes sir, thank you, sir, and a good night to you and Miss Lockwood," Duran said.

When they had walked a few steps more, Mersey turned to face Steele. "John, we need to help them, and the others in Cabin Town."

"Please trust me, Mersey. We'll find out what happened here. Give me a chance to sort this out."

Mersey's father jerked the door open when he heard footsteps on the boardwalk. When he saw her tear-streaked face and her disheveled appearance he said, "Come here, daughter," and he opened his arms to her.

Mersey looked up at Steele. "Please stay," she said, and then she stepped into her father's arms.

"Father, I'm sorry I didn't tell you where I was going," she said into his chest.

Graylon Lockwood patted his daughter's shoulder.

"All is forgiven," he said. "This time," he warned. Then to Steele he said, "Please come in, Major. Let's have a hot cup of tea, and you can tell me about it."

As Mersey recalled the events of the evening, she was not aware of the subtle reactions shared by her father and Major Steele when she recounted Curly's words that Captain Kendrick was not there to protect her, that Master Sergeant Jennings had their backs.

Steele noted that Mersey shivered after telling him and her father about the encounter with Curly and Jocko, and Steele thought she might be in a state of mild shock. He retrieved a shawl from a hook by the door, and draped it over her shoulders. She pulled it close around her, and gave him a grateful look.

"I agree with Major Steele, Mersey, about the escort, so please heed my wishes," her father said. "You escaped serious injury tonight, but I trust you will make no mistake such as this again."

"Father, I promised Alameda and the children that I would help them in the evenings to keep up with their studies," she said.

"Commander, I will see to her escort, if you will allow me," Steele said.

"Then you must join us for dinner, Major," Lockwood said, and when Mersey's head snapped up, he added, "An early dinner, tomorrow night. The Major and I may still have some questions for you about tonight, but they can wait until morning, my dear. Please try to get some rest now."

After Mersey left the room, Lockwood thanked Steele again for what he had done to protect Mersey.

Steele's emotions were still so tangled about Mersey and his part in aiding her that he only managed to mumble something about duty and honor.

The commander studied him for a moment, and then nodded.

Steele told Lockwood about Kendrick's order to be notified anytime Mersey went to Cabin Town, and about Master Sergeant Jennings' near-insubordination when told to arrest the men. He acknowledged that one would expect Jocko and Curly to be surprised to lose their two to one advantage over him in the fight, but the surprise he had seen in their eyes when Pou Nachay had stepped up beside him had seemed like more. He would check, but suspected he would find that the schedule had been changed at the last minute. The men plotted their assault while Pou Nachay was scheduled to be on patrol.

The commander agreed that they needed more information and investigation, before confronting Kendrick and Jennings, and that they would discuss this again after Kendrick gave them his reports.

December 12, 1862
Fort Garland

"Good evening, John," Mersey greeted as Steele accompanied her father into their small dining room Steele stepped forward, and returned her greeting. Her father watched them with a bemused expression, and she had to admit, she was looking forward to this dinner with equal parts anticipation and curiosity.

Steele's uniform had been brushed clean and his boots gleamed with high polish. He smelled of soap, and shaving cream, and leather. His dark hair was combed back, as it had grown longer, and curled a little at his nape. His cheeks were smooth, she noticed. He must have shaved a second time today.

He had taken extra care in his appearance, as though this casual dinner had mattered to him. And if she would admit it, it had begun to matter to her too.

She had prepared roast beef, buttered baked potatoes, cooked sliced carrots, fresh baked rolls, and she had made an apple pie to be served with cooled whipped cream for dessert. She knew the meal smelled very appetizing, but the anticipation she felt was centered upon the table.

She had set the sturdy wooden table with her mother's favorite white lace tablecloth. And then she had added the most glorious mismatch of china that she had ever devised. A man would have to be blind not to notice. Mersey struck a long match to light the tapered bees' wax candles at the center of the table, but John stepped up beside her.

"Allow me, Miss Lockwood," he said, and she handed him the match.

Her eyes were drawn to his hands as he cupped the flame. His fingertips were calloused, the nails clean and trimmed short. His hands were tanned and broad and strong, steady and sure in their movement as he lit the tapers. And then her eyes went to his face, watching his concentration, until his eyes met hers, and she looked away.

"Thank you," Mersey said as he snuffed out the match. "Won't you sit down, Major," she invited, gesturing toward the chair opposite her father's.

But he moved behind her chair, and helped her be seated. She thanked him again.

The commander opened a bottle of red wine, moved to fill the three lovely but very different wine glasses on the table, and then he took his own seat.

"Mersey, would you please say grace for us?" the commander said.

Mersey nodded, reached for her father's hand, then turned and met Steele's eyes with a questioning look. He smiled and turned his hand palm up as it rested on the table. She placed her fingers lightly in his palm, and then his fingers curled around hers.

"Heavenly Father, we thank You for Your guiding light in all things, and for the loving care You give us. Help us to walk in the path of service and duty with honor and compassion, to give the best of ourselves to those around us in need, and to always look for the good in others. Please protect our men in uniform," she said tightening her grip on Steele's and her father's hands, "As they protect all of us. Amen."

"Amen," Steele and the commander echoed, as Mersey raised her head and looked at Steele when he didn't release her hand.

It occurred to Steele that in the past month, he had experienced a greater uplift of mood and emotion in the company of this woman than he had felt in the previous year. She was desirable to him, in all ways.

His eyes held hers for a moment longer as he held her hand, and then he said, "Thank you, that made me feel more at home than you can imagine."

Mersey felt her heart warm at the tenderness she saw in Steele's expression. He was a remarkable man. He was a natural protector, a warrior, a man of strong conviction and self-assuredness, and yet he could still see things through another's eyes. And there was a vulnerability to him, a longing for home and the family that he had been honor-bound to leave behind.

She felt drawn to the complexity of his character, and she was coming to care about him, to care for him. She looked at the table and at her mismatched settings, and she felt herself a great fool for her *test*.

She had used this little exercise to keep men at arm's length, but now, with John Steele sitting next to her at their table, she wondered if it would still matter to her if this man noticed or cared not at all.

But was any man worth the loss of her independence? Aunt Andrea didn't think so, and Mersey knew her aunt's arguments by memory for she had heard them on numerous occasions. *A woman should retain her right to make her own decisions, achieve an education so as to support herself without dependence on the approval of a man*, Aunt Andrea had expounded.

Aunt Andrea held men's archaic views that a woman know her place, that a woman's place is in the home, in righteous contempt. That a woman should only leave her home on three occasions, when christened, married, and buried, were fighting words if spoken to Aunt Andrea. And at age thirty one, vivacious Aunt Andrea celebrated being firmly *on the shelf.* She prided herself in the success of thus far avoiding the Great State of Matrimony, though she had a long-standing social relationship with Mr. Zander, a very nice, attentive and attractive, educated and liberal gentleman.

Her Aunt had confessed to Mersey once that Mr. Zander had a valid argument in favor of marriage, as she could then bring into the world a number of enlightened offspring to better balance the, as yet, unenlightened. Aunt Andrea had nevertheless often used Mersey's mother as an example of the price of loving a man, letting that love conquer all, forfeiting dreams to allow the goals of the man usurp one's own, and suffering for it in the back of beyond, in places like Fort Garland.

Mersey only wished she could hear her mother's side of it, to know if her mother had ever regretted her decision to marry the man she loved, to follow him, to bear a child for him. Her mother had been an accomplished pianist, and had taught Mersey to play. Had her mother given up her dreams? Or had she replaced them with new ones?

Her thoughts were brought back to the present when the commander cleared his throat.

"Well now, let's eat. I'm starving," he said. "But first, a toast to life, may it be long, and contented."

"Here, here," Steele said, and three mismatched crystal glasses clinked together.

Steele felt Mersey's eyes on him as the food was passed and plates were filled. He had noticed the clever setting of mismatched china, and knew a trap had been laid, but he kept his eyes and expression neutral. He didn't stop to consider why it was so important to him that he pass this test.

On the other hand, he knew any gentleman worth his salt must compliment the meal. He could likewise fail *the test* if he neglected to remark on Mersey's efforts to create this masterpiece of imperfection. The commander seemed to be watching him with some expectation, and gave him a small encouraging nod. He must say something and the time was now.

Steele reached for his napkin, stalling he knew, rehearsing his comment in his head, then he took a breath. He smiled what he hoped was a beguiling smile, and said, "Miss Lockwood, I must compliment you on your table arrangement, a most charming selection, and all of my favorite colors are here, the colors of a beautiful sunset."

Mersey gaped at him, eyes wide, speechless for a long moment, and then at last she stammered, "Thank you, these are my favorite colors too."

The commander cut a bite of roast, feigning disinterest, but grinned at his daughter's expression, and he winked at Steele when he also complimented Mersey on the savory meal.

The Commander agreed, and with a self-deprecating smile admitted, "Mersey learned to cook from her Aunt Andrea, my sister. If I cook, you need a sharp knife to cut the gravy."

Steele smiled. "I rather like to cook," he said, "Though I don't get much chance anymore."

He caught Mersey's surprised expression, and then she said, "If you have the inclination, feel free to commandeer my kitchen."

"I'd like that," he said, and his eyes met hers.

The commander chose that moment to volunteer himself and the major for kitchen duty, and Mersey left the room to gather the school lessons that she would take to Cochetopa and Antera.

****

As the two officers washed and dried, Lockwood said, "We received word that Seagram, the general leading the Texas Volunteers, has left Fort Thorn and is marching north along the Rio Grande. His scouts have been seen as far north as Fort Craig."

"Do we know his numbers, Commander?" Steele asked.

"Nothing reliable, and please call me Graylon in my home," Lockwood answered. "I can't imagine how Seagram is supplying his forces. They can't bring them along the Santa Fe Trail past Fort Union. That much is clear."

"Is he getting supplies from the area as he moves up the river?" Steele asked.

Lockwood answered, "There is very near nothing to forage in New Mexico this time of year. Winter stores will be close to depleted, and new crops won't be planted for months. Most small farms can produce what the families need to live on, but nothing more. There may be some cattle and wild game, but the temperatures are still very cold, and there is still deep snow, even in the valleys. The way north from Texas on the Rio Grande between Fort Fillmore and the town of Albuquerque is two hundred miles of hostile wilderness, including a desert passage known as the *Journey of Death*."

Lockwood paused for a moment then continued. "The majority of the people who live in New Mexico are poor, so there is very little to commandeer, and no large cities to capture and plunder. The supplies in the abandoned forts have been moved or destroyed."

Lockwood shook his head. "Reports say that Seagram had to abandon some of his own supplies because he didn't have the animals to pull the wagons. Without those wagonloads of supplies, he had to move his troops north in snowstorms, without tents, extra clothing, or bedding. His choices were to move forward and fight, stay where he was and starve, or retreat."

"He has chosen to move forward and fight," Steele said, and Lockwood nodded, his expression grim.

"We received orders today from General Canfield to send as many infantry volunteers to Fort Craig as we can spare and still keep this fort secure," Lockwood said.

"With your permission, I'll speak to Captain Roberts tomorrow, have him ready his company," Steele said.

"Yes, I believe that would be prudent. I'll send an orderly as a messenger to Fort Craig at daybreak to let General Canfield know of our intentions," he said.

The men finished their kitchen duty in silence, each lost in thought.

The Way of Things

The following Monday morning, Mersey had begun class when Cochetopa threw open the door to the school room. Antera stood behind him. Mersey started to ask him why he was late, when she realized that Alameda had said that he wouldn't be there at all. And then she looked at his face. He looked terrified. Both children were flushed and out of breath.

Mersey asked two of the older children to take over class, grabbed her cloak from the hook, and hurried out the door with Cochetopa and Antera.

"What's happened? Is it your mother?" she asked.

They nodded.

"Is she having the baby?" Mersey asked.

They both shook their heads.

"The men hurt her," Antera said on a sob.

"Let's go," Mersey said, grabbing their hands, and they sprinted to Pou Nachay's cabin.

Mersey followed the children through the door and then into a bedroom. Alameda lay in the bed, her hand resting on her pregnant belly, her face turned toward the wall. When they entered, she turned to look at them, and Mersey gasped.

She had been beaten. Her eyes were black and blue and swollen, her nose bloody, her lips split and swollen. She had red finger marks on her cheeks and neck, and bruises on her hands, wrists and forearms where she must have tried to defend herself.

Mersey turned to the children.

"Cochetopa, I need a bowl with water and some clean towels. Can you get them for me? And Antera, would you find your mother a clean nightgown?"

The children nodded and ran to the shelves in the hallway, getting the items, happy to be doing something to help their mother. Cochetopa poured water into the bowl from a pitcher. Antera opened a small wooden trunk and got a clean gown and towels. Mersey wet the cloth, and with gentle strokes, cleaned the blood from Alameda's face.

She sent the children into the other room before helping Alameda out of the blood spattered dress she was wearing, and into the clean gown. Mersey almost sobbed at the bruises on Alameda's thighs.

"Was it Jocko and Curly?" Mersey asked.

Alameda hesitated, then nodded.

"The other night, Pou Nachay asked if it was them. Has this happened to you before?"

Alameda looked away, swallowed, and nodded again. When she looked back, her eyes were bleak. When she spoke, her speech was soft and not quite clear through the swelling in her lips, and Mersey had to lean close to hear.

"It is the way of things," Alameda said. "Men are stronger than women, and some men will take what they want. It was so with my mother. When my mother was a maiden, it was her monthly woman's time, and so she was bathing alone at a stream. An Apache brave was spying upon her Ute village, and he saw her. He wanted her, and he stole her from her family, and took her to his village."

Alameda paused and asked for a drink of water. Mersey found a cup, poured water from the pitcher, and helped Alameda to drink a few swallows.

Then Alameda continued. "My mother told me that she did not want this man for a husband, and she was a maiden, but he took her, and it was the way of things."

She paused again, and then took another sip of water when Mersey offered it to her.

"My uncle and his good friend followed after the Apache man for over a year, searching for my mother at every camp they found. My uncle vowed to find her and steal her back, and bring her home. He made his friend promise to care for her if something happened to him, and when they found her, they waited, and waited, until they could steal her back. But my mother's Apache husband discovered them and fought my uncle and killed him. Then his friend killed the Apache warrior."

Alameda closed her eyes. Mersey thought her too exhausted to continue, and was about to slip away to arrange transport for Alameda to the infirmary. But after a moment, Alameda spoke again.

"My mother had Pou Nachay by then," Alameda said. "He was not much older than a newborn babe. She told my uncle's friend that she loved her son and could not leave him. It was not the fault of the babe that he was born, and that there was good in him. The babe was the grandson of an Apache chief, but she would give him a Ute name, and he would walk the Ute path. My uncle's friend agreed, and brought Pou Nachay with them, and my uncle's friend soon after married my mother. My uncle's friend became my father, and what my mother had said was the truth. There is only good in Pou Nachay, and he walks the path of a Ute man."

Mersey knelt beside the bed.

"So you told no one, not even Pou Nachay, because it was the way of things?" Mersey asked.

"Yes," Alameda said. "And there is only good in this child too. I feel the truth in this."

"Did the men ever threaten or hurt the children?" Mersey asked, terrified of the answer.

"No," Alameda said. "I told them if they touched my children, I would tell Pou Nachay, and he would kill them."

"Why didn't you let Pou Nachay protect you too?" Mersey asked.

"Because they are white men, and he is Ute. If he killed them, he would be hanged." She shook her head. "I could not let that happen, though he raged at me to tell him."

"And Master Sergeant Jennings, he is a white man. Why did you not tell him?" Mersey asked.

Alameda met Mersey's eyes. "It is because he is a white man," she said.

"I'm going to get my father, and we'll get you moved into the infirmary. I'll take the children with me now if you want," Mersey said.

"No, they will be fine here now. Thank you for coming," she said.

Mersey nodded. "Pou Nachay?" She asked.

"Out on patrol," Alameda said.

****

Steele sat at the commander's desk reading the ledgers that Lockwood had asked him to review. Everything appeared to be in perfect order, making Kendrick's false accusations even more of a mystery.

He didn't know Kendrick well, but this seemed out of character for the man. He looked up when he heard the door to the commander's quarters open and then heard Mersey's voice. Wasn't this a school day?

He stood.

"Is my father here, Lieutenant?" Mersey asked, and there was urgency in her voice.

"No, Miss," Lieutenant Hawkins said, "But..."

"Will he be back soon?" she asked, sounding even more urgent.

"No, Miss. He went to survey the gorge, and won't be back until near dark, and..." he began.

But Mersey was out the door.

Steele stepped out of the office and walked to the door. When he opened it, he saw Mersey enter the school house. Maybe he was wrong about the sound of her voice. Maybe she was just excited about something. He returned to his desk, feeling uncertain. He didn't realize until just then how much he wanted her to come to him when she was troubled.

Several minutes later, the door opened again.

"Miss Lockwood," Hawkins greeted.

Steele saw Mersey all but run past the open office door without a glance. And when he saw her face, he knew something was very wrong.

The door opened once again, and Hawkins greeted a sergeant named Orin Bell. He was the blacksmith and everyone called him Smithy. Smithy appeared at the commander's door and wrapped his knuckles against it, though Steele saw him there.

"Come in, Sergeant Bell. What can I do for you?"

"Well, Major Steele, about that, uh, it's about Miss Lockwood," he said.

"What about Miss Lockwood?" Steele asked.

"Well, sir, I'm not sure what to make of it."

"Make of what, Sergeant?"

Steele remembered Mersey's face just moments ago, and fought the need to go to her and find out what was troubling her. Bell reclaimed Steele's attention.

"You see, she just paid me a visit…." Bell said, then hesitated.

"And?" Steele prompted, his sense of unease building.

"Well, sir, when she first started talking to me, I thought she was asking me to build a cabin out of iron, or another Merrimac battleship, or something." Sergeant Bell scratched his head. "She was upset and talking so fast."

Steele nodded. "Go on," he said, feeling ready to shake the information out of the man.

"What I figured out was that she wanted iron bolts made for all of the cabin doors in Cabin Town, windows too, and maybe iron doors and walls, sir. So I thought I'd check with you to see what I was supposed to do."

"Let me get back to you on that, Sergeant. Thanks for checking with me," Steele said, placing his hand on the man's shoulder and escorting him from the room.

****

Steele could hear Mersey moving around inside the dining room, so he knocked on the closed door.

When she didn't answer, he announced, "I'm coming in, Mersey," then he stepped into the room.

Mersey was pacing like a caged lioness. She glared at him, and he knew, as her father had once described, she had moved beyond tears to steam.

He had prepared a few thoughtful, encouraging opening statements to get her to tell him what had driven her to order a battleship from the blacksmith, but when his eyes fell on a plate full of muffins on the table sitting next to a .45 caliber pistol, all of his preparation went out the window.

"Is that gun loaded?" he heard himself ask.

She all but snarled at him, only glancing at him in her pacing.

"Yes, and the muffins will soon be decorated with arsenic frosting, so now that you have seen them, I will no doubt be at the top of your suspect list."

"Alright then, am I to understand that you are contemplating murder as well as manning your own battleship?" Steele asked. "This is the Army you know, not the Navy,"

His attempt at humor fell appallingly flat in her state of distress. Mersey avoided his eyes and kept pacing, as if she were lost in her own private world.

"Mersey, stop pacing and look at me!"

She looked up at him then, meeting his eyes, and the terrible pain he saw in hers struck him like a blow. He watched her stopped pacing and an ocean of tears threatened to fall from those lovely eyes.

Mersey was afraid to let go. She held herself rigid, fighting the need to let John take this terror from her, to place her burden on the strength of his broad shoulders. She was the person that Alameda had taken into her confidence, the one Alameda trusted to keep it. But she needed someone to keep Alameda and the children safe. She couldn't protect them on her own. Not even Pou Nachay could protect them, not alone. She couldn't keep Alameda's confidence and keep her out of harm's way.

John stood before her, capable, powerful, wanting to help, and with the authority to get it done. She needed John. She needed the strength and resolve etched in his handsome features, needed his focused intelligence, his unrelenting determination to protect, his iron will to serve.

Once she admitted that to herself, her body threatened to collapse, and when he spoke again, it was her undoing.

"Can you not tell me what is troubling you so?" he asked, his eyes dark with concern, the fierceness of his expression softening, "can you not trust me?"

As Steele had seen her father do, he opened his arms, and when she rushed into them, he wrapped her close to his chest as her tears began to fall.

As she clung to him, her face buried against his chest, her sorrow seeped into him, her grief became his, her tears and warm breath binding him to her, filling his heart, and he wanted to hold her close to him forever, wanted her to belong with him, and he wanted her to feel about him the way he was starting to feel about her. Her lavender eyes looked up at him now, and as he looked back into her eyes, he knew he would move heaven and earth to do anything that she asked of him within his power to provide, and the realization almost took him to his knees.

In that moment he made a vow, that he would never relinquish the care of her, the protection of her, unless to someone more able than himself. It was as simple and as life-changing as that. His need to keep her safe surged over him, not just for the soldier, but for the man. No matter if she didn't return his feelings, anything in his power to do for her, he would do.

He rocked her in his arms, stroked her hair, murmured soothing words, and then she began to talk to him. She held him tight as the story spilled from her, and he felt his rage burn and his blood run cold.

When she finished, she asked, "Will you go with me to bring her to the infirmary? I believe she is too weak to make it on her own."

"Yes, sweetheart, of course I will go with you," he said as his gentle hands wiped tears from her cheeks.

Mersey wondered if he realized that he had spoken an endearment to her, spoken it in a deep, soft drawl that had thrilled her heart. But she couldn't think about it now. Alameda needed them.

Mersey took John's hand and led him to the door. In silence, they donned their coats. As they opened the door to leave, Mersey looked up at John.

"I'm a dead-on accurate shot with a pistol at fifty paces. Father taught me. I just wanted you to know that."

Steele nodded. They left together for Cabin Town.

Making It Right

Alameda was settled in the infirmary, resting, being cared for by the doctor, but she hadn't answered any of Steele's questions. She either didn't know the answer or was refusing to answer questions that could explain Kendrick and Jennings' involvement.

Steele had confided to Mersey that he suspected the captain and the master sergeant were being blackmailed or taking bribes, or both, to look the other way when the volunteers strayed from rules of conduct, but it couldn't be proven yet. He was also making it an imperative to find out how Jocko and Curly had escaped the jail.

After leaving the infirmary, Mersey walked to the stables. She wanted to find Sergeant Sandoval. She found Sergeant Bell at his bellows, heating a horseshoe over the fire. He wore a heavy glove that extended to the middle of his left forearm, held the red hot curved piece of iron with tongs and pounded the now pliable metal with a small sledge hammer held in his ungloved right hand. He was shirtless. A leather apron covered his chest and the front of his trousers, his suspenders hung at his thighs, his massive arm muscles gleamed with sweat from the heat of the fire, and his upper body was coated with black ash.

Sergeant Bell looked up when Mersey entered, smiled when she waved, and returned to his task. She wondered if he had begun working on the iron bolts for the women's cabins in Cabin Town.

Major Steele had agreed to have the bolts made for the doors and windows as soon as possible, and had provisioned that the cabins were to be rebuilt in a barracks style to increase security, and also add chimneys and stoves and better flooring for warmth.

Images of John had been invading her thoughts, remembering the strength of his arms when he held her, making her feel protected, almost cherished. He didn't seem to mind her tears, didn't tell her to stop, just tried to comfort her, to listen and then take action to make it better. She was learning to trust him.

His handsome face and the way he looked at her with his intense gray eyes were starting to invade her dreams as well. She didn't know what to make of his mismatched china comment. His compliment had fitted her sentiments as exact and perfect as she could have imagined. But her father acted a little too proud of himself when she mentioned it to him, and she suspected that she had been out-maneuvered.

Sergeant Sandoval and a private named Brooks stepped out of the last horse's stall on the right, closed the gate and then saw Mersey waiting near the first stall. Private Brooks' eyes widened and he started to say something, but Sandy stayed him with a hand held up.

"Miss Mersey, now come away from that stall, nothing to be alarmed about, but just move away," Sandy said.

Mersey glanced into the stall and met the big liquid brown eyes of The Black. The Black looked back at her, pounded one hoof on the ground and snorted.

"I think he smells the apples in my pocket," Mersey said, reaching inside her cloak, and offering a small dried apple to The Black on her flat palm through the separation in the wooden fence.

The Black sniffed it, then snatched it so quickly that Mersey's eyes widened. "Well," she said, looking back at Sandy, who looked like he was staring at a grizzly bear.

Sandy kept his voice low and calm. "Miss Mersey, please step away from that gate. That one is as black as the devil, and acts like him most of the time. I ain't ever seen him let anyone but the Major within three feet a' him, let alone…. Just come away from him, please, Miss," Sandy repeated.

Mersey moved toward Sandy, away from the stall. "And now you know that the secret to make him act like a sweetie is to bribe him with apples," she said.

Sandy looked doubtful. "Could be, Miss," he said. "Now, just what are ya needin' here with the likes of us?" he asked.

"I want to take a buggy to San Luis, one with a back platform, and I'm not…." she began.

"…S'posed to leave the fort without an escort," he finished for her.

"How….?" she began again.

"That ship done sailed, Miss. The word is all over the fort, and we're s'posed to know where you're headed and why and how long you will be gone."

"Who…?" she asked, but Sandy interrupted again.

"The Major done already been in here," he said, then smiled at her exasperated expression. "It ain't no trouble getting' an escort for ya. Why I 'spect these young fellas 'ull be trippin' all over each other ta do the escortin'." His smile widened. "Ya said ya be needin' a buggy?" he asked.

"Yes, a buggy with a back platform. And to answer your other questions, my Aunt from Massachusetts sent me a sewing machine and a big box of thread and fabric, and the South Patrol yesterday brought a message from Don Ricardo's store in San Luis that the machine was left there by mistake, and that I can come pick it up," she said.

"It's a buckboard that ya be needin' then. 'Bout five hours round trip, I reckon," Sandy said.

Mersey nodded. "It's a new Wheeler and Wilson, with four-stroke motion and locking stitches, and it can sew two hundred fifty stitches a minute, Sandy," she said with a small smile.

Yesterday, she couldn't wait to show the machine to Alameda, who would get ten times the work done in the same amount of time. Mersey had planned to loan it to her. But all the joy she had felt for the machine had gone out of her when Alameda was hurt, a joy Mersey was slow to recover. Maybe there was still a chance for joy in the new machine when Alameda's good health was restored.

"That there sewin' machine sounds right handy, Miss. Two hundred fifty stitches a minute, that's somethin' fer sure," Sandy said. "I wonder, can it sew leather bridles an' cinches? I work these ol' fingers ta the bone tryin' to run a needle through them tough pieces of leather."

"As soon as I get it, and learn how to use it, we'll find out," Mersey said.

"We'll get that buckboard hitched up for ya right away, Miss, and find ya an escort," he assured her.

"There's a new foal, a pretty little filly just like her mama down there in that last stall if ya want to take a peek at her while ya wait."

"Yes, I'll do that, thanks, Sandy," Mersey said, then walked toward the last stall.

Some moments passed and Mersey began to wonder if something had come up that needed Sandy's attention more than she needed the buckboard. She left the stall, locked the gate, and had a near collision with Master Sergeant Jennings. He looked to be in a rush, and he was watching her in an assessing way that made her feel uneasy. Mersey started to walk down the center path between the stalls, but the master sergeant blocked her way.

"Please excuse me, Master Sergeant," she said.

"I don't think so, ma'am," he said. "I'm obliged to be the one to take you to Don Ricardo's store."

Mersey was sure that a master sergeant didn't need to be taken from his post when any soldier would do just fine as an escort, and Master Sergeant Jennings had always acted like she was a pain in his backside. It didn't make sense that he would volunteer.

"Thank you for your offer, Master Sergeant, but the trip will take half a day and I'm sure Major Steele…." she began.

"Would like to ask me a few questions right about now, and I can't….I need to find those two deserters and bring them back. Maybe I can redeem myself in this mess, but I can't do it from inside a jail cell in Fort Leavenworth waiting to hang. You helped get me into this, and now you're going to help me get out," he said to her.

Mersey's eyes widened, and then she looked down the path, but saw no one, not Sandy, not Private Brooks, and even the blacksmith was no longer at the bellows.

Jennings was studying her. "Just in case you think there will be someone to come along and rescue you, I sent the men on errands that will keep them busy for a while. They might have been led to think that they were needed right away at the practice field," he said and shrugged. "A small exaggeration, but then I needed to get out of here unobserved."

He glanced at the horse hitched to the buckboard, then turned back to Mersey and said, "And taking you to Don Ricardo's store just gave me the perfect cover to get out of here."

Mersey felt the skin prickle on the back of her neck. "Master Sergeant, I don't understand what you're talking about. My trip can wait. I am sure...."

"You don't understand?" he gave a harsh laugh. "When I took Jocko and Curly to the guardhouse that night, I told the guard that they were just there to sleep it off, that they'd been drinking, and as soon as they were sober, they could be let go."

She gasped. So they hadn't escaped. They had been released.

"That's right, I disobeyed a direct order, and the Major, no doubt, knows that by now, but I had good reason. You're the cause of all of this, you and your interfering ways. I'm through here because of you, and now I'll be on the run and hunted, unless I can find where Jocko and Curly are holed up and bring them back to pay for what they did, or die trying," he said.

Mersey startled as Jennings grabbed her arm and began pulling her down the path. Though his grip was not painful or brutal, he was such a strong man that her efforts to resist were ineffectual.

"And now I've got you for cover. You're coming with me. You won't be hurt if you do as you're told. I'll let you go as soon as I get a head start. That Pou Nachay can track a snowflake in a blizzard. I got to get to those men before he does." he said. He must have seen the panic on her face because he added, "Don't even think about screaming for help. I swear I'll shoot to kill anyone who tries to stop me."

"That would only get you into more trouble, Master Sergeant. Can't you just explain and maybe I can help…." Mersey said, trying to delay him.

"It's too late for that," he said, His voice held a miserable, bitter tone, maybe even regret.

"You have no idea what you did, getting those men into trouble. You upset a fine balance, and any control I had over those lawless men slipped away. They were swearing revenge, but I thought they were too drunk to remember," he said. "Men like that never admit that they did anything wrong, only blame others because they got caught."

They were nearing the buckboard and Mersey saw that another horse's reins were tied to the back of the platform, a horse belonging to Jennings, she was sure.

"I would have stopped them, Jocko and Curly, if I'd known what they planned to do. It was too late by the time I found out. I was too late, and they were on the run. What you don't seem to understand, ma'am, is that many of our regular army were called back to fight in the East, and some of our good men left to fight for the South. Now we are relying on a bunch of volunteer soldiers. All of those volunteers are good fighters, but they're former miners or trappers or prospectors, men whose dreams of treasure never panned out. Maybe they lost their land, or just lost their way."

He was quiet for a moment, but then he looked at her. He looked defeated, and he seemed to be rambling in his speech, rationalizing his actions.

"I was doing the best I could, but most of them don't care about rules or laws, or even what their Creator might think of them. They lived too long in the wilderness, answering only to Mother Nature, and it took compromise to keep them in line," he stated.

"Your compromise was to let them terrorize and force themselves on a woman who wasn't willing, instead of going to the women who were," she said. "Alameda lived in fear of them. They raped her."

Jennings' face lost all color. He looked stricken. "I heard rumors, but I wasn't sure," he said. "Alameda never came to me. Certain women in Cabin Town ease the needs of the men, and keep those men from threatening the women in the fort." He shook his head, slowing as they reached the buckboard, then he added, "She's a Native Indian."

"That doesn't change what happened to her," she said.

"Not to you or me, but those men, as with many of the rest of them, when they encountered any Native Indians in the past, those same Indians were trying to kill them. Those men had no respect for the woman, or Pou Nachay, for that matter, but I would have kept them away from her if I'd known. But it's too late for that now." He met her eyes. "Ask Captain Kendrick. They threatened him, too."

At her questioning look, he nodded.

"With you," he said, "They threatened Kendrick with harm to you. It was pitiful how easy it was to get to him. All anyone had to do was look at his face when he looks at you to know he would do anything to protect you. He knew he couldn't protect you all the time, especially since you insisted on visiting Cabin Town, insisted on trying to improve things. You have no idea how dangerous it is there for anyone who tries to interfere."

Mersey wanted to keep Jennings talking, slow him down, prevent him from taking her out of the fort, but she must not endanger anyone else. He threatened to kill anyone who got in his way. He said he wouldn't hurt her, that he would let her go, but he was determined and desperate, and volatile.

"I'm sure if you told all of this to my father that…."

"No," he said as he dragged her forward again. "No more talking. Get into the buckboard, now!"

He was hurrying, and he was nervous, his voice was gruff and threatening, and it had an effect on the mare hitched to the buckboard that he should have anticipated. When he released the knot tying the reins to the hitching post, the mare shied away from him, and he had to let go of Mersey to grab the bridle and try to calm the animal.

In his moments of distraction, Mersey backed away from him toward the stalls. Jennings and the buckboard were between her and the stable door. She wouldn't make it past him if she ran. She opened the stall nearest her and closed the gate, then she huddled into the shadows in the corner of the stall.

When Jennings once again had the mare under control, he glanced at the empty pathway, and started glancing into every stall, skipping the first one when he recognized the horse that occupied it and working his way down.

"If you don't get out here now, I'll set this place on fire, killing you and every animal in here. Do you hear me! Get out here now!"

Mersey froze. He wouldn't do that would he? That would bring everyone running, but then it might be easier for him to escape.

Instead, she heard him at the end of the stalls, and he started opening gates, yelling, "Get! Get!"

She heard the repeated cracking of a whip. Horses raced passed her hiding place, as one by one, they were driven from their stalls. If she tried to flee the stables, frightened horses would trample her before she reached safety. She crouched low and moved with slow cautious footsteps toward the horse standing in the center of the stall.

When she reached him, she petted his nose, spoke in soft, crooning tones to him, easing him toward the gate. She grabbed a handful of his mane, placed the toe of her half-boot between the fence slats, mounted him bareback, and lay low against his back, her face against his neck.

****

"On whose authority were the prisoners released, Corporal?" Steele asked, feeling his anger surge.

"Prisoners, sir?" the corporal stammered. "Master Sergeant Jennings told us that Jocko and Curly were drunk and needed to sleep it off, that they could be released as soon as they sobered up. We didn't even lock the cell and they left as soon as they woke up. We weren't told that they'd been arrested, sir."

As Steele strode out of the guardhouse, he met Sergeant Sandoval and Private Brooks coming back from the direction of the training field.

Sandy was muttering something about a wild goose chase when Steele asked, "Sandy, have you seen Master Sergeant Jennings?"

"Yes sir," Sandy said. "He was just at the stables, and I'll swear he sent us on a snipe hunt. Told us and Smithy we was needed on the trainin' field. Didn't make much sense at the time, and made less sense when we seen Captain Kendrick and he said he ain't sent for us when Jennings said he had."

Sandy scratched his head. "He probably ain't still there, though, said he would escort Miss Mersey to Don Ricardo's store in San Luis." He looked at Steele's face. "Somethin's wrong here, ain't it?"

Steele nodded. "Private Brooks, check with the sentries to see if they've left the fort. Sandy...." he said, but it wasn't necessary to finish. They were both running toward the stables.

****

Mersey stroked the horse's neck, keeping him calm, when Jennings wrenched the gate open.

"Hee-yaw! Get!" he roared and cracked the whip.

The horse bolted through the open gate with Mersey clinging to him. They had almost made it to freedom when Jennings saw Mersey's skirts draped over the horse's back, and at the last possible moment, he grabbed the bridle, pulling the horse's head around.

The horse wrenched back, dragging the big man out the stable door and into the open ground surrounding the stables. But Jennings didn't let go, and when the horse threw back his head, he lifted Jennings off the ground. Then with one powerful whip of the horse's neck, Jennings lost his grip, hit the ground and skidded to an abrading stop.

Jennings started to get to his feet. The horse whinnied and reared, rolling his front hooves like sharp, airborne pistons.

Steele and Sandy stopped dead in their tracks at the unbelievable sight before them.

Mersey was riding The Black, bareback, holding her body close against his back, her face against his neck, hands buried in his mane. Mersey's hair was flying loose as The Black reared, readying to crush the man who was struggling to stand up.

"Jennings! Freeze!" Steele shouted. "Stay down!"

Jennings turned toward Steele's voice just as The Black's hooves came down, hitting Jennings square on the upper back, knocking him to the ground, and then Jennings lay unmoving.

The Black danced back, his head lifting and dipping, his eyes on the man on the ground.

Steele stood still, not wanting to startle his enraged horse. "Easy boy, easy," Steele said, extending his hand palm up.

The Black looked at Steele then, recognizing his master's voice, and walked forward. Reaching Steele, he stopped, and waited to be petted, but after only one stroke, his master moved to his side, and The Black turned his head to watch his master lift the woman from his back.

Mersey clung to Steele as he held her crushed against his chest. He felt the tears on her soft cheek as it rested against the roughness of his.

"Thank you, Dear God," he breathed, and could say nothing more.

****

Alameda watched Jennings walk into the infirmary unaided and escorted by two guards. He turned his pain-filled blue eyes to look at her, and she cast her eyes down.

His back was bleeding from an injury. He carried himself with a stiffness that told her it hurt him to move. He groaned when one of the guards pushed him on his shoulder to sit down on the bed. Then shackles were attached to Jennings' ankles, securing him to the bed frame.

"Sorry, ma'am," a guard said to Alameda. "We'll make sure that a privacy curtain is placed between you and this prisoner. You will be safe, ma'am. A guard will be present at all times."

The doctor entered the infirmary. He looked first at Alameda, then at Jennings. He moved to Jennings and asked what happened.

"I was trampled by a horse, sir," Jennings said.

"Just on your back?" the doctor asked.

"Yes sir," Jennings said.

The doctor nodded, and started to remove Jennings shirt. Torn pieces of his shirt were imbedded into the wounds, and adhered to the cuts with dried blood. Jennings gave a small cry when the doctor attempted to rip the torn shirt from the first wound, and fresh blood began to flow.

Jennings gritted his teeth and struggled to control his reaction to the pain. The first cut revealed on his upper back was deep, curved to the precise size of a large horseshoe. The surrounding skin was swollen and discolored in massive purple and blue bruising.

Alameda couldn't stand the suffering she could see and hear being inflicted on the master sergeant, no matter her feelings for him, and she knew how to help ease his pain. She had regained some of her strength, and her own bruises had faded. She pulled back her covers, and climbed out of bed. When she moved to stand beside the doctor, he turned to her in surprise.

"Ma'am, what are you doing?" he asked.

"If you but soak the cloth in warm water for a few minutes, it will come free and not cause more damage to the injury," she said.

She kept her eyes downcast, but when she glanced up, Jennings was staring at her, looking….grateful. She looked away. She swayed from her exertion, and the doctor helped her back to bed.

"Don't worry about this man. Please, just rest."

Alameda settled back onto her bed. Her breath caught as she felt the muscles in her belly cramp. She wasn't ready, not in body or mind to begin her labor, but she knew that was not a choice she had the power to make.

Hidden Strength

Sweat beaded on Alameda's forehead. She gasped in agony. The brutal, burning contractions racked her belly, gripping her with a thousand pins and needles, robbing her breath, and forcing a sob from her throat. How many hours had she been at this? It felt much longer than with Antera, or even her first time with Cochetopa. Though she struggled to endure each one, she knew these contractions were not strong enough. Was something wrong with her baby, or with her? At least there was no bleeding, she thought, not yet.

The doctor had just left, and Mersey had come to sit with her. It was kind, but Alameda preferred to be alone, preferred to find a private place, as the labor of birth was between a woman and her baby.

When the contraction eased, Mersey asked, "Would you like a sip of water, Alameda?"

Alameda accepted the drink of water and asked, "Are my children here?"

"They are waiting outside. Would you like to see them?" Mersey asked.

"Yes," Alameda said. "Just for a minute, and not when I have a pain through my belly, but not yet. I want to speak to you about something."

Mersey nodded.

"This baby, she is having trouble coming," Alameda said. And when Mersey smiled, she added, "Yes, I believe she is a little girl. I want her name to be Salayah, for my good childhood friend, who always got me into happy mischief. Please remember. If the child is a boy, Pou Nachay will name him."

"Alameda, please don't talk like…."

"Pou Nachay will need help with the children," Alameda said. Her eyes met Mersey's and held. "It would be best if he would claim a wife, but he says he will not do that until he can provide the right home."

"You have my promise," Mersey said, fighting her tears, her heart breaking. "I will remember the name Salayah, and I will help Pou Nachay with the children in any way that I can."

****

The doctor, an Army captain named Forrester, had short, thick blond hair, and he was young. His slender face was unremarkable except for his intelligent, perceptive pale blue eyes that he shielded behind wire-rimmed spectacles. His long white doctor's coat hung loose on his thin build. He looked tired and defeated as he addressed the Indian scout.

Mersey watched Pou Nachay's face become a mask of stone as the doctor spoke.

"Your sister hasn't recovered enough from her injuries. She is too weak to deliver this baby," the doctor said. "There is a procedure that I explained to her, and having this procedure done is what she says she wants. The baby's heartbeat is strong. With the procedure, the baby can live."

"What of my sister?" Pou Nachay asked.

"This surgical procedure is to save the baby. It is performed when the mother is dying trying to give birth. Without it, both will die. That is why I have come to you. As her only adult male relative, I need your permission. Otherwise, I cannot act on her wishes alone."

"What is this procedure?" Pou Nachay asked.

"It is called a Caesarian Section. I will make an incision, that is, I will cut open her belly with a knife to take the baby from her womb," Forrester said. "I will do everything I can to save your sister's life, but no woman has lived after this procedure"

Pou Nachay bowed his head. "Do as my sister wishes"

The doctor nodded. "I will prepare an operating room."

****

Jennings sat upright in his bed. It hurt too much to lie down. The guards had moved to stand near the door. They didn't have the guts to stay close to a woman in the throes of labor.

He couldn't help overhearing what the doctor said to Alameda, and what she had said to him. The fact that the decision was up to an adult male relative instead of the woman herself gave him pause. What would he decide in this terrible situation if it were left up to him?

He knew this woman as a quiet seamstress and laundress who took pride in her work, and did a good job for the wage she received. Her beadwork could be described as beautiful. From the time that he had first seen her, when she had come with Pou Nachay to work at the fort, she had invaded his thoughts more than he cared to admit to himself. He had heard others call her *The Indian Princess*. Though it was said to belittle her, it was somehow fitting. She was, in her own graceful. gentle way, regal. He had never taken his garments to her to be washed, because having this pretty young woman tend to his things had seemed too personal. He would think about it too much, that her slender hands had touched his things with care. He was a rough man, he knew that about himself, much too rough and callused, inside and out, for a peaceful, quiet woman such as Alameda.

Now, because he hadn't protected her, had failed to keep her safe, this quiet woman was facing her death in a losing battle within her body to give birth.

She must hate him, hate the very sight of him, hate everything about him, hate his guts.

He could work with that.

He was a drill sergeant above all.

Jennings reached up, gritting his teeth against the pain the movement caused him, and moved the privacy screen from between them, and then moved it again to hide his intentions from the guards at the door, though they were facing away, trying to distance themselves from this woman's suffering.

When Alameda looked up at him, then away, he felt as if The Black had struck him again. Her mental and physical agony had been there for him to see in her dark eyes, and he braced himself for what he was about to do to this lovely, fragile creature.

"I know you don't know me. I am Seth Jennings."

Alameda blinked up at him, tears glistening in her eyes. "I know who you are, Master Sergeant," she said, and turned her head away from him again.

"I couldn't help hearing what the doctor said to you. I want to know why you aren't fighting harder for your life."

Then almost too low for him to hear, she said, "I don't want my baby to die."

"That doctor doesn't know everything," Jennings said. "He doesn't know you. What right does he have to tell you that you are too weak to have this baby?"

"The muscles in my stomach don't push hard enough for the baby to come out," she said.

"Find that strength," he said. He reached across the space and took her hand. "Squeeze my hand as hard as you can."

She squeezed.

He snorted.

"If that's all you've got, that doctor might be right. Try again, harder, think about how you felt when Jocko and Curly…." His voice drifted off, but he saw her eyes flash, and her lips firm, and she tried again, harder this time.

"That's better," he said. "Think about how you felt when you thought they could hurt your children."

She scooted a little closer to the edge of the bed to grip his hand tighter. She looked up into those clear blue eyes, and squeezed his big hand, and then she squeezed it again involuntarily as another contraction began, and she moaned, her breath coming in, then held, then gasped out, again and again.

When the contraction subsided, he said, "I would like to help you. I was raised on a farm in Indiana, and we raised lots of animals. I helped with many a difficult birth. It's not so different with people. Will you let me help you try?"

She nodded, her eyes caught in the bright blue intensity of his.

He pointed to his shackles. "I can't reach you"

"I'm not sure I can walk," she said, "And your shoulders…."

"Don't worry about me, this is about you. If you sit, I'll help you stand, and I can lift you over here."

She gave him a small smile. "I have reached a very large size," she said.

"You'll be light as a feather to me," he said as he helped her to sit up.

Then she leaned on his arm to stand, and he did indeed lift her to lie next to where he sat on his bed.

"I need to touch your stomach," he said, trying to soften the roughness of his voice, to restrain the forcefulness so innate to his character.

She hesitated, then she nodded.

He felt the shape of the baby in her stomach with his strong, warm hands. "You have pushed him deep. Now you just need to push him out," he said.

"Her," she said.

He grinned.

"Her," he said, and he began to massage her belly. "Tell me as soon as the pain comes back."

"Now," she groaned, throwing her head back against the pain.

"Alright, do you feel like you want to push?"

"Yes," she panted.

"Think about what you would like to do to Jocko. Think about it, hold your breath, and bear down," he said. "Now push!"

His hand rested on her belly where her muscles quivered with the strain, and he knew the doctor was at least partially right. Her muscles were fatigued, and this needed to be over quick if she was going to live.

When the contraction receded, he said, "Rest now, relax your breathing, save your strength for the next one."

They waited in silence, each deep in their own thoughts.

"Now," she said again, but he already knew. He had felt her abdomen begin to tighten.

"Think about Curly, think about that lousy, sick, heartless, filthy, worthless, mean…." he said, and he grinned when she growled.

"Bear down, now push, hard, breathe, again, bear down, push, harder, harder."

As Alameda rested, Jennings thought he could feel that the child had moved lower in her abdomen, and he felt hope.

A few moments later, Alameda took a breath, and nodded at Jennings.

"My turn," he said, his voice low and tense, his expression fierce. "Think now of me not protecting you, walking away when I should have helped you, leaving you to two sick, coldblooded…."

"No!" she growled, and half sat up to bear down, supporting her weight on her arms.

"Yes," he said. "I didn't stop them, they hurt you and I let them…."

"Noooo!" she said again, and she gave a battle cry, then caught her breath and pushed with every fiber in her body, and the baby's head crowned.

Breathing hard, sweat dripping from her brow, she pushed again, and again, and then with Jennings' support, she reached down, and eased her own child from her body, as she had done twice before, as the women of her People had done for centuries.

The unmistakable cry of a healthy newborn baby, a beautiful baby girl, resounded through the infirmary. And then the room filled with people, the guards, then

Pou Nachay and Mersey, and then the doctor rushed in. The guards threw back the privacy screen and wrestled Jennings to the floor, though he didn't fight.

The doctor stared at the baby with an amazed expression.

Pou Nachay took the baby from Alameda's trembling hands, and she collapsed back on the bed, breathing hard. She turned to look at Jennings who lay on the floor, his blue eyes gentle on her face.

"Thank you, Seth," she said.

"You're welcome," he said.

"What happened was not your doing," she said. "I believe you would have stopped them, had you known."

"Why didn't you come to me?" he asked, his eyes holding hers.

The doctor interrupted before she could answer.

"I need to get everyone out of the room and let me examine this patient," he said.

Pou Nachay laid the baby girl in Alameda's arms, touched his sister's cheek with shaking fingers, and then left.

The guard unlocked the shackles on Jennings' ankles, told him to get to his feet, which he did with careful, painful movement. Then the guard ordered the master sergeant from the room.

Mersey kissed Alameda's cheek, and went to get clean towels and more blankets, as tears of relief streamed down her face.

Quest for Justice

Mersey knocked on her father's office door. When her father called to her to enter, she stepped into the room. Her father stood, as did the two other men in the room, Major John Steele, and Captain Charles Kendrick.

"Father, you asked to see me?" she said.

"Yes, Mersey," the Commander said. "Please sit down, my dear." And when she sat, the men sat too.

"I asked you to join us because Major Steele and Captain Kendrick wanted to hear your concerns about what happened with Alameda and with the things that happened to you that led to Master Sergeant Jennings' arrest. I had discussed with them your testimony, for lack of a better term, and Captain Kendrick wanted to speak to you about his own involvement."

Kendrick spoke to Mersey as he leaned toward her, his expression intent, his brown eyes searching hers, his hands opened palms up.

"I wanted you to know that everything I did was intended to keep everyone at the fort safe. I know it was blackmail, but I was trying to do the right thing."

"Master Sergeant Jennings said something about you being threatened that harm could come to women of the fort," she said.

Kendrick gave a small smile. "Some of the men threatened you, Mersey, and…" he paused, glancing at the Commander. "I felt protective enough of you that I agreed to overlook….certain things. The men were sometimes insubordinate, grossly insubordinate. They were drunk and disorderly and failed to be at their posts, sometimes for a few days or more."

"And you allowed this, so that they wouldn't do me harm?" she asked.

Kendrick looked at the Commander again, and at Steele, then he faced her again and continued.

"I felt ill-equipped to continue to protect you. I couldn't go to your father, as his safety was also a part of the threat, and I....wrote reports to my uncle at Fort Union, making false accusations that made it seem....that your father was ignoring his duty."

Mersey stared at Kendrick. "But why?" she asked. "How could that possibly have helped?"

"I hoped that more officers would be sent in support of the commander, regulars, not volunteers, and my uncle sent Major Steele with a company of regular cavalry, exactly what I had hoped," he said.

Except, Kendrick thought, what he hadn't thought to expect was that the Major would be young, unmarried, the very embodiment of all things manly and gentlemanly, and possess an irrepressible dash of southern charm. Steele had ridden in like a fairytale knight in shining armor on a...well, black horse, but that was beside the point. That the Major would singularly, though subtly, lay siege to win the heart of the fair maiden that he had his own heart set on, the one he may have sacrificed his career to protect, was the most agonizing irony.

Mersey turned to Steele then. "You knew about these accusations against my father from the beginning?" she asked.

He nodded, his eyes unreadable, his jaw tight.

"This brings us to the discussion regarding Master Sergeant Jennings," the Commander said. "You asked that his charges be reconsidered, lessened, perhaps dealt with by some sort of community service. Please, state your case, my dear."

The men waited.

"Master Sergeant Jennings helped Alameda through her childbirth. When the doctor was ready to cut her open, do a Cesarean Section to save the child at her request, guaranteeing her death in the process, Master Sergeant Jennings bullied her, in true drill-sergeant fashion, into fighting for her life," she said.

"Major Steele made the point that in consequence of Master Sergeant Jennings' disobeying a direct order, Alameda was assaulted, and then in his attempt to desert his post, he endeavored to kidnap you in the process. The Major asserts that these crimes cannot go unanswered, Mersey."

Mersey looked at John.

"Mersey, disobeying an order doesn't always have dire consequences, but soldiers can't pick and choose which ones they will obey."

She turned to her father, appealing to him. "He wanted to make it right. He was trying to make it right by going after Jocko and Curly. He planned to find them and bring them back to make amends for what he did. How can there be justice if there is no allowance for that, father?"

She looked at Kendrick. "He was convinced that he was doing what he had to do, Charles, just as you were."

And to John she turned imploring eyes. "Is there nothing that can be done to save him from prison or worse? Alameda believes that he saved her life, John, that his actions led him to be there when she needed him most," she said.

The image of The Black as he reared with Mersey clinging to his back appeared in John's memory. His heart tripped in mid-beat as if seeing the image for the first time and the image twisted his insides. She could have been thrown and injured or killed, or The Black in his distress could have gone over backward, falling, crushing her, crippling or killing her. He wanted to remind her of what could have happened to her when she had tried to escape Jennings, or if Jennings had changed his mind, or had lied about letting her go free and unharmed, but instead, he said, "He will have to stand trial, Mersey, and until then remain in jail. With your testimony and Alameda's, if you both will be allowed to testify, we believe he may receive leniency, but we can't guarantee it."

Mersey stood and turned her head away from the men to try and hide her tears.

"Mersey wait, please," Kendrick moved to stand beside her. He placed his hands on her shoulders, and dipped his head to catch her eyes. "I plan to give testimony as well, about the situation he was in with the volunteers."

"Thank you," she said. Then she left the room.

All three men stood in uneasy silence for a moment after Mersey left, each wanting to follow after her, to try to comfort her, but each knowing that there was little more that could be said, that there was little more they were able to do.

****

Mersey entered the guardhouse with a basket filled with baked treats and a flask of warm tea. The guard stood up from the wooden chair on which he had been sitting. An open deck of cards sat on the small table. The floors in the guardhouse were made of wood planks, and a cot with a wool blanket and thin pillow was placed against the wall in a corner of the room. A small open fireplace was built into an outside wall, its heat taking some of the chill from the room.

"Miss Lockwood," Private Decker said. "What can I do for you?"

And then Alameda, babe in arms, followed Mersey into the room.

The young soldier acknowledged her. "Ma'am," he said, and tipped his hat.

"We brought something for Master Sergeant Jennings," Mersey said. "Would we be permitted to see him?"

"Sorry, Miss," Decker said. "The cells are all full and the hall is narrow. The master sergeant is in the last cell and I can't let you walk down that hall. I'd be happy to give him whatever you brought."

Through the doorway into the hall, Mersey could hear the sound of chains dragged across a wooden floor, followed by the sound of a heavy ball rolling. Now that the fresh air from their entry was gone, the guardhouse smelled of unwashed bodies, and misery.

Mersey set the basket on the small table and set out the contents of apple scones and tea. "There is perhaps enough here for everyone, yourself included, but if there are extra, we would like them to go to Master Sergeant Jennings," she said.

The private nodded, and thanked Mersey.

Then Alameda asked, "Are his injuries healing? Is there anything Master Sergeant Jennings needs?"

"Blankets, ma'am," a Spanish accented voice called from the hallway. "And maybe some of that good ol' Kentucky creek water, if'n ya know what I mean. It's powerful cold here at night," he said, then laughed a raucous laugh.

"Quiet, Manuel," Decker called out, then turned back to Mersey and Alameda. "The doctor checks on the master sergeant every day, and we have blankets, but the nights can be bitter, it's true. The warmth from the fireplace doesn't reach far down the hall."

"If we brought wool scarves, hats or socks for the prisoners, would that be allowed?" Alameda asked.

"I can clear it with the lieutenant, but I reckon just the hats and socks," Decker said, "And I'll ask if Master Sergeant Jennings can be moved to the forward cell so you can visit."

"Thank you," both women said, and then they left the guardhouse.

Rumors

Captain Kendrick led the patrol out of the gates. His orders from Colonel Lockwood were to investigate the report of an attack on a whiskey wagon that had come into the valley from the Sangre de Cristo Pass. The wagon had two broken wheels as a result of the peddler's attempt to make an off-the-trail run for it over very rocky terrain. The reports indicated that the attack on the wagon was by a small band of Apache braves, but the report also indicated that two white men may have been involved.

Rumors of Jocko and Curly's whereabouts abounded, from every peak and crevice of the valley. It kept the patrols racing about the valley, but the patrols were always too late, the fugitives seeming to vanish into thin air like so much smoke.

Kendrick and the patrol rode north for several miles. They could see the ruins of Fort Massachusetts that had been established in the summer of 1852. With walls ten feet high, made of pine logs cut from the nearby mountains, Fort Massachusetts had been a sturdy structure, and had quartered one hundred fifty men. Master Sergeant Jennings had been one of those one hundred fifty.

Following the Christmas massacre at Fort Pueblo in 1854, the men of Fort Massachusetts had launched a campaign against the Indians involved in the massacre, and in six months the Indians were caught and their lands ceded.

In 1858 when Fort Garland replaced Fort Massachusetts, some of the timber from the old fort had been moved to help build the new one.

The relocation had occurred to achieve a better strategic position for protection of the many trails and mountain passes into the valley, as well as closer proximity to the town of San Luis.

Passing the ruins of the fort, the patrol turned west and then rode north until they reached the great sand dunes. Rolling hills and five hundred foot peaks of glittering sand shifted with the winds against the foothills of Mount Blanca. On the northeast border of the dunes, where Medano Pass opened into the valley, Kendrick spotted the broken-down whiskey wagon. A grizzly-bearded, bow-legged, round-bellied man who walked like his boots hurt his feet, stepped away from the wagon with a shotgun resting in the crook of his arm, and greeted the patrol.

"It's 'bout time you fellas got here. Name's Peddler Pete. I been waitin' here like a fish in a barrel, figurin' them braves would be comin' back to finish the job. I got pots and pans and blankets, but I only carry one spare wheel, and two are broke."

"Well, Peddler Pete, I'm Captain Kendrick of the U.S. Calvary at Fort Garland. We've brought you two wheels for your wagon, and our orders are to get your wagon up and going again, and to escort your whiskey wagon out of the valley. Your cargo is banned here," Kendrick stated.

"Whiskey? Who said anythin' 'bout whiskey? I'm a li'jit businessman. but if you and yer men might be interested in making a little deal…." Pete said. He stroked his beard, and a speculative gleam lit his eyes.

"Sergeant!" Kendrick called out. "Let's get those wheels replaced and get this li'jit businessman on his way back from whence he came."

"Yes sir," came the reply. The men dismounted, and unloaded the two wagon wheels that had been roped to a mule.

"Now, Mr. Peddler Pete," Kendrick said taking a pencil and paper from his inside coat pocket. "While my men are restoring your wagon, tell me everything you remember about this attack."

December 25, 1861
Christmas Day Celebration, Fort Garland

"Mersey, I'm going to be late. I need to be on time to the parade grounds," Colonel Lockwood said.

"I'm finishing this angel costume, father. I need one more minute," Mersey said, her speech somewhat garbled because of the pins she held with her lips.

"Mersey," he repeated. This time he rolled his eyes and paced the room three times across and back.

"There," she said. "I'm done."

"I'll get your cape," her father said, and hurried to the front door. Mersey followed.

"You look beautiful, Mersey. You remind me so much of your mother," he said.

"Thank you. I wish I had clearer memories of her."

"You are as intelligent, kind, and caring," he said.

"And the tears?" she asked.

"She was the same, and you are as compassionate and brave as she was."

"Brave, father? I am the coward of the county," she said, and laughed.

"You have courage in your very marrow," he said.

Lockwood opened the door of the commander's quarters for her, and they stepped onto the boardwalk. He then moved forward and directed his attention to the mounted men in formation facing him.

"Atten-hut!" was the command from Lieutenant Hawkins, and the cavalry company saluted him.

Major Steele sat upon The Black in the lead position, flanked by Captain Kendrick, then the lieutenants, and sergeants in front of their squadrons.

Lockwood returned the salute to Major Steele first, then turned right to left maintaining the salute, and when he dropped his arm, so did the companies.

The day was cold but sunny. Families and civilian staff of the fort surrounded the parade ground, all dressed in their holiday best. Claps and whistles and cheers followed the salute as the bugle sounded and the drills began.

An infantry sergeant marched onto the field and faced the infantry. He barked commands for intricate maneuvers, first with marching steps, then with rifles. The crowd was dazzled.

Mersey had never seen this kind of skill performed at Fort Garland, and her eyes went to the man she considered to be responsible for the changes, Major Steele. He sat on The Black in perfect stillness, back straight, head high, watching the maneuvers with analytical eyes. Just then, his eyes cut to her, met her gaze, then snapped back to the field.

When the infantry finished, the sergeant led their march from the field.

The bugle sounded again and Steele whirled The Black to face the cavalry, then Kendrick and the lieutenants wheeled their mounts and faced the mounted men.

Sergeant Barrows began shouting commands.

"Platoons, columns of four!" the sergeant shouted.

The platoons separated into side by side columns of four.

"Right wheel, March! Counter wheel, March!"

The men wheeled their mounts to the right, then left, in synchronized whirls, then faced forward.

"First Platoon, individual lines, oblique march right! Second Platoon, individual lines oblique march left!" he shouted.

The riders led their horses in alternating succession crisscrossing from right to left and left to right through the lines, the distance precise and lines clean, the horses' reins held in the left hands, the right hands resting on the thighs, knees tight, and spurs exacting.

Mersey clapped at the impressive maneuver.

Barrows ordered, "Single rank formation....right dress front....draw sabers....present sabers.... break right....charge!"

The breath of both men and horses clouded the frigid air as the cavalry followed each precise command, then charged their mounts across the parade ground bringing the thunder of hoof beats, the hooves throwing back ice and snow and sod as they galloped out the gate to the field where the soldiers manning the artillery waited beside the cannons.

Commander Lockwood mounted his horse, which had been saddled and waiting, then he joined Major Steele to lead the other officers from the fort.

Mersey walked to stand beside Alameda and her children. Salayah was cradled in Alameda's arms and bundled against the cold. Pou Nachay, as a scout was considered a civilian employee and didn't take part in the exercises. He stood with his hand on Cochetopa's shoulder. Antera stood next to Alameda.

Steele rode forward to join Lieutenant Hawkins near the artillery. Both officers dismounted.

Seven of the infantry stepped forward with rifles and followed commands for a twenty one gun salute.

Hawkins stepped up then and began shouting commands. Three twenty-four pound cannons and four twelve pound howitzers boomed, were shoved back into position, then in quick succession, repositioned, reloaded, boomed again, repositioned, reloaded and boomed a third time, demolishing targets in succession at one thousand, seven hundred fifty, and five hundred yards, answering the twenty one gun rifle salute.

The smoke cleared. Barrows shouted, "Atten-hut," and Colonel Lockwood rode front and center.

"Well done, Soldiers!" Lockwood shouted. "Merry Christmas! God be with us all here at Fort Garland." Then he nodded to Sergeant Barrows.

"Dis….missed!" Barrows bellowed, and a loud cheer erupted from soldiers and observers alike.

****

Everyone began moving off of the practice field toward the fort. They planned to enjoy the holiday feast prepared by the Ladies of the Regiment. They walked across dozens of footprints, hoof prints and wheel prints indented the light covering of snow over the dormant grass of the field.

Mersey heard hoof beats behind her, and turned to see Steele rein in The Black and then dismount. She smiled and walked to join him as Alameda, Pou Nachay, and the children continued toward the fort.

Mersey reached into her coat pocket, retrieved dried apple pieces, fed them open-handed to The Black, and then stroked his nose.

"Now some of his behavior is starting to make sense," Steele said.

When she looked up at Steele, his expression was questioning.

She asked, "Are you wondering if I approve of the precision exercise? Do I think it passed muster?"

His grin was almost boyish as he ducked his head, and then looked away.

Mersey reached up and patted his broad shoulder, bringing his eyes back to her.

"I've never seen the men perform better, John, and you've accomplished so much since you arrived."

"Thank you," he said. "That's good to hear."

She studied his face, his fierce eyes, then she said, "One thing you might not know you've accomplished is that everyone is safer because of you."

Steele's brows drew together and he frowned. He reached to stroke The Black's neck before turning back to face her. He cleared his throat.

"Mersey, that day in your father's office, when you learned about Captain Kendrick's letters to Colonel Anderson," he paused. "I want to talk to you about what information I was given before coming here, and what I observed while being here."

Two little girls skipped by Mersey, laughing and sliding on the slushy ice churned up by the drills. They looked school age, and Mersey thought she would recognize them if they had been less bundled.

"Race you," one of them said, and started running.

"Hello Miss Lockwood," the other little girl shouted, waving a mitten-covered hand as she ran.

As was inevitable, both children lost their footing on the slushy surface, and fell flat, hitting their knees, chests and noses in quick succession. Both children started to sob and cry.

Mersey hurried to the children, helped them up, and brushed off the slush.

Steele rushed after her and The Black trailed him.

"My knees hurt," the smaller child said, big tears falling down her cheeks. "Would you carry me?" she asked Mersey.

Mersey recognized the little girls now. They were the Noland children, Clara and Polly.

"How about I carry you?" Steele asked, squatting to her level.

Polly looked at Steele, grabbed the edge of her slush-covered dress and swayed back and forth.

Mersey would swear that the adorable little girl batted her eyes at him. Steele looked smitten, and Mersey grinned.

"Alright," Polly said, and lifted her arms to him.

Steele settled her against one shoulder, and then Clara reached up and took his free hand and Mersey reached back to take The Black's reins.

"I'm going to be Baby Jesus' mother Mary in the Christmas play today," Clara announced looking up at Steele. "Miss Lockwood put all the girls' names in a hat and then she had Cecil draw, and Cecil picked my name and then I picked Rudy's name from the boys' hat to be Joseph."

"And what are you going to be in the play?" Steele asked Polly.

"I'm going to be an angel," she said, batting her eyes at Steele again.

"I'm sure that is the perfect part for you," he said.

"You're so handsome," Polly said to Steele.

Steele glanced at Mersey, who watched them in obvious amusement, then he smiled at the little girl.

"Why, thank you," he said. "And you ladies are all very beautiful. I'm a lucky man to be escorting you," he said in his most charming drawl.

The two little girls giggled. He thought he heard Mersey sigh, and hoped that meant she interpreted his compliment to include her. He threw her another glance, but now she was looking straight ahead. How was a man to interpret a woman's sigh, this woman in particular? Mersey was a fine and pleasant mystery to him, a mix of contrasts. She was ferocious and tender, objective and passionate, and the most complex part, she was independent and yet so vulnerable. Could she ever need a man like him, or want him, or….

"There you two children are," Aggie Noland said, "I've been looking for you everywhere."

Lieutenant Noland's wife approached them at the front gates of the fort, a look of relief on her face.

"Mommy," Clara said. "We fell down!"

"I see that," Aggie said taking Polly from Steele and setting her on the ground.

"My husband was directing moving the cannons into the fort. I took our baby inside. These two ran ahead and I thought they were going to our quarters, but here they are. Thank you for looking after them," Aggie said.

"It was our pleasure to accompany them," Steele assured her, tipping his hat.

Aggie grasped her daughters by the hands.

"We'll see you later at the play," Mersey said.

Aggie nodded and the little girls waved as the trio walked further into the fort.

Steele looked at Mersey. He wanted to talk to her uninterrupted and in private, and the opportunity had escaped him. Now the activity all around them in the fort made him hesitate to continue his explanation.

"You are coming to the Theater for the festivities later, aren't you?" she asked.

"I'm looking forward to it," he said. "I need to get The Black to the stables and check the duty rosters, but I hope to be on time. I wouldn't want to miss little Baby Jesus' mother and an angel in the play."

"You fell in love. I knew it," she quipped. "I saw it the moment it happened."

Mersey smiled at his surprised expression, but he recovered, and turned to fully face her. He took a step closer to her, forcing her to look up at him.

"Did you now, Miss Lockwood," he said, aware that she was teasing him about little Polly Noland, but choosing to misunderstand.

Mersey froze as his deep drawl cascaded over her, his gray eyes glinted dark as gun-metal, but her father's voice saved her from stammering a response.

"Major," Commander Lockwood said. "I want to congratulate you on the men's performance today."

Steele saluted, then said, "Thank you, sir."

"At ease, Major," the Commander said after returning Steele's salute, and then he directed a curious look at his daughter and the major, wondering if he had interrupted something.

Mersey said, "If you gentlemen would excuse me, I'd better get to the Theater."

Both men responded with courteous remarks.

Steele's eyes followed Mersey as she moved away, a telling look that the commander didn't miss. So that was the way of things, Lockwood thought, at least as far as the major was concerned. He doubted the major knew how apparent his feelings were. But Mersey's feelings, when not about concern for others, were not so easy to read. Lockwood hid his grin. It would be interesting to watch the major's campaign to attain Mersey's affection, but gaining her affection would be a skirmish. Getting Mersey to relinquishing her independence would be a crusade.

****

The fort Chaplin held a short religious service in the Theater before the dinner. Everyone attended including Jennings and the other prisoners under guard from the guardhouse.

Mersey sat at a long table with the school children and their families, speaking soft encouragement, anticipating their nervous excitement for the school Christmas play, trying to keep their jitters, and hers, to a minimum. When the meal was finished, Colonel Lockwood announced that the play would begin in ten minutes, and the children and Mersey scrambled for their costumes and then their places.

Antera was an angel, too, and she retrieved Salayah to play baby Jesus, and when she first held the baby in her arms. Antera said in a proud clear voice, "Behold, I bring you tidings of great joy," and she laid Salayah in a straw-filled basket before continuing with her part.

Cochetopa was a wise man and looked convincing in his costume. He told a story about a long journey to find the Savior.

Jennings sat across the room from Alameda, but when Antera laid the baby down, Alameda looked over at him.

Jennings' bright blue eyes were intent on the baby, but then his eyes met Alameda's. His expression was filled with such regret, such longing, that she almost looked away, but couldn't. She smiled at him instead, and returned to watching her children.

The children had a good time doing the play. There were a few botched lines that elicited good-natured chuckles among the gathering, as well as ornery sheep whose capture by the wise men and shepherds would have been given a high score at any rodeo event. All in all, it was a success for Mersey's first school Christmas play, and she told the children how proud she was of all of them, and they grinned and giggled at her praise.

Finally, before going back to their quarters, Mersey asked everyone to participate in carols of the season. She asked her father to lead the carols and she played the piano. They started with The First Noel, then Hark the Herald Angels Sing, O Come All Ye Faithful, and ended with God Rest Ye Merry Gentlemen, the commander's clear tenor leading all of those participating. Those who had gathered stayed to enjoy the company, and devour punch and cookies. The children were getting sleepy, partly from the let-down of the excitement of the day, and partly because the hour was getting late. Mersey helped the children get into their winter coats, praising each of them for their performance in the play.

Again the commander watched Major Steele track Mersey with his eyes, even changing stance or position so that he could keep her in view as he stood with the other officers, conversing and enjoying the activity around him.

As the last of the families left, Mersey walked to her father.

"Do you wish to stay a little longer?" she asked.

"Not if you are ready to leave," he said, watching Major Steele approach them.

"Sir," Steele said.

"Did you enjoy the program, Major?" Lockwood asked.

"I can't remember when I enjoyed one more," he said, and then he smiled at Mersey. "The Christmas play was very well done by the children."

"Thank you," she said, smiling back at him. "And some of it was completely unrehearsed."

He chuckled, then he dipped his head closer to Mersey, his eyes intent on hers. "I was hoping there would be dancing tonight."

The commander smiled. "We save dancing for New Years' Eve, Major. And I'm not sure Mersey saved enough energy for that. She would like to call it a day, it seems."

"Oh, but I will stay if you're not ready to leave, father," she said. "I'm sure I can…."

"Miss Lockwood, please allow me to escort you home," Steele said.

"I would appreciate that very much," she said. I find myself on the brink of falling asleep on my feet. I worked late last night to finish the costumes."

"And early this morning," Lockwood added, his expression stern, but his eyes twinkled. "We were in danger of being late to the parade grounds because she was finishing the last costume." He patted Mersey's shoulder. "I'll be along in a few minutes."

The commander gave Steele a meaningful look.

Steele nodded, and then grasped Mersey's elbow, and they turned together toward the door.

Snow was beginning to fall, and the night was quiet and peaceful. They crossed the parade ground to the Commander's quarters in silence, and then Steele drew Mersey to a stop.

She turned to him, her eyes questioning.

Steele said, "I wanted to speak to you alone, to explain…."

"Please come inside, John. It's turning bitter cold out here," she said.

He nodded, and opened the door for her to enter. They stood in the lamplight inside the hallway, and John spoke.

"Colonel Anderson received letters from Captain Kendrick accusing your father of indifference and lack of leadership in defense of the fort and the area settlements. He claimed the essential fortifications against a Confederate threat were ignored. Colonel Anderson insinuated to me that your father would soon be facing mandatory retirement based on these accusations," he said.

He watched Mersey's face for reaction, expecting shock or outrage, but she kept her eyes steady on his.

"You had been designated to take his place?"

He nodded, and she knew from his expression, from the shadows in his eyes, that this was true.

"What I discovered here at Fort Garland was not the chaos that I expected, but a well ordered fort and command, with the exception of the misconduct by the volunteer soldiers," he said.

"What happens now, for my father?" she asked.

He shifted, and seemed to study the closed door to the commander's office a moment before speaking.

"I discussed this all with your father, and I want you to know that I did my utmost to present the facts as I understood them, without prejudice, in the report I sent to Colonel Anderson. Kendrick also sent a report explaining his actions." Steele threaded his fingers through his hair, his expression entreating her to understand. "I'm sorry, Mersey, I…." he hesitated, his drawl becoming more discernable in his speech. "I didn't seek a position to displace your father. I would never do anything to cause your father distress, but like so many things, the final outcome has never been within my control, but in the hands of those superior to both your father and me."

She nodded and turned away.

He reached out and grasped her elbow. "Do you believe me, Mersey? Do you believe that I didn't seek advancement through your father's displacement?"

Mersey could tell by John's earnest expression that her answer was important to him.

"I believe you, John. I believe that you are here through no ambition of your own, and I believe that whatever happens next for my father, it will be alright. I have been with him many times when he has left a post or position when he valued, even loved, his work. He accepted his call to serve elsewhere or in another capacity. He has always done so with valor." She placed her gloved hand on his arm. "I see that same gallantry in you, John, the same resolve, the same acceptance and willingness to serve."

John looked relieved, and pleased, and the tight set of his shoulders relaxed.

"Thank you, Mersey. Your good opinion of me means more than…." John began as Commander Lockwood entered through the front door.

John bit back his frustration. He never seemed to get enough time with Mersey to finish a conversation.

"I'll take my leave of you. Thank you for your gracious time listening to me, Mersey. Good night," John said, "and good night, Commander Lockwood."

"Good night, Major," Lockwood said.

"Good night, John, and it was kind of you to escort me home," Mersey said. "Thank you."

John stared at Mersey for a moment, his eyes full of deep unreadable emotion. He nodded, turned and left the house, clicking the door closed behind him.

After John left, Commander Lockwood stood staring after him.

"Father, what is it?" Mersey asked.

"I'm trying to figure him out," Lockwood said.

"In what way?" she asked.

"Why he asked to come out West, for one thing," he said. "Major Steele has all the potential and connections that a man could want to advance back East, and yet here he is."

"Can't a good man want to come here? You're here, father," she teased.

He chuckled. "You are right of course, my dear. Many a good man would want to come here."

December 31, 1861
Fort Garland

On New Year's Eve morning, Mersey was walking back to the commander's quarters when she was hailed by a young woman riding in a horse-drawn buggy along the parade ground. Mersey called out a greeting as the buggy was pulled to a smooth stop next to the boardwalk.

"Rosa, Don Ricardo, how wonderful to see you!"

"We were on our way to pick up my Aunt Rita from her ranch and thought we would deliver your sewing machine, since you haven't been able to come to get it yourself," Rosa said.

Though Rosa didn't mention any of the recent problems at the fort, gossip in the small community was a rapid and efficient form of communication.

"Thank you for being so kind and thoughtful. I didn't mean for you to go to so much trouble...." Mersey said.

Don Ricardo smiled and held up his hand in a dismissive gesture. "Please, Miss Lockwood, it was our pleasure and no trouble to us at all you see, as we planned to come this way to pick up my sister for my family's New Year's celebration."

At age nineteen, Rosa was Don Ricardo's oldest daughter, and she helped every day in her father's store in San Luis. She and Mersey had become fast friends in their brief encounters when Mersey visited the store. Rosa was sweet-natured and smart, with a quick smile and beautiful, dark, expressive eyes. Rosa seemed only to become nervous and flustered when Captain Kendrick accompanied Mersey to the store.

As if thinking of him brought him forth, Captain Kendrick exited the front door of the commander's office. He greeted Mersey first, his eyes lingering on her face, and then his regard shifted to Rosa, who blushed and spoke a shy greeting.

Mersey watched the exchange, and a plan began to take form in her head, a plan that would not include her being the only unmarried woman at the dance. Her feet would thank her later.

Mersey said, "Rosa, why don't you and your Aunt and Don Ricardo join us this afternoon for the New Year's Eve party and dance? We have plenty of room and an excess of refreshments, and you would be most welcome."

Don Ricardo began to decline when Rosa turned to him with beseeching eyes and he relented.

"We would be happy to accept," he said and then he gave his daughter a warning glance. "But you must remember, I promised your mother that we would be home before your brothers and sisters go to bed."

Captain Kendrick spoke then. "I would be honored if both of you ladies would save me a dance."

Mersey smiled at him, and Rosa blushed again, and said, "Oh, most certainly, Captain."

Kendrick nodded and said, "Until later then. If you will please excuse me, I must be about my duties."

Don Ricardo stepped out of the buggy and walked to the back to lift the sewing machine.

"I'll just be a moment, Rosa," he said, then asked, "where do you want this, Miss Lockwood?"

As Mersey led Don Ricardo into the house, she said, "Rosa, please, when you return, you all must come here to freshen up."

Mersey felt a little self-satisfied with her plan as she stood next to John, sipping punch and watching Rosa surrounded by young officers vying for her attention. No one seemed to command her attention more than Captain Kendrick. An unexpected result of her plan was her father and Rosa's Aunt Rita standing close together exchanging polite conversation.

Observant of Mersey's every mood, Steele followed her eyes to the two young officers and the lovely, dark-haired store-keeper's daughter.

Mersey said, "She's pretty, isn't she."

"Pretty enamored with Captain Kendrick," Steele said, watching for Mersey's reaction.

She frowned, "Do you think he is smart enough to notice?"

"His eyes are open," Steele said.

"Yes," she said. "But it is the heart that must see."

Steele stared at Mersey, wondering what her heart would see when she looked at him.

After a moment she asked, "My father looks to be having a nice time, too, don't you think?"

Steele glanced at the commander and back at Mersey, and he raised an eyebrow. "Matchmaking today, are we? You remember that saying, the one about leading a horse to water…?"

He watched her frown again as the music began to play. Steele took the glass of punch from her hand and set it on the table. "Dance with me, Mersey," he said offering her his hand, and when she took it, he led her to the dance floor.

For several moments, they danced without speaking, Mersey watching the other couples with interest, and Steele watching her. She was friendly and welcoming to everyone, but she was still a very private person. He felt she was coming to trust him, to feel safe with him, maybe depend on him a little, but he wanted to know everything about her, her hopes and dreams, and if he could possibly fit in with them.

"Do you want children of your own, Mersey?" he asked before he could stop himself.

She looked startled for a moment.

"I want to teach," she said.

His eyes searched hers. "It wouldn't be unheard of to teach and have children of your own."

She tripped, but he steadied her.

Mersey felt taken off guard by this question. Why had she never asked it of herself? Did she know the answer? She and Aunt Andrea had discussed many things, but most were centered on education, self-sufficiency, and independence. She had been led to believe that a career and having a family were in direct opposition of each other, her mother being the prime example. Mersey pictured John as he had carried little Polly as if he held a child in his arms all the time, and she could imagine him holding a child of his own. Were her dreams so shallow that she had never considered all the possibilities? With a man who valued her independence as she did, could she have both? She stared at John for a long moment, at his expression that seemed guarded, at his eyes that seemed to hold promise.

"I guess I would like to imagine that…."

Kendrick tapped Steele's shoulder. "May I cut in?"

John swallowed his exasperation, nodded, stepped aside, and watched as Kendrick swept Mersey away. It was clear that his question about having children of her own had taken Mersey off guard. He needed to slow down, or he might frighten her away.

As they danced, Kendrick asked Mersey, "Would you step outside with me? There is something that I want to speak to you about."

Mersey looked up at Charles' expression, and Randall's earnest face appeared in her memory. The memory brought with it a feeling of apprehension, but she said, "Of course."

Steele watched Kendrick drape Mersey's coat over her shoulders and open the door for her as they stepped outside. Had she seemed nervous? Should he go to her? Or was it his own jealousy, his own uncertainty of his place in her feelings that he was responding to? He started toward the door but was intercepted by the commander and introduced to Rita. Steele gritted his teeth at their abominable timing.

Kendrick stopped Mersey with a hand on her arm and she turned to face him.

"Miss Lockwood," he said, and then cleared his throat. "Mersey, you must know how I feel about you, that I am serious about wanting us to have a future together."

Mersey tried to hide her dismay as he continued.

"I feel that we are well suited for a life together. With your background, you will be the ideal wife for any officer, for me, I mean. I had hoped to give you more time, but I can wait no longer to speak of this. I want you as my wife, Mersey, and I am sure that my mother and your father will approve the match."

"And if I wish to continue teaching?" she asked.

He hesitated before saying, "I suppose that I could consider it a topic for discussion."

Mersey had no desire to hurt this man.

"Charles, do you love me?" she asked.

He frowned. "I think that you are beautiful and desirable, and we have been friends for months now. I am very fond of you. I believe that we will grow to love each other in time."

"Charles, do you believe that you deserve more than someone you think would be an ideal officer's wife? Don't you want to marry someone who is head over heels in love with you?" she asked.

He shook his head. "We are so well suited…."

"Not to me, Charles," she said.

He closed his eyes. Then he nodded. "I pray that I have not distressed you…."

Mersey placed her hand on his arm. "Charles, you are a wonderful man. Whether you believe it or not, I believe that you deserve a woman who is crazy about you. She's out there waiting, maybe even close by."

Charles' head came up as the door opened, and Mersey heard Steele ask, "Mersey, is everything alright?"

"Yes, quite alright, John. Shall we go back inside, Captain?" and she accepted Kendrick's arm.

January 22, 1862
The Ancient Trail, Los Caminos Antiquos

Lieutenant Hawkins entered Colonel Lockwood's office. He came to attention and saluted. "Sirs!"

Lockwood, Steele, and Kendrick all looked up.

"Do you have something to report, Lieutenant?" Lockwood asked.

"Yes sir. With the southwest patrol, the scout believes he has picked up the trail of the fugitives Curly and Jocko, sir. The pair must have been holed-up somewhere for weeks because we hadn't found a trace with the heavy winter snow, and now someone or something must have rooted them out because they are on the move again."

"Pou Nachay?" Steele asked.

Hawkins turned his attention to Steele.

"Yes sir, and I had to do some fast talking to get him to agree to come back for reinforcements and supplies and not go after them on his own."

Steele rose to his feet. "If Pou Nachay thinks he found the trail, this is no wild goose chase. What men and gear do you need, Lieutenant?"

"A platoon with rations and supplies for a week," Hawkins replied, "And the raft, sir."

Steele lifted an eyebrow.

Kendrick explained. "The Rio Grande River south and west of here is wide, and at some times of the year, too swift and deep for horses to cross because of snow melt, so we use a raft." Kendrick looked at Hawkins. "Is the river unfrozen, Lieutenant?"

"At the place where the Los Caminos Antiquos, *The Ancient Road*, he translated for Steele, crosses the

Rio Grande, the river is a combination of frozen and flowing water about two hundred fifty feet wide and ten feet deep. Some of the wild life have attempted to cross and were trapped in the ice. Pou Nachay thought the horses might not be able to cross, even with a leading rein."

"With your permission, Commander," Steele said, first addressing Commander Lockwood then turning to Hawkins. "I'm coming with you, Lieutenant."

Lockwood nodded. "Permission granted. That will be all for now," he told the officers. "We'll continue this discussion upon your return, Major."

Steele and Hawkins saluted, and when Lockwood returned the salute he said, "Dismissed, Gentlemen, good luck."

****

Steele observed as the raft was loaded on a wheeled platform hitched to two teams of six oxen. It was fifteen feet wide and thirty feet long, made of twelve inch diameter logs fastened together with thick, tightly-wrapped rope. The logs were double deep near the outer edges and in the center to add buoyancy. Pulleys were attached to iron rods on the four corners of the raft. Thick ropes were coiled next to the rods and secured with leather straps. Long poles were tied to the platform, as well as oars.

With Pou Nachay in the lead, the platoon of soldiers left the fort riding south following the Los Caminos Antiquos trail. The terrain around the trail supported few trees, and only the yellow or tan tops of sage brush and other shrubs, and tall salt grass were visible above the drifted snow. Antelope and deer were seen on the plains on occasion, and a few small adobe homes could be seen as well. Some homes were close to the trail, others stood in the distance, identified by wood smoke from a chimney. Snow-covered peaks towered on the horizon in every direction from the valley floor.

That night as they camped, Steele approached Pou Nachay who sat on his bedroll somewhat separated from the rest of the camp. Pou Nachay was a quiet man, and Steele wondered if the man preferred his solitude and thus kept himself apart from the men, or if he felt he was an outsider.

Soldiers could be cliquish, and the patrols often had to pursue and fight against rebel Native Indians. At best, this could engender only a fragile trust between these men of different cultures. Since this Civil War began, Steele had himself felt the outsider when his fellow officers recalled his background, and he had discerned a refined caution in other officers' manners, at times even polite withdrawal.

Pou Nachay rose to his feet as Steele reached him. They greeted each other and Pou Nachay invited Steele to sit. They sat cross-legged in the Indian style facing each other. The light wind smelled of snow, of spruce and pine, of horses and wood smoke.

Steele decided to broach the subject. "You do a good job as scout for the patrols and for these men. Do you feel accepted among them?"

Pou Nachay glanced at the men at the campfire. I am my job to them. I am Scout. It is enough for me."

Both men sat in silence staring at the night sky.

"The moon is full tonight," Pou Nachay said. "My people call the full moon of January the Wolf Moon.

The winter is long, and the wolves come closer to the villages now because they are hungry."

He looked Steele in the eyes.

"I am hungry like the wolf, hungry to find these men who hurt my sister. Under the Wolf Moon, I could be hunting them. All men should respect a woman's right to choose her man in her own time. That right should not be taken from her because men are stronger."

Steele nodded. "How shall we do this? So that we follow you as you hunt them and yet communicate? You will need to rest to stay alert, and to defend yourself if you need to. We can help you with that."

Pou Nachay nodded. Together, they made a plan.

The next day they awoke to a world of surreal white and mist. Every bare twig and blade of grass tripled in size under the burden of thick diamond-bright frost. The mountains around them became invisible behind a heavy fog, and the breaths of the soldiers and the animals puffed white with exhales in the windless bitter cold dawn.

The troops returned to the trail when the warmth of the rising sun lifted the fog and the frost fell from stalks and branches like snow. Then ten miles further south, the platoon reached the town of San Luis.

The town consisted of a variety of small and medium-sized wood and adobe buildings distributed along two blocks of storefronts bordered by wooden boardwalks. The streets were of hard-packed earth and clay, with intermittent potholes and imbedded rocks of various sizes.

The buildings on either side of the main street consisted of a church with a small graveyard enclosed by a white picket fence, Don Ricardo's grocery store, a blacksmith shop, and a leather goods store on the right. On the left stood a town hall, a barber shop, a veterinarian office, and two saloons. Behind the businesses on either side of the street, houses of similar construction were scattered, one or two stories tall, with lean-tos or small barns attached or nearby.

Chickens, sheep, horses and a few cattle were fenced in small pens. Small stacks of hay or dried grass were stacked close by. The larger animals were thin, and lacked luster to their coats, a sign of a long and lean winter.

At the church, the Los Caminos Antiquos turned west following along a narrow dirt trail between a rocky ledge and a shallow, tapered ravine, before stretching again into grassy and shrub-scattered plains. When they neared the river hours later, the patrol heard the howling and yipping of wolves and the frantic bugling calls of an elk.

The banks of the Rio Grande dipped abruptly below the level of the trail, and the men discovered that a large bull elk was caught in the ice more than half way across the river. The animal had broken through the ice when attempting to drink, and had been unable to escape the freezing water before becoming entrapped and frozen from the chest down, leaving only its head free to defend itself from the pack of hungry gray wolves besieging it. The wolves' lighter weights were supported by the thick ice.

The pack was large. They had spread out and were attacking from every direction. The elk's massive rack of horns rotated with the movement of its head, attempting to keep the wolves at bay.

When one of the more aggressive wolves caught and held a point of the elk's rack in its teeth, Hawkins reached for his rifle.

Pou Nachay looked at Steele.

Steele nodded. "Hold, Lieutenant, the sound of a rifle shot is unmistakable and will be heard for miles around. It will give away our position, though no one may be close enough to see who fired the shot. It will nevertheless put the men we are after on the alert, if not on the run."

"Yes sir," Hawkins said, "But...the animal is about to be ripped apart fighting for its life. Is it not more humane to spare it the suffering."

Just then, with a powerful jerk of its head, the elk tossed the wolf onto the ice bank, where it yelped and skittered until it regained its footing.

Steele sat back in his saddle. No doubt the injured elk couldn't last much longer. It would be crippled from the damage to its body from freezing regardless. He shared Hawkins difficulty watching this regal animal's futile fight for its life against a superior force, and stand by doing nothing.

"I'm thinking we can use the elk meat ourselves, extend our rations for at least another day, and spare this creature some fear and torture from being eaten alive by wolves. I'm open as to how we can do that without telling the whole valley who and where we are. Any suggestions, Pou Nachay?" Steele asked.

Pou Nachay gave Steele a nod, then slipped down from his horse and walked to a stand of willow trees near the riverbank. He reached under his serape and pulled a large, serrated hunting knife from the sheath at his side. He cut a medium thick branch of willow, judged its length, cut again, then notched both ends of the branch. From a leather pouch tied to his belt, he removed a long cord of sinew, secured an end of the sinew to one notched end of the branch, bowed the branch, and then secured the sinew to the other end.

Next he cut several shorter willow pieces, notched one end and carved the other to a point, fashioning arrows. Securing the notched end of the arrow in the sinew cord, he drew back the bow, and sent the arrow flying toward the wolves, skimming the lead wolf by the fur of its neck.

The wolf yelped in surprise, then turned its yellow predatory eyes to the men, seeming aware of them for the first time.

There was no wind, or very little to speak of, and what there was must have put the men downwind, or the pack had been too deep into the drama of the kill to be diverted from their goal. But the men had the wolves' attention now. The alpha wolf lowered its head, rumbled a threatening growl from deep in its throat, and bared vicious canines at the unwelcome intruders to the scene.

Pou Nachay sent two successive arrows flying, both aimed in the direction of the alpha, sending him scampering away and the rest of the pack followed. Then Pou Nachay walked with slow, well-placed steps across the ice to the trapped animal. He dropped to one knee. His lips moved as if in prayer before he nocked an arrow, drew back the bow, aimed, and released the arrow into the tortured animal, ending its suffering.

Pou Nachay harvested the meat. Hawkins ordered the men to set the ropes and pulleys to float the raft.

They made camp on the second night into their journey on the east bank of the Rio Grande. Pou Nachay had butchered the elk and the men ate elk steak with their cornbread and coffee.

Steele noticed Pou Nachay seemed restless. Though he stayed still and quiet, his eyes were on the horizon, scanning, searching. Steele felt it himself, as if the opportunity for apprehending the two fugitives was slipping away from them through their slow, organized pursuit.

The following morning, after testing the raft without a load, the second trip carried one supply wagon, three men and three horses. Pou Nachay held his horse's reins and stood at the front of the raft beside the oxen, his eyes on the landscape beyond. When the raft met the far riverbank, he disembarked, mounted, and began his search for any sign of Curly and Jocko.

Steele ordered half the platoon to stay with the raft and keep it secure for their return. Pou Nachay doubled back at intervals to bring the caravan along in his wake as they continued southwest, staying just south of the Conejos River. He later brought word of two men who had camped in the area who were suspected of poaching sheep and chickens from the few area inhabitants. There was a rumor that two scruffy men on cavalry horses had tried to abduct a young woman from the small adobe chapel in Conejos, but they had been driven off by the men in her family.

Reports of the fugitives were vague in location or of a timeline too late to be helpful, and again, Jocko and Curly seemed as elusive as smoke. On the fourth day, they reached the foot of a high mountain pass going south into New Mexico Territory, and they watched a heavy gray cloudbank approach them from the west. Pou Nachay returned to the caravan at noon, and he reported to Steele.

"They have gone south into the mountains," he said, his disappointment and frustration revealed only by the fierceness in his eyes. "If we try to follow, we will be caught in those mountains in a storm without enough supplies."

Steele nodded. "I understand and I'm sorry. We came close, but not close enough. We won't stop our pursuit. We'll get it done, just not today."

Then Steele called to Hawkins to turn the caravan around. They were headed home.

February 19, 1862
Confederate Camp, 20 Miles South of Fort Craig

"What is it, Major Franklin?" Seagram asked the Arizona Rangers' Commander.

"Sir, I know a way around Fort Craig."

"Let's hear it, Major. We can't seem to draw them out to fight. They are entrenched in that fort with heavy artillery, and their supplies will last six months. We can hardly lay siege with only two weeks' supplies of our own."

"Sir, you may recall that I once owned an express company and I know this land as well as anyone except the Apache. If we swing east around the fort, we can access a river ford at Valverde, six miles north of Fort Craig. It is passable for wagons, though risky. There are deep ravines and sand drifts and steep walls up from the river bed. The seventeen miles around will take us two days, but the river bed is dry. There will be no water along the way for the men or animals. It's a bit of a gamble, sir."

Seagram was thoughtful a moment, then he said, "Yes, a desperate one without water for two days. The Army Corps of Engineers have declared that way impassible. If we do this our line of communication will be cut off, as well as our only way of retreat south to Mesilla," Seagram said as he poured himself a glass of whiskey.

Franklin waited, seething inside. They had left more than half of their supplies, including tents, bedding and extra clothing, abandoned at Fort Thorn because they lacked the animals to pull the wagons.

They lacked the animals to pull the wagons because the animals had died of disease or malnutrition from lack of supplies. Even so, their supplies for the men and animals would not be this desperate had Seagram had their cavalry in place to intercept the seventy supply wagons that had, several days before, reached Fort Craig.

"Very well, Major. If you think you can get around Fort Craig, by all means get it done or we'll never take Fort Union," Seagram said, waving his hand in a dismissive gesture.

"Yes sir," Franklin said.

March 6, 1862
Fort Garland

"Major Steele and Captain Kendrick reporting as ordered, Commander," Steele said as he and Kendrick stood at attention in Lockwood's office.

"Sit down, Gentlemen," Lockwood said, and when they were seated, he continued. "Our infantry company of volunteers under Captain Roberts returned last night. With them came orders that we are to move half our forces to Fort Union in support of that location against the Confederate advance. Our troops from Fort Craig were defeated by the Confederates at Valverde, and have retreated."

Silence followed the announcement.

Half their forces, Steele thought. They were already short-handed with the extended patrols to keep the settlers and the small town of San Luis safe from the ever increasing number of raids by the Native Indians, and from following up on sightings of the two fugitives. And he had been told that even by valley standards, this winter had been hard.

"According to Roberts' report," Lockwood said, "On the 21st of February, the Confederate Army of New Mexico had taken an eastward route around Fort Craig following the Rio Grande River, a route considered impassible. The Commander of Fort Craig, fearing that the Confederates were trying to seize the high ground that overlooked the fort, sent forces to intercept them. Two companies of infantry regulars and two of volunteers were sent, as well as five companies of regular cavalry, one of volunteers, and two artillery batteries with a total of six guns."

"They found the Confederate army camped on a small, flat, dry riverbed of sand bordered by a steep plateau, and near a thick stand of cottonwood trees."

"Were our Union forces facing superior numbers, Commander?" Kendrick asked.

"No, but the Confederate army, a company of Arizona Rangers, took a defensive stand in the cottonwood trees, making good use of their long rifles until their reinforcements could arrive. We were unsuccessful in gaining the steep plateau to use our sharpshooters," Lockwood replied. "Our artillery was superior, but even after sending several messengers across the icy river, the cavalry commander failed to advance to a most strategic point."

At the men's questioning looks, Lockwood said, "I can only imagine that he was unsure of the numbers he faced. His delay in movement allowed for the arrival of two regiments of the Texas Mounted Rifles. Then Fort Craig sent two more battalions of infantry, who had to wade through chest-deep, ice cold, rushing water to reach the battlefield. After that, something terrible and remarkable occurred in which our own volunteer infantry under Captain Roberts took part."

Lockwood stopped his speech and rubbed his eyes with his thumb and forefinger, then spoke in awe.

"For whatever mistaken call to duty, a company of sixty-five Confederate Lancers rode to their deaths against our musket and artillery fire."

Steele sat still, barely able to draw breath.

"How could they have been ordered to charge against modern weaponry?" Kendrick asked. "I thought Lancers were only for parades."

"Unknown, but it was sickening to hear our volunteer infantry boast of what they called more fun than a turkey shoot." Lockwood said. "Then another Confederate mounted company charged our twenty-four pound cannons, and after that we outnumbered the Confederate army five to one. They were low on ammunition. Most of their mounts had been killed."

"How then could we lose the battle?" Kendrick asked frowning.

"Well," Lockwood said. "Though their losses were high, they were well trained against cannon fire. They just kept charging, and then when they were able to get close to the artillery, the majority of our Union New Mexico volunteers deserted, just turned and ran. The Confederates excelled in close combat."

"They captured our guns," Steele said.

"Yes, and turned them on us," Lockwood finished.

A moment of silence followed, then Lockwood spoke again. "You two will take half the battalion with you to Fort Union as we have been ordered. This will include Captain Roberts and a company of volunteer infantry. We have ten days to prepare."

"Yes sir," Steele and Kendrick responded.

Lockwood stood and paced. "I intend to keep most of the family men here, so as not to separate them, but I'm sending Mersey with you. With half the battalion gone, we will be short-handed in the extreme. I want her safe at Fort Union."

Kendrick said, "I'm surprised that she agreed to a disenrollment of the school."

Lockwood gave a wry smile. "I wanted her to go back East to stay with my sister near Boston, but we compromised," he said, "For now."

Not back to Boston, not yet, Steele thought. He felt as if he were being torn in half. The thought of not being close to Mersey caused such an intense sense of loss that Steele admitted that he could wait no longer to tell her what she meant to him. He must try to keep her with him. He must tell her that she owned his heart, and soon, before the world ripped them apart.

Before he could stop himself Steele asked, "A compromise, sir?"

"Alameda and the children will go to Fort Union as well. Alameda wishes to be there to speak on behalf of Master Sergeant Jennings, if it is allowed."

"We will be taking the prisoner with us then, sir?" Kendrick asked.

"Yes, Captain," Lockwood said. "It's better for everyone involved to move this process forward, to have Jennings face the accusations and state his defense with no further delay."

March 15, 1862
Leaving Fort Garland

Mersey and Alameda were finishing the packing for themselves and the children. Baby Salayah was asleep in a cloth carrier wrap on Alameda's back.

"Seth will be traveling with us when we travel to Fort Union," Alameda said.

Mersey nodded, knowing that Jennings was facing court martial. If convicted, he faced imprisonment, if not worse, for his failure to follow orders. They were in a time of war, and punishment could be extreme.

"Will you still speak well of him when he is in trial?" Alameda asked.

"Yes, I will, Alameda," Mersey said. "Has he spoken to you about what may happen at his trial?"

"Yes," she said, "I cannot let myself think that he might lose his life."

Mersey put her arm around Alameda's shoulders. "You have come to care for him very much, haven't you?" she asked.

Alameda's expression became joyful then, and she nodded. "When I first met him, I thought him a hardened man, and a man who hated the Indian People. Now I believe that it is violence he hates, not the color of someone's skin, and there is more to him. He has much to give."

"We must trust that those who hear what we have to say will listen with openness, that they will see the good things that Master Sergeant Jennings has done, and in what he tried to do," Mersey said.

After Alameda left, Mersey sat for a moment on the bed. It must be exhaustion, this feeling of dread.

This was not the time to let courage desert her. Her father had pulled rank on her, informed her that she couldn't stay at the fort without his permission, and he would withdraw it if she didn't agree to go to Fort Union *temporarily* for the duration of the war in New Mexico. He had at first asked that she return to Massachusetts and stay with Aunt Andrea, but Mersey hadn't wanted to give up her school. No amount of reasoning or pleading would dissuade him. 'Going with the troops to Fort Union should ensure that she, Alameda and the children, would have better resources and increased safety.

And so she had agreed.

She wanted to hold onto the resentment she felt at having her decision taken from her. But she had seen the regret in her father's eyes, and had known that he suffered too because of her leaving and because of the circumstances that drove it. He would miss her as much as she would miss him.

At Fort Union, she would have Alameda and the children's comforting company. She rationalized that the sacrifice of her dreams at the school was so much less than what was asked of so many others, but she mourned the loss anyway. She prayed that this war would soon be over, and she resolved to help those affected by the war if she could. She acknowledged that she was glad to be going where John would be. Being close to him was important to her. They were getting to know each other and the more she got to know him, the more important became. She could admit how much she had come to care for him, depend on him. Was it so unthinkable that he could come to depend on her too?

What would independent Aunt Andrea say to that?

Memories of John invaded her thoughts, the safe haven his arms, the warmth of his touch, the soothing deep drawl of his voice, the intense emotions that showed only in his eyes, and Mersey frowned as she realized that being parted from John would cause her heart to ache. Was this love, she asked herself as she drifted off to sleep.

March 21, 1862
Confederate Headquarters, Santa Fe

General Seagram of the Confederate Army of New Mexico sat in the drawing room of a spacious hacienda that he had commandeered as his headquarters. The Confederate forces had taken control of Santa Fe ten days ago, five days after the Union forces previously occupying it had determined the city indefensible and retreated to Fort Union.

"What is it you need to tell me so urgently this time, Major Franklin?" Seagram asked.

"Sir," Franklin said. "We have word that several Colorado companies of cavalry and ten companies of volunteer infantry may in the near future reinforce Fort Union. The companies were sent from Denver by order of the Secretary of the Territorial Governor of Colorado, and from Fort Lyon in the east and Fort Garland in the northwest by order of General Canfield. Soon we will be positioned between superior forces in Fort Union and Fort Craig. We will be cut off should they decide to leave their forts and march on us."

Seagram took a swallow of whiskey, and smiled at the young dark-haired woman who sat next to him.

"Well then, Major, it sounds as if we will be obliged to take some action," he drawled.

"May I be of service, sir, to retrieve our men from where they camp with the horses in the mountains? I believe that Fort Union is the weaker of the two forces at present."

Franklin didn't add that the only hope the Confederates had for victory in New Mexico was to seize Fort Union before the reinforcements arrived to secure their large stores of supplies, supplies the Confederates were in desperate need of. Their current meager supplies would only last a few more weeks at best. In the mountain camp, many of the men had become ill from respiratory ailments after sheltering in inadequate tents, and wearing clothing inadequate for the bitter cold winds. Men and animals suffered and died from too little food to sustain health and no medicine to treat illness.

Men of one mounted company had given up their mounts, their own personal mounts, under promise of repayment that they would likely never see, in order to keep another company fully mounted. If wars could be won by sheer determination, self-sacrifice and will, these men deserved victory.

"Bring them down from the mountains, Major, and I will inform the other officers to take our army north to Fort Union through Glorieta Pass," Seagram said.

"Yes sir, thank you, sir," Franklin said, saluted, and left the room.

Steele's Promise

Steele halted the caravan as one of the forward patrol approached.

"Major Steele," the private said. "There are two armies about to collide at Apache Canyon on Glorieta Pass. We need to hurry if we're going to join the boys from Fort Union, sir."

Steele looked back at the line of wagons. Sandy drove the ambulance wagon full of supplies, its square shaped, canvas-covered top rippling in the breeze. Mersey sat on the bench seat in the front beside Sandy. The children and Alameda must be settled in the back.

"I'll stay with them, Major," Kendrick said following his gaze. "I can keep them safe here, or take them on to Fort Union. Jocko and Curly are still at large, and there is suspicion that they may have headed this way."

"I share your concern, Captain, but I will need to depend on you to lead the cavalry while I stay with the artillery," he said. Then Steele looked around him.

"Pou Nachay?" Steele called.

Pou Nachay rode forward.

"Is there any way for the women and children to reach Fort Union without going through Glorieta Pass?" Steele asked.

Pou Nachay shook his head.

Steele said, "Pou Nachay, I'm leaving you to find a safe place for the women and children, and wait for my return. Are you familiar with this area?"

Pou Nachay nodded. "I will stay on the trail along Apache Creek, until we reach Johnson Station south of here. I will camp near the creek. I will keep them safe."

"When will you reach Johnson Station?" Steele asked.

"We should reach the station tomorrow before nightfall," Pou Nachay said. "The mules have reached their limit today." Pou Nachay looked around them. "I will camp near that alcove for the night," he said, indicating a large deep indent in a formation of boulders.

"Good," Steele said. "Our plan will be to collect you at Johnson Station."

Steele turned The Black and rode toward where Mersey waited on the wagon. Alameda and the children had poked their heads out behind Mersey and Sandy, likely curious as to why they had stopped.

When Steele reached Mersey, he rode close to the wagon and she gasped as he lifted her, setting her in front of him on The Black. He held her close, secure and safe, against his chest.

The Black stepped sideways balancing the weight, and then looked to his side at the woman his master held. He nickered and looked forward again.

"John, what are you doing?" Mersey asked, clinging to his shoulders.

"Making you a promise," he said. "We are going on to Glorieta Pass and you can go no farther without being in the middle of a fight. It seems the Civil War has reached us now. You, Alameda and the children are under Pou Nachay's care, and I promise to return to you just as soon as I can. I am coming back for you, Mersey."

Mersey looked at John's fierce expression, his earnest eyes, and placed her hands on either side of his face.

"You will please be very smart and be safe, and…"

"Mersey, there is so much that I want to say to you, but now is not the time. I want you to know that you have come to mean everything to me, and I…." but he couldn't finish.

Her eyes were bright with tears, though she smiled at him as she tried to mask her worry for him, for all of them.

"I'm holding you to your promise to return to me just as soon as you can, John," she said.

And then she kissed him, just a sweet, tender caress of her lips on his, but he took control of the kiss as she leaned into him, and he held her like he would never let her go.

Mersey's heart thrilled with his kiss, a kiss filled with longing and hope, and deep sentiment, and she kept kissing him, hoping her kiss revealed all of her feelings for him. When she drew back from him, both of them were breathless.

"Ah, Mersey," he said, his voice full of tenderness, their warm breath fogging the cold air between them. "I knew a kiss would feel like this with you. I love you, Mersey."

Melting inside, but speechless at his unexpected words, Mersey stroked his rough beard-shadowed cheek and stared into his eyes.

"See you soon," he said.

His eyes locked with hers as he gave her a quick kiss, lifted her back onto the wagon and rode forward.

Mersey stared after him, and then Captain Kendrick rode up beside her. Sandy had jumped from the wagon and untied his horse's reins from the back of the wagon. He rode up beside them now.

"Can you handle this wagon alone, Mersey?" Kendrick asked.

"She can handle the wagon," Sandy said and winked at Mersey. "Just remember what I taught ya, Miss. Keep 'em steady, and call 'em mangy critters every now and again. They'll think I'm still drivin'."

"Captain Kendrick, move the company forward by two's, double time!" Steele shouted.

Kendrick looked at Mersey, his eyes warm. "Take care, Miss Lockwood," he said.

"You, too, Captain," she said.

Kendrick glanced behind him then shouted to Steele, "What of the prisoner, sir?"

"He comes with us," Steele ordered. "Let's move!"

****

Pou Nachay rode back to the wagon as the troops and caravan wagons moved forward, vapor from the horses' nostrils clouding the air. The guards passed the wagon with Jennings between them.

Jennings' gaze searched the wagon until he saw Alameda, and his eyes met hers. His look said farewell, hers said take care, and then he was gone.

Pou Nachay pointed to a mass of boulders. "We will stay here for the night. There will be some shelter for us there," he said.

Mersey followed his point, and sighed with relief. As exhausted as she was, she knew Alameda and the children had to be more so.

Mersey drove the wagon into the open space near the rocks. Pou Nachay took the bridles and unhitched the team of two mules.

****

Pou Nachay knew this area well. As a youth he had sat many times with people of the pueblo in their kivas and heard their histories. Before Santa Fe and the Santa Fe trail, the Pecos Pueblo had called this area their home for generations. A few hours ride from this location, and twenty years ago, they had abandoned their homes and left a mission in ruins.

Two centuries ago, the Spanish Conquistadores and missionaries had come. Then after a century of the missionaries' attempts to convert the pueblo people to Christianity, after a century of oppression and disease and starvation, the people of pueblos across this land rose up in a coordinated revolt, driving the Spanish from New Mexico, and tearing the mission to the ground.

The Sangre de Cristo Mountains had been fertilized with blood, and it seemed this was destined to continue.

****

Once they were settled and had a fire going, Pou Nachay removed the heavy cotton wagon cover and draped it over posts to shelter one side of the wagon.

Pou Nachay knew the danger of building a fire when camped in hostile territory, but it couldn't be helped. They would die if they couldn't keep warm. The supplies in the wagon included blankets, corn meal, coffee, dried pork and beef, cooking utensils, bandages, and Mersey's sewing machine.

Mersey and Alameda retrieved the supplies they needed from the wagon and started a meal of bacon and skillet corn bread. Mersey melted snow in a coffee pot for drinking water.

Pou Nachay walked the perimeter in widening circles checking for any sign of a threat. He was squatted on his heels studying the rocky snow-covered ground when distant sounds of rifle fire reached them, coming from southeast of their camp.

It's started, Mersey thought, and she closed her eyes in a silent prayer for John and the soldiers.

But Pou Nachay's attention was fixed southwest of them, past a grove of trees and up a ridge, in the opposite direction of the rifle fire. He stood and took a few steps in the direction of the trees, and then stood still as he studied the sky, watched the flight of birds, and seemed to listen to the wind. After a few moments, he walked back to their fire.

"Will you be alright if I leave for a while?" he asked the women.

"What is it that is worrying you?" Alameda asked.

"Something is out of place," he said. "There is no threat to us close by, but I need to go take a look." He gestured southwest. "Up there. I will be back in a few hours. I will not let the camp out of my sight as I search." Then he turned to leave.

"Pou Nachay," Mersey said. "Take this with you."

She handed him bacon and cornbread wrapped in a cloth, and gave him some warm water in a cup.

Rifle fire was heard again in the distance and then cannon fire joined it.

"I'm terrified for them," Mersey said to Pou Nachay.

He took a drink of the water, but didn't speak.

"Do you think it will be over tonight?" she asked "that the Major will be back for us tonight?"

Pou Nachay shook his head. "No, not tonight."

March 26, 1862
Glorieta Pass, Santa Fe Trail, New Mexico
Day One

Steele led his fifty mounted cavalry and thirty infantry into the Union camp near Apache Creek. Chaos was evident in all quarters. The camp had been unprepared for this battle. How could that be with another army a stone's throw away? Had there been no forward patrols? Rifle fire erupted to the south.

"Soldier, where is your commander?" Steele shouted at a soldier running toward the canyon.

The soldier halted. "The command tent on that flat clearing, sir," he pointed to a tent fifty yards away.

"Who is in command? Is it Colonel Anderson of Fort Union?" Steele asked.

"No sir, a colonel from Denver, Colonel Whitmire. He looked south. "And Major Parody rides yonder"

Steele looked down the canyon and saw a large man leading at least a hundred mounted men at full charge, their horses jumping a deep, narrow chasm where the bridge had been destroyed.

"Sir?" the soldier questioned.

Steele nodded. "As you were, Private." and the soldier ran to join others of his company. Steele faced Captain Kendrick. "Have the mounted volunteers stay here until I return. When our artillery arrives, be ready to ride."

Steele rode to the command tent, dropped The Black's leading reins to the ground, and introduced himself to the soldier outside the tent, requesting to speak with Colonel Whitmire.

Permission was given for Steele to enter.

"Major Steele," Whitmire said, jumping to his feet answering Steele's salute. "Are you reinforcements from Fort Union?"

"No sir, we were called from Fort Garland to serve at Fort Union, and were on our way there when our forward patrol discovered your eminent encounter with the Confederates, sir," Steele said.

"Yes, well, we weren't expecting to encounter the Confederates here, but in Santa Fe. We had sent no forward scouts. The Rebels surprised us. It seems that we surprised them as well down in that narrow canyon. How many men are with you, Major?"

"Fifty mounted, thirty infantry, and we brought two mountain howitzers, sir," Steele said watching the colonel who looked more like an accountant than a soldier. The man was flustered, and lacked the calm resolve of a man familiar with battle command.

The sound of cannons joined the distant rifle fire, shaking the ground and pummeling the sides of the canyon a little too close for comfort.

"This terrain is not conducive to battle strategy, too many frozen ravines and steep cliffs. The forests are nearly impenetrable and I can't seem to get any estimates of their forces," Whitmire mumbled as he sat at his desk, his head resting in his hands.

"Sir," Steele said. "My men and I can do the reconnaissance and acquire the information you need. And if you will permit me, sir, I can position my two cannons on the plateau just south and east of this position, and counter their cannon fire."

"Yes, yes, Major, I would be grateful for that, and do it with the utmost haste and report back to me," Whitmire said.

Steele exited the tent, remounted The Black, and returned to his men.

"Major," Kendrick said. "The rifle fire is coming closer, and the cannon fire has caught dry trees and leaves on the hillsides on fire. We can hear wounded calling for help. What are your orders, sir?"

Steele looked around at the steep rocky ridges jutting up from the canyon, the thick underbrush, and at the smoke from the tree and brush fires that was beginning to obscure their visibility.

"Detail the men you need. Move every wounded man out of harms' way, do you understand?" Steele asked meeting Kendrick's eyes. "We will not stand by and let any helpless man be burned alive."

"Understood, sir," Kendrick said.

"Then take your mounted south into the canyon. See what you can observe about the Confederate forces and send a messenger back to Colonel Whitmire there in the command tent. Then report to me or Lieutenant Hawkins the same information. Engage the enemy forces if need be, but we need critical information of their numbers and locations, especially their cannons. Draw their fire to get their location, but stay within cover and out of range."

"Yes sir," Kendrick said. He detailed a dozen men to locate wounded and bring them into the camp. To the others he shouted, "Forward! Follow Me!"

Steele dismounted and led The Black to where Lieutenant Hawkins waited with the wagons.

"We need to get the howitzers to the flat tops of those two ridges above us south and east," Steele said. "We should be able to fire to our advantage from there."

"Yes sir," Hawkins said. "We're going to need to tie the cannons to the mules."

"That we will, Lieutenant. Will you see to it?"

"Right away, sir," Hawkins said, and began marshaling his men.

"Sir," said a young soldier coming toward. Steele

"Yes, Private Decker."

"Sir, Private Duran and I are guarding Master Sergeant Jennings, but we'd like to help if we can," Decker said. "All of us, sir."

Steele glanced at Jennings who sat on horseback, shackles on his wrists, and he accepted the man's silent entreaty.

"All of you, come with us," Steele said to Decker. "Help with the cannons."

"Yes sir, thank you, sir," Decker said.

The two mountain howitzers had been lowered from the wagons and were being wheeled by four men to where soldiers were standing ready to disassemble the guns and tie them to the mules.

Hawkins said, "We're only going to get partway up the ridge with the mules, sir."

Hawkins tilted his hat back as he considered the ridge, and squinted into the sunshine, looking up at the steep, narrow path leading to the rocky plateau seventy-five feet above them, jutting nearly vertical.

"And," he continued. "Someone is going to have to free-climb the last twenty-five feet or so of this cliff face, then anchor the ropes so we can pull the cannons up. It's going to be tricky to get those heavy guns off of the mules while standing on that narrow trail, and then rig the ropes to winch them up the rest of the way."

"Yup," Steele said. "Would you have a man retrieve that grappling hook?" he asked.

"Yes sir, I'll make sure we bring it along," he said.

Hawkins turned to supervise the soldiers as they prepared the mules to carry the cannons. Each cannon needed three mules for carriage, one for the barrel, one for the undercarriage, wheels and levers. A third was needed to carry two ammunition chests.

The narrow ridge trail leading up to the plateau wound a little north as well as west. It was rocky, with patches of small loose gravel. The north facing areas were shaded from the sun, and there, the trail was covered with ice. They climbed until it was too narrow for the mules to continue. Steele retrieved the grappling hook and commanded, "Stand back."

"Major," Hawkins said. "I should be the one to…"

"No, Lieutenant, the first try is mine. If I fail, it falls to you, no joke intended." Steele grinned. "Be ready with all the rope we have. I will pull it up and tie it so that others can climb up. I want at least six men on the plateau with me to steady the lift of the cannon. We're protected from rifle fire here behind this cliff face, but we'll be in the open up there. Tell them to keep their heads down."

Steele moved to the outer edge of the trail, swung the hook like a lasso, then aimed it upward and let go. He tried twice before hitting the top of the plateau, and a third time before tugging it back to catch on something invisible, and with luck, immovable.

After testing its stability to hold his weight, he wrapped the rope around his waist, slipped another coil of rope over his shoulders, and started to climb. Despite the freezing temperatures, Steele felt sweat bead on his forehead. His fingers and toes clutched every rock projection and protruding root available on the rock face. His hands were cramping, his muscles aching and trembling with his exertion, and it felt like it was taking forever. From his elevated position as he climbed, he could see lingering smoke from the cannons and thicker smoke from the brush fires below. He could make out fallen men and horses as they lay on the ground, some still as death, others writhing as if in agony.

He forced himself to concentrate on every finger-hold and toe-hold, to stay on task, because he wouldn't be able to help anyone if he didn't get those cannons into position. It took him long minutes to reach the top of the plateau, and then he dropped the rope. Once additional ropes were attached from below, Steele pulled up the lengths of rope, secured them to the sturdiest trees close by, and dropped the rope ends to the men ready and waiting below.

"Six men are coming up the ropes, sir," Hawkins yelled. "Then we'll tie the first cannon."

As six men cleared the edge of the plateau, the sniper fire began, and they all dropped to the ground. They'd been spotted.

"Ready the cannon," Steele shouted down.

Steele directed the men with him on the plateau to wrap the ropes around boulders and sturdy trees, then drop the rope ends to the men waiting below. After securing the first howitzer with the ropes, making a fulcrum and hitching two mules with the ropes, Hawkins and his men began to hoist the five hundred pound cannon, in manageable pieces, up the last twenty-five feet of the seventy-five foot rock face.

As Steele waited on the top of the plateau, he watched the battle play out south of his position. Some of the cannon load being fired must be filled with incendiary materials, as well as gun powder and musket balls, because the snow had been melted by the heat of the cannon blasts, exposing the dried leaves and twigs underneath the snow pack. Those same exposed dried leaves and twigs were smoldering and then catching fire as the wind blew past.

Dozens of dead and injured horses were scattered across the canyon. Some were bleeding from massive wounds, mortally wounded, and others, eyes wide and panicked by the smell of smoke, were struggling to stand, their broken legs buckling, compounding their injuries. Steele could hardly bear it.

Then in the brilliant blaze of the sun, he was filled with horror as he saw new brush fires approaching some of the wounded.

"Hawkins!" Steele shouted down. "There are more fires! We have to move the wounded men!"

A bullet whizzed by Steele, and then a cannon shot hit directly below him on the cliff face, shattering rock and shrubs, sending sparks and debris hissing and pinging down to the ground. His eyes stung and his lungs burned from the smoke as he scrambled for cover. He lifted his head, looking for tell-tale smoke from the cannon, but couldn't pinpoint it. He needed to take out those guns. He needed a target.

The men below fought to hold the cannon steady and keep it from crashing against the cliff as it swung on the rope above them, every man straining under the weight. Now, the wounded still coherent began to scream in earnest, afraid of being burned alive.

"We can't let go, sir! The cannon will be damaged or it will fall and crush us!" Hawkins shouted back.

Then Jennings stepped forward, grasping the rope and wrapping it around his forearms. He pulled, growling with the strain, his massive muscles bulging, taking the slack for two men.

"Go!" Jennings gasped to Hawkins.

Hawkins, Duran, and Decker ran into the heavy, toxic smoke calling out for men to answer them, frantic in their desperate search to find the wounded men before the fast-moving fire could reach them. When a man answered, the rescuers strained to locate the direction of the call. One after another, they scooped the men onto their shoulders, or worked together to lift and carry them, or hobbled with them, or dragged them near the clearing below the men hoisting the cannons. In a matter of minutes, twenty men were rescued from the spreading brushfires. Duran stayed with them, getting them water and applying bandages as Hawkins and Decker returned to Jennings.

From above, Steele looked away from the horses screaming in pain and terror as the fire engulfed them, knowing there was nothing he could do, nothing anyone could do to save them. Steele thought of the affection he felt for The Black. He fought sadness at the loss of the animals in the canyon below. Steele had no sooner watched the wounded below him be carried to safety when movement erupted from the thick stand of trees forty feet away from him on the plateau, accompanied by gun smoke, fierce Rebel yells, and a barrage of bullets.

"Hold the guiding ropes!" Steele told two men.

Jennings looked up at the sounds of pistol shots and shotgun blasts.

"Lieutenant, you need to get more men up there!" Jennings shouted. "Help the major and the men. They're under attack on the plateau, sir!"

Hawkins looked at him blankly. "How?" he asked.

"You, Decker, and Duran need to get up there. Go up the ropes," Jennings said. "Tell the mule handlers to hold the mules steady. Do it now, sir!"

Hawkins gave the order, then he, Decker and Duran began to climb, pulling past the cannon pieces suspended as if weightless against the cliff.

****

Pistols empty, outnumbered and overrun, Steele and his four men battled the Confederates. They fought now with fists and sabers to keep the enemy soldiers from capturing the two men gripping the ropes at the top of the plateau. Steele took a glancing blow to the side of his head from a rifle butt. Stars exploded behind his eyes and he fell to the ground, losing his hold on his saber. In his peripheral vision, he saw two of the Confederates rush past him toward the defenseless men holding the ropes steady.

"Look out!" he shouted to them, grabbing for his saber, struggling to gain his feet, but despairing. He would be too late to aid them.

The Confederates grabbed the soldiers who couldn't let go of the ropes to defend themselves. Just as it seemed the men would be overcome, Hawkins, Decker, and Duran pulled themselves up over the edge of the plateau and charged the Confederates, pistols firing at close range. The Confederates turned and retreated into the trees from which they had come.

When they were able to get the cannons maneuvered onto the plateau, and the men began to reassemble them, Steele led twenty men into the trees in pursuit of the Confederate soldiers who had charged them, to assure that they were not still a threat to them and the artillery. After moving one hundred yards into the trees and no engagement from the Confederates, Steele signaled for the men to hold their positions.

A man emerged from the trees on Steele's right, and he looked surprised for a moment as he stared down the line of men. The man wore a tattered and ill-fitting blue infantry coat, and buckskin pants. He carried a shotgun instead of an Army rifle, and he only briefly met Steele's eyes.

Steele didn't recognize him, but knew that in battle and on unfamiliar rough terrain such as this, men often became separated from their companies.

When the man moved away from them going right again, and back through the trees, Steele said, "You be careful now, those fellows from Texas will shoot you."

The man answered, "Thank you, sir, I surely will be careful."

Steele watched the man disappear into the trees, thinking about the ill-fitting blue coat and reports that the Confederates had come poorly dressed for the weather, and thinking that the man's speech reminded him of his own when he tried to cover his drawl.

Gray Eagle

Pou Nachay returned to camp carrying a boy of about twelve or thirteen years of age with a bullet wound in his left shoulder. He laid the shivering, half-conscious boy down close to the fire near Alameda and Mersey. Alameda gave Salayah to Cochetopa to hold.

"How did you find him?" Alameda asked. "Did you have to shoot him?"

Pou Nachay gave her a look. "I didn't shoot him."

"Then who shot him?" she asked. "His clothing looks Apache. He's too young to be out here on his own, isn't he?"

Pou Nachay shook his head.

"He may have been separated from a hunting party. He wears no war paint, or none remains. He might have been on a quest of manhood," he said and shrugged. "I need to find out if he knows where the men are who shot him."

"Let's get a look at the wound, get him warm, and maybe then he can tell you," Alameda said.

An unmistakable sound of a turkey gobble sounded in a stand of shrubs nearby.

"Turkey," Cochetopa said, then listened, "more than one."

Pou Nachay smiled at Cochetopa and nodded, and slipped away from the fire. Mersey and Alameda wrapped the Apache boy in a blanket before looking at his shoulder.

"The bullet went through his shoulder," Mersey said. "We need to clean it well. He must have crawled to some hiding place, judging from the stains on his clothing, and tried to pack some dry moss into the wound to help stop the bleeding. Smart boy."

He was looking at them now, his dark eyes wary, his shivering not as severe.

"Uncle taught me some Apache," Cochetopa said. "Should I try to speak to him?"

Alameda looked at Mersey, who nodded her agreement. Then Alameda said, "Ask him if he would let us clean his wounds?"

Cochetopa chose his words carefully, and then the boy nodded. With quick efficient motions, Mersey cleaned and bandaged the wounds. The boy stared at her face as she took care of his shoulder. She smiled at him when she noticed the intensity of his dark-eyed gaze, thinking that he wasn't convinced that he should trust her, but then he smiled back at her.

"Cochetopa, would you ask him if he would like a drink of water and something to eat?" Mersey asked.

The boy nodded again to Cochetopa's question, and sat up, bracing his weight on his uninjured shoulder. Pou Nachay came back then with two turkey carcasses, gutted, plucked, and ready to roast on a spit.

"You must teach me to do that, Uncle," Cochetopa said. "We didn't hear you hunt them."

Pou Nachay nodded. Then he turned a questioning gaze to the Apache boy.

In Apache he asked, "What is your name?"

"Gray Eagle," the boy answered.

"How did you get wounded?" Pou Nachay asked.

"Two men shot me and stole furs from me, and took my horse."

"Did you know them?" Pou Nachay asked.

"No," Gray Eagle said.

"Did you see their camp?" Pou Nachay asked.

Gray Eagle pointed and Pou Nachay nodded, as if he already knew, and the boy had confirmed it.

Pou Nachay looked at Alameda.

"I need Cochetopa to keep the horses and mules fed and watered, and to help gather enough dry branches to keep the fire going tonight," he said.

Alameda took the baby from Cochetopa and nodded, understanding that Pou Nachay meant he wouldn't be back until morning.

Pou Nachay looked at the turkeys roasting on the spit and then at Cochetopa. "The smell of meat may bring predators. Keep the fire well supplied."

"What kind of men would shoot a boy, steal his things, and leave him for dead?" Mersey said.

She looked at Pou Nachay's fierce expression, and she knew without him having to say it aloud, two men, Jocko and Curly. Pou Nachay was going alone after Jocko and Curly.

Mersey started to protest, but Alameda stopped her with a hand on her arm and shook her head.

"Pou Nachay knows what he is doing. He will not want you to question his decision," she said.

Mersey asked Pou Nachay for his army canteen and filled it with warm water, and put more food in a cloth wrapper. She offered it to him, and he accepted.

****

Pou Nachay tracked back to where he had found Gray Eagle and glanced toward the moon-lit snow-covered hills. Steady falling snow was filling the hoof prints of three horses, two horses carried riders and one horse was being led. The hoof prints headed toward a slender thread of smoke from a campfire. Pou Nachay felt caution holding him back, though he was always cautious. This was different. If something happened and he couldn't return, five people, now six including the Apache boy, would be unprotected and defenseless from too many possible threats. But he couldn't chance Jocko and Curly surprising them in an ambush. He must act first before the two men discovered him and his precious cargo.

Even now he questioned the wisdom of bringing the injured boy back to their camp. The People of his father, the Apache, were volatile, and no matter his good intentions, no matter that the boy's wound had nothing to do with him, the Apache could target him and those under his safekeeping for retribution of what had happened to the boy.

Pou Nachay shouldered his rifle and followed the trail. It would take him an hour to reach the campfire, and then he would decide what to do. The men deserved to die for what they had done to Alameda. He would not kill them. He wanted no confrontation with them. He planned to cripple them and keep them away from those under his protection.

He was a Native Indian, and it was becoming a white man's world. If he killed the men, he wouldn't have time to make their bodies disappear. But if he could do what he planned, the criminals would soon be battling for their lives against Mother Earth.

****

Mersey dreamed a storm's massive waves crashed against a brittle straw house at the edge of an ocean.

Inside she huddled wet and cold in a corner as the house broke apart, wind wailing into the breach, and she awoke to the sound of the howling of wolves.

Cochetopa and the Apache boy were awake, talking, feeding the fire, their eyes watching the dark beyond where yellow eyes reflected in the fire light. Cochetopa turned to her.

"The wolves don't come closer, Miss Mersey," Cochetopa said. "We're keeping the fire high."

"Good job," she said, and smiled as she noted that two of the turkey legs had been devoured.

It was snowing now, and Alameda, Antera, and the baby were sleeping. Mersey drew the blanket closer around her, and moved to sit beside Alameda and the children, making sure they were covered under the canvas shelter. That was when she felt the quiet. All sound of battle had ceased, and she wondered if John was alright, prayed that he and the men were alright, and Pou Nachay.

****

Jocko snickered, "What do you mean you can't say for sure that little Apache boy was done in?"

"It don't matter none anyways," Curly defended. "Knocked out and bleedin' is as good as done in with the ground frozen and it freezing so hard at night. Then there's hungry wolves and bears around to smell the blood, and we needed to make tracks, and fast, before any more of them Apache showed up."

Jocko's eyes scanned the perimeters of the camp where the firelight faded into darkness, uneasiness crawling up his spine, and he took another drink from the half empty bottle of whiskey.

"Them Apache are like ghosts. Ya can't hear 'em or see 'em half the time," Jocko said scowling, his speech slurring from the whiskey he had consumed.

Curly said, "You're just spooked. You can't hear 'em or see 'em 'cause there ain't any Apaches out there. We should be more worried 'bout Pou Nachay trailin' us. He'd likely slit our throats for what we done to his sister. But she needed to be taught a lesson for causin' us trouble when we was just havin' a little fun. And we got a good head start, and we'll soon be in Santa Fe."

Curly looked around at the darkness, then back at Jocko. "Hey, that there's our last bottle. Pass it back over here 'fore you drink it all." Curly shivered and pulled his collar up higher. "It is miserable cold out here. Let's finish this bottle and get some sleep, and when morning comes, we'll get so long gone, it'll be like we just up and disappeared."

"I'm tellin' ya, I'm not spooked. Somethin's out there. I can feel it waitin' fer us to fall asleep." Jocko stood, weaving and unsteady, and peered into the darkness beyond the firelight. "We ain't lived this long by not listenin' to our guts."

Curly got to his feet. "Alright, alright, let's go take a look see once around the camp, and then get us some shut eye. There, are ya happy now?"

Pou Nachay knew that Jocko and Curly would find him if they circled the camp. His best option had been a surprise attack, but that advantage was leaving on the wind. He watched Curly reach for his shotgun. He readied himself, hoping they would start their search with their backs to him, but luck was not with him. They walked straight for him.

Curly led the way, pausing and turning to taunt Jocko who stumbled along after him. Pou Nachay shifted his weight forward onto the balls of his feet, and his muscles tensed. This wasn't going the way he planned, but he would take these men down, and then pray that Mother Earth would finish the job.

But there was always Coyote, the trickster of legend to his People, who might let these men live to torment him. If his plan failed, he prayed that the snow cover his tracks and not lead these two evil men back to the women and children.

****

When Mersey woke again, Pou Nachay was back, sitting by the fire, and the boys were asleep. There was dried blood on his knuckles and a bruise on his cheek.

He glanced at her and gave her a reassuring nod. She handed him a blanket, and she fell back to sleep.

March 27, 1862
Apache Canyon
Day Two

The next morning they followed the trail along the bank of the frozen Apache Creek. Mersey held the reins of the wagon and Antera sat beside her. Alameda and the baby were in the back of the wagon with the injured boy. Cochetopa rode the boy's Indian pony beside Pou Nachay, and led two other horses. The two new horses had Army saddles. No one asked where they had come from, and Pou Nachay, a man of few words, didn't offer to explain.

The trail was arduous over the rocky snow-packed ground and progress was slow. After traveling for over an hour, they reached a rough-timbered bridge over Apache Creek that had been scorched and damaged. Heavy smoke from cannon fire lingered in Apache Canyon like a fog, stinging their eyes and making them cough, drifting and clearing in the light wind, only to settle around them again, limiting their ability to judge their surroundings. Alameda had the children cover their noses and mouths with scarves, and she covered the baby's face with the blanket.

Smoke from the cannons was a dreadful reminder for Mersey that John hadn't come back for them. Though there didn't' seem to be any fighting today, she was unsure what that could mean. Were they taking care of the dead and wounded, or were they strategizing and repositioning, or was the battle over? If so, had they won the day?

Won the day, Mersey thought with a grimace. The expression sounded profoundly wrong to her, placing war at the level of a morbid game, as if to capture a flag, as if there could be an across-the-board winner and loser, as if the tragedy of life-changing injuries or of the incalculable sorrow for loss of their fellows could be diminished when the collective force had ultimately won the day. It was individuals who lived or died, unique potentials that were gained or lost, personal hopes and dreams saved or sacrificed that must be measured at the end of the day.

Mersey's heart ached for John, regardless of the day's outcome. He had fought for the Union against soldiers loyal to the South, his birthplace, his home. He would feel the loss for both sides of the conflict.

The wagon crossed the battle-scarred bridge over Apache Creek without mishap. Pou Nachay rode to the wagon and looked at Mersey, seeming to make a decision based on that look.

He said, "We'll stop here for rest for an hour and then we'll move on to Johnson Station."

"Thank you, Pou Nachay." Mersey said as she pulled the mules to a stop, looped the reins over the post and rubbed her shoulders. "Rest is welcome."

Mersey had driven the wagon for a few hours, and her whole body ached. Yesterday, she had listened with absent-minded courtesy to Sandy as she rode beside him, her mind wandering to other things. Now she realized that he had been demonstrating the basics of driving this wagon, instructing her. She needed to remember not to say yes to questions asked of her while daydreaming.

Before this journey, she had driven horses and buggies, but she had found a new respect for drivers who drove teams of mules. The muscles in her upper body were strained from the near constant pulling on the reins, holding back the mules from a too rapid descent down the slopes, and from snapping the reins when they climbed too slowly. Her lower body was strained from bracing her feet against the footboard, half-afraid that she would be pulled forward enough to fall head first from the wagon with the jostling changes in speed, and be trampled or run over.

She wondered how long it would take her exhausted body to recover from the dipping and shuddering and side-shifting of the wagon as its wheels accommodated the rough, rocky terrain. She realized that she was still bracing herself against the sway, and she could still hear the creaking of the wagon in her ears, though she was now sitting still.

Mersey glanced along the canyon and thought she might have seen a small group of men, men who had to be soldiers, moving further south, away from where she sat in the wagon. She couldn't tell the color of their uniforms from this distance.

The men appeared as apparitions walking slowly, silently, through the lingering drifting smoke and smoldering ash, stopping, as if searching, sometimes lifting something from the ground, but always moving on. They were looking for wounded, she thought, or maybe they were marking bodies for a burial detail.

What a blessing it would be that she could be asleep, only dreaming that she was awake, and none of this was real, just a nightmare.

Mersey prayed for peace.

Pou Nachay dismounted, his eyes alert and scanning the smoke-shifting terrain all around them. He helped Mersey down and she walked around to the back of the wagon and held the baby as Alameda climbed out of the covered wagon.

As if by rote, Pou Nachay started a fire, and Mersey retrieved the supplies to melt snow for drinking water and put together a meal for them. Pou Nachay carried Gray Eagle into the trees to allow the boy to relieve himself, and then brought him close to the fire. Alameda had placed blankets over gathered piles of fallen leaves to help provide comfort and warmth for them while sitting on the frozen ground.

They sat together, talking, consuming their meal, until a muffled turkey gobble sounded, the location elusive, but close by. Pou Nachay looked up, then stood up, and walked away from their campsite, trying to stare through the smoke into the trees.

"Will he hunt more turkeys?" Mersey asked.

"This time, Miss, it wasn't a turkey that made that call," Cochetopa said, his voice lowered. "We must be quiet and still."

Pou Nachay moved further away, and now the turkey calls seemed to be coming from points of a circle around him, the callers concealed in the dense underbrush and forest, the sounds misleading in the low visibility, but he knew where to walk to intercept an approaching war party of Apache. Twenty warriors on horseback rode out of the smoke and stopped before him.

Pou Nachay had no doubt that many more were hidden around him. They must have observed him when he carried the boy into the trees. Pou Nachay scolded himself for his carelessness in showing the boy kindness. Kindness did not always bring reward.

One warrior rode in the front and center of the warriors and wore the markings of the chief.

"We search for a boy," he said to Pou Nachay in Apache. "His name is Gray Eagle. He is my son. If he is returned safely to us, you will be left unharmed."

"We found a boy, wounded, but not by our hand," Pou Nachay said. "He is weak from his wound, and he rests with us. We have cared for him. But we will not turn him over to you unless he requests it."

The chief glanced at the visible few who were huddled at the campsite, and smirked. His expression revealing that he didn't think Pou Nachay had a prayer of trying to stop them if they decided to be less courteous.

"You speak our language, yet you wear the clothing of a white soldier," he said, indicating the coat Pou Nachay wore.

"I am Pou Nachay. My mother taught me. She was Ute, my father Apache. I am scout for the fort, north and west over the mountains."

"I know of this fort," the chief said. "I will speak to the boy." He signaled for the warriors to dismount.

Pou Nachay looked toward the small camp a hundred feet away. The women and children sat huddled and partially hidden by the wagon. He couldn't risk revealing the prize they were, and how inadequate he was to defend them.

"I will bring him to you," Pou Nachay said.

The Apache chief cocked his head, perhaps wondering at Pou Nachay's hesitancy to let him enter their camp, but nodded his agreement.

Pou Nachay walked back to the camp, and knelt at the boy's side.

"Wake," he said, and the boy's eyes fluttered open to look at him. "Your father searches for you. Do you want to go with him?"

"Are you certain it is my father?" the boy asked.

"He is leading a war party of Apache. He called you by name," Pou Nachay said.

"I am the son of a chief," he said. "It would be a coup for our enemies to take me."

"They are a superior force," Pou Nachay said.

The boy looked at the women and children gathered near the fire and nodded.

"Then take me to them," the boy said bravely.

Pou Nachay nodded, lifted the boy to his feet, then into his arms.

The Apache chief watched Pou Nachay and the boy approach, and leapt from his horse to take the boy from Pou Nachay, and then he lowered the boy to the ground and knelt beside him.

"I feel great joy that you are alive, my son," he said, holding the boy to him.

"Father, I feel joy to see you, my chief. I felt I would not see you again until we met in the land of the Great Spirit."

"Are these people responsible for your wound?" the Apache chief asked, looking at the boy's bandaged shoulder.

"No, it was two white men," the boy answered.

"Were they soldiers?" the chief asked.

"I am not sure. They wore some soldier clothing, but they were dirty and unshaven. They shot me and stole the furs I carried. They left me for dead, but this man found me," the boy indicated Pou Nachay. "He found me and brought me here."

"Where are the men now?" the chief asked.

"The man," Gray Eagle indicated Pou Nachay again. "He found them."

Looking at Pou Nachay, the chief asked, "Where are they?"

Pou Nachay gestured southwest and then he said, "On the mountain. When those men next awaken, they will find that they have traded their boots and horses for the furs they stole, though they will find the furs are gone as well," Pou Nachay said. "All are the boy's to take with him."

The Apache chief nodded and the boy smiled.

Pou Nachay had also relieved Jocko and Curly of their rifles, but those he would not offer to the Apache. If Jocko and Curly could defy Mother Earth and make it out of the mountains alive, they will have suffered, and would lose their unprotected feet to the bitter cold.

"Did these people treat you well? Are they to be left in peace?" the chief asked the boy and gestured to Pou Nachay and the people in the camp.

"They saved my life," the boy said, "Though I would take the woman with eyes the purple color of mountains at sunset as wife."

"He just said what?" Mersey whispered to Cochetopa who had been translating.

"It's what I would ask for, if I were him," Cochetopa said with a shrug.

"Would you now," Mersey said with a small smile, remembering the two young Townsends on the stagecoach and wondering why marriage was on the mind of so many young boys.

The Apache chief spoke.

"The chief said that the boy couldn't yet protect a wife," Cochetopa said.

"That's good," Mersey whispered.

"But that he, the chief could. A month ago he lost his second wife to fever," Cochetopa said.

"Oh dear," Mersey said.

The chief spoke again, and Mersey saw Pou Nachay grow even more alert, something she hadn't thought possible.

"The chief asked to see the woman with the purple eyes," Cochetopa said.

Pou Nachay spoke then.

Mersey looked at Cochetopa.

"My uncle said that you are the woman of a powerful warrior of high rank in the white army," Cochetopa said.

Was that what Pou Nachay believed? Or was it a tactic to protect her? Mersey frowned. Did she belong to John? Either way, she couldn't worry about it now. Everyone waited while the chief thought this information over. He cocked his head.

"Where is the powerful white warrior?" he asked.

"Close by," Pou Nachay said, and waited, unmoving, but watchful.

A trick by a trickster, Pou Nachay thought, a half-truth, an attempt to instill caution that an aggressive move toward them would soon bring retribution. Pou Nachay knew that the chief was smart enough to recognize it, and call his bluff, but he hoped that, for once, Coyote was done tormenting him, and would stand beside him instead.

Baby Salayah slept. Mersey, Alameda, Cochetopa and Antera sat frozen, and for long moments, the only sound was the crackling of the fire, as if time had slowed and all of nature held its breath. Smoke from the battlefield drifted around them as the wind seemed to shift, sometimes obscuring the warriors, and though he stood closer to the camp, obscuring Pou Nachay.

As with the wind, something shifted in the chief's eyes, his dark eyes seeming to harden with cunning, and with something more primal and dangerous as he surveyed the wagon, the mules and horses, and the women and children. His relaxed posture altered as he glanced around him, as if weighing the possible truth of Pou Nachay's words, his gratitude for the safe return of his son all but forgotten, replaced by anticipation of an easy victory and spoils.

The chief's gaze moved over his warriors and some intangible, invisible knowledge passed between them, some unseen signal, but something that alerted Pou Nachay as well, because his eyes locked on the chief.

Mersey glanced at Alameda who was hugging Antera and Salayah close to her chest, her eyes wide as she watched her brother.

Mersey remembered then that Pou Nachay and Alameda's mother was taken by a man such as these warriors, and suddenly Pou Nachay looked acutely, perilously alone.

The grave danger to Pou Nachay as he stood ready to defend them with his life hit Mersey like a lightning strike, stealing her breath, tripping her heart, and she felt very afraid as the world around them shifted again and more armed Apache warriors crept out of hiding.

In a smooth motion, Pou Nachay lifted his rifle and pointed it toward the chief as the warriors closed in on him from all sides. The men were tense, silent and still for a long moment, waiting.

Pou Nachay's eyes stayed on the chief.

The chief broke eye contact with Pou Nachay, gestured something to the warriors and they lowered their weapons and backed a little away, but stayed within striking distance.

Then one warrior stepped forward and spoke to the chief with some urgency. The chief's eyes cut to Pou Nachay, and then dropped to the rifle Pou Nachay held in a steady grip aimed at his chest. He nodded to Pou Nachay.

Mersey was so frightened for all of them that she could barely breathe to whisper, "Cochetopa, what did the warrior say?"

Cochetopa grinned at her. "He said white soldiers approach."

Mersey wanted to feel relieved, but the tension surrounding Pou Nachay remained.

"How many?" the chief asked his warrior.

"Twenty more than our number," the warrior said.

"On horseback?" the chief asked.

"Some, but others are on foot," the warrior said. "All are wounded."

"Good," the chief said. "Mount up. We will outrun them."

The chief lifted his son onto his horse, climbed up behind him, and as sudden as they had appeared, the Apache rode away.

****

Mersey let out the breath she had been holding. It would be alright now. The cavalry had returned. She said a prayer for John that he was safe and whole, because if John was with these soldiers, it meant that he was injured. *All are wounded* the warrior had said. There were medical supplies in the wagon, She could help care for their wounds. It would be alright now.

She waited, expecting Pou Nachay to return to Alameda and the children and their campsite, but he stayed in the clearing. She watched him lower his weapon, but he didn't relax his guard as he turned to face the wooded area behind him.

As the Apache disappeared to the north, twenty soldiers rode out of the woods from the south. Thirty approached on foot, some supporting each other. Two ambulance wagons followed.

"Hold there," a voice commanded.

"Oh, thank heaven," Mersey said, knowing that voice.

It was John. He was alive and he had come back for them as he had promised. She jumped up and ran toward him.

"I'm so glad to see…." Mersey broke off her greeting, hesitating, and her smile faded as she looked up into that familiar face.

Something stayed her speech, something about his expression as he sat his great horse in the shifting smoke and light. There was interest in those intelligent gray eyes watching her, but no recognition.

The horse he rode was not The Black, but a beautiful russet-colored thoroughbred.

And the uniform was wrong….

Not The Black….

Not....John.

"Who are you?" she whispered.

But he must have heard.

"Captain Jordan Steele of the Seventh Texas Mounted Rifles and the Confederate Army of New Mexico, ma'am," he said, and as Mersey continued to gape at him, he tipped his hat in a chivalrous gesture. "From your expression, I believe you may have been expecting an army of a different color," he stated with a wry smile. His eyes moved to Pou Nachay where he stood holding his lowered rifle, watching them with silent scrutiny. "May we be of service, ma'am?" asked the man with the memorable deep drawl.

Mersey was too stunned to respond.

Jordan Steele.

John's brother, his twin.

A Confederate Cavalry Officer.

Here.

If Jordan was curious about her odd behavior toward him, he was too much of a gentleman to show it, and he had already guessed that she was expecting Union soldiers. He held the reins of his great horse in his right hand. There was dried blood on the left shoulder of his gray uniform and his left arm was in a sling. A bloody bandage was on his left thigh and the wound seeming to still be oozing blood. Jordan leaned back in his saddle in a manner so like John that Mersey continued to stare at him. He looked at the encampment and the supply wagon. Then his alert consideration settled again on Pou Nachay.

Pou Nachay met his gaze steadily, and if he was as surprised at Jordan's appearance as Mersey, he kept it hidden.

Mersey looked at Alameda and the children, who seemed as captivated by Jordan Steele as she was.

Jordan signaled to the men on foot.

"This band of wounded that I now command is headed for Johnson Station. It looks like ya 'all will be coming with us," Jordan said in polite speech as the infantry soldiers approached Pou Nachay and demanded that he surrender his weapons. "And we will be most appreciative of any supplies you could spare that you carry in that wagon," he said.

Mersey found her voice then.

"Of course you are welcome to any of our supplies for yourself and your men who need care for your wounds, Captain," she said as she watched Pou Nachay put his rifle and hunting knife on the ground.

Pou Nachay stood proud and straight as the soldiers confiscated his weapons, but his eyes were on Alameda and the children. Mersey knew how important it was to him that he be able to defend his family, and had they just traded one threat for another? Pou Nachay had to be trusting, as she was, that these soldiers were disciplined enough not to harm them.

A few of the soldiers dismounted to escort her, Alameda, and the children to the wagon, leading them to the rear of the wagon as one of the infantry soldiers climbed onto the driver's seat. Pou Nachay remained on foot and under guard.

She wanted to speak to Pou Nachay, but how could she with him under guard? Pou Nachay had chosen not to speak to Jordan about John. Should she tell Jordan about his brother? Would that be the right or the wrong thing to do? She missed her father very much at that moment, but maybe even he wouldn't have the answer to her question. For now, she would keep John a secret.

As Mersey stepped to the back of the wagon, she heard a faint call coming from somewhere near the battered bridge. Staring through the smoke, it moved with the wind and she saw a man, a soldier, who lay trapped under his horse. He seemed to be looking at her. He moved his arm and waved for her to come.

Without hesitation, she turned and started walking toward the man.

"Ma'am," the soldier closest to her said, stopping her with a hand on her arm. "You must get into the wagon."

Jordan rode to where she stood. He looked toward the bridge in the direction she had been walking.

"Is there something wrong here, ma'am?" he asked, alert that there could be enemy soldiers nearby.

"Someone is there, hurt, near the bridge. He is calling out. Can you not hear him?" she asked.

"Our ears are all still ringing with gunfire, ma'am, but we will oblige you and check," Jordan said.

He is as gallant as John, she thought, and she wouldn't have believed that possible of anyone until now. She watched his careful dismount. He must be in significant pain with his wounds, but he didn't let it show. She could see subtle differences now. He was leaner than John, but powerfully built, and he looked pale and exhausted, as if he had been through hell.

He took her elbow and walked with her toward the bridge, limping slightly on his left leg. When she got closer, she gasped. A young man watched her as if willing her to come to him. He looked nowhere else but into her eyes. The man had to be severely injured as he was trapped in such a way under his dead horse that he must be crushed below mid-chest. His back must be broken.

The horse laid dead, its body torn open by cannon fire. It must have reared up and fallen over backward onto this soldier in its death throes, injuring him beyond all hope of healing. How was this man still breathing? She glanced up at Jordan. His jaw was set in a tight line.

"Ma'am," the soldier said, his voice weak, almost breathless. "I seem to be trapped….under Old Jumper here….a finer plow horse….you never did see….but it seems….he was unsuited for battle….didn't…like the cannon fire at all, ma'am."

Mersey knelt beside the young man and touched his cool face with gentle fingers. He clutched her hand to his cheek and closed his eyes with her touch.

He said, "I was afraid to blink, afraid….you'd disappear….if I closed my eyes, but you're still here."

Mersey looked up at Jordan.

"I need Pou Nachay," she said. "He will know how to…." *what? Unbury this soldier from the crushing weight of the horse? And then what?*

Pou Nachay was beside her then, kneeling on one knee. He looked at the fallen soldier, then the horse and the ground around them, knowing it was frozen.

"I will dig you out," he told the man.

The young man seemed to notice for the first time that there were others there beside Mersey.

"I'd be….right grateful," he said to Pou Nachay. "Cap'n," he said respectfully to Jordan, and Jordan nodded in acknowledgement.

It was then that it dawned on Mersey that the man wore gray.

The young soldier looked at Mersey again.

"The burial detail….didn't help me, couldn't hear me….callin' from here, I reckon. You, pretty lady, heard me calling….when no one else did."

Pou Nachay retrieved shovels from the wagon and together with two other soldiers who seemed to have less disabling wounds, carefully dug the frozen ground around the young Confederate soldier. Then Pou Nachay took hold of the man under his arms and eased him from under the animal.

Mersey's breath caught as the soldier's body was exposed, revealing a large open abdominal wound.

"I need bandages from the wagon, if you wouldn't mind getting them," she said to Pou Nachay. "Alameda knows where they are kept, and I also need some clean warm water from the pot."

He nodded, and a soldier escorted him to the wagon. Mersey knelt again beside the young man, and Jordan knelt beside her, though she knew it must hurt him to do so.

"My name is Mersey Lockwood," she said to him. "What is your name?" she asked.

"Corporal Vance Hicks, Miss Lockwood, of the Arizona Rangers, at your service," he said, his breathing though still weak, was easier now. "But I'd be pleased if you'd call me Vance. I surely miss having a pretty girl call me Vance."

"I would be delighted, Corporal, to call you Vance," she said. "And you must call me Mersey."

"Mersey," Vance repeated. "That's a right pretty name."

"Thank you," she said.

Pou Nachay arrived then with a package of bandages and a container of water, and handed both to Mersey.

"I will bring a stretcher," Pou Nachay said to Mersey, and she thanked him again.

Mersey turned to the young man and said, "Let's see what we can do to get you cleaned up, Vance."

Mersey was amazed that the wound wasn't bleeding. The position of the fallen horse must have put pressure on the wound, keeping this young man from bleeding to death, and he must not have felt the pain of the wound because it was below the level of the injury to his back. He had to be unaware of either life-threatening injury.

Mersey cleaned and began to bandage the wound, though she knew it would be for naught. The bowel had been ruptured, and was leaking dark bloody material. It was a gift that Vance couldn't feel the pain. Her hands were shaking, and Jordan reached out to steady her hand and help her wrap the wound.

When they finished, she said, "There, all done for now, but we must try to keep the bandages dry."

"You have the most tender touch, ma'am," Vance said. "I didn't feel a thing."

Mersey forced a smile, but Vance took her hand.

"I know what shape I'm in, ma'am. I had a horse fall on me once before, and broke all kinds of bones. Some are likely broke again, but I can't feel anything below my heart. I just hoped to have someone to talk to, and not have to get on with this all alone."

Mersey's eyes filled with tears, and then the tears began to fall, but she held fast to her smile.

"I would love to listen and talk all you want, Vance. We'll get on with this together," she said.

"Can we get him to the wagon without hurting him?" she asked Jordan.

Jordan was staring at her, his gray eyes full of something like approval, and perhaps gratitude, and even admiration.

"We'll get it done," he said and gave the order.

Pou Nachay arrived with the stretcher.

Most of the men were in such imperiled physical condition with uncared-for wounds, exposure to bitter weather, infection, and poor nutrition, that Mersey worried for everyone's safety who tried to move Vance. If not for Pou Nachay's strength, they would not have gotten it done.

Mersey had returned to the wagon to prepare some comfort for the soldier, and to enlist Alameda's help in caring for him, and soon they were on the move again toward Johnson Station. It took more than an hour for them to reach Johnson Station where they were met by a handful of Confederate soldiers who had been left with the task of guarding the supply wagons at the station, and seeing to the care of several hundred horses and mules stabled in a large corral. There were more than two dozen supply wagons standing idle around the fenced corral.

Jordan ordered the guards to find blankets and bedrolls in the supply wagons, and to carry or assist the more seriously wounded in the ambulance wagons to get settled inside the station house.

The guards agreed, but one of them informed Jordan that the wagons held mostly munitions, the personal belongings of the soldiers, some food, and little else.

Mersey looked at Jordan's stalwart expression.

"We will share the food and supplies in our wagon. Even with this number of men, we have supplies enough for a few days," she said.

Frowning, he asked, "What of you and the Indian family? You will need more than a few days' supplies to complete your journey."

"We have Pou Nachay," she said. "We won't lack what we need."

The wagon she had driven had supplies intended to provision the Fort Garland soldiers on their march to Fort Union. To use the supplies otherwise, it might put the Fort Garland soldiers at risk, but it couldn't be helped. She could only hope that the supplies brought from Fort Union to this battleground would be sufficient for Fort Garland's men as well.

The stage house at Johnson Station was a large, one story adobe structure. It seemed to have been abandoned in a rush, as it had a good supply of wood for the fire, and a storeroom full of supplies. The station manager must have decided that it would be safer for him and his family to be somewhere else.

When the wounded had been moved and settled, Jordan told Mersey that he had started attending medical lectures before the war broke out. Though he wasn't a doctor, he had medical knowledge and since he had been wounded himself, he had been given the order to bring these soldiers and ambulance wagons to Johnson Station and to turn it into a field hospital.

"Shall we start with you then, Captain Steele, and see to your wounds so you can help the others?"

"We will see to them first," he said with a polite dip of his head. "We'll start with Corporal Hicks."

Looking at Jordan's pale skin and the dark circles under his eyes, Mersey bit her lip to stop herself from arguing. She retrieved supplies from their wagon to help Jordan while Alameda settled her family in the front corner of the room.

She asked Alameda to prepare a large amount of nutritious soup with their food supplies. She planned to see that Jordan had a bowl of hot food as soon as he would agree to accept it.

March 28, 1862
The Battle of Glorieta Pass
Day Three

After the unannounced and unplanned cease fire of the day before, Steele and Kendrick regrouped their men. There were still fifty able-bodied men in their company. Not nearly enough for the job ahead of them, Steele thought, but they would have to be, wouldn't they.

"Find as much cannon rope as you can," Steele said to Hawkins as they began walking toward the mountain howitzers. "And find Sandy so we can pack the mules."

"Yes sir," Hawkins said as they passed a large group of men camped fifty yards distant.

Steele heard someone shout his name and then a man jogged forward.

"Major Steele," the man said and saluted.

Steele recognized the young man from Fort Union.

"Lieutenant Corbin," he greeted returning the salute.

"Major Steele, sir," Corbin said, and then he glanced at the encampment before he continued.

"We've been forgotten back here, I believe. We are supposed to be reserves and we've been sittin' here on our duffs waiting to be called. The men have been complaining, saying that they've got an itch to fight that ain't gettin' scratched, sir. These men know what they're about. Some are old timers that fought in the Mexican-American war, sir, and some are part of the Colorado Volunteer Infantry's First Regiment. When their regiment of nine hundred fifty men got the order from Lewis Weld, the Territory of Colorado's Acting Governor, they marched four hundred miles from Denver to Fort Union in thirteen days in this winter weather, marching the final ninety two miles in thirty six hours during a blizzard. That has got to be one of the greatest marches in history," Corbin said, and then he snapped to attention. "And I've been training hard myself. Isn't there anything we could do for you, sir?"

Steele hid his grin. Old timer indeed. He was old enough himself to have fought in the Mexican-American war, but he had been a first year cadet at West Point at the time. What Corbin had described may be one of the greatest marches in history.

"That does sound like it deserves something. How many men are with you, Lieutenant?" Steele asked.

"Two hundred, sir," Corbin answered.

"Tell your men to get ready to scratch because you're coming with us. Do you or any of your men know artillery?" Steele asked.

"I know some, sir, and we have at least two others who have worked it," Corbin said.

"Good," Steele said. "Get them and then join us on Artillery Ridge."

"Artillery Ridge, sir?" Corbin asked.

"That's what I'm calling it," Steele said. "Meet us by those howitzers, and I'll tell you what we're planning and what we need."

"Yes sir, right away, sir," Corbin said, his excitement obvious, and he dashed away.

****

Quiet men huddled together in the chill morning wind. Sporadic gunfire erupted in the canyon below.

"This is the plan," Steele said. "Captain Roberts and his men will be part of the infantry who will be charging the main Confederate force in the canyon. Colonel Whitmire will be leading the cavalry protecting the right flank of the artillery. Captain Kendrick and our cavalry are with them. Those of us not manning the artillery will take to the woods to protect the artillery's left flank. Hawkins, you will stay and be in charge of Fort Garland's artillerymen and our two howitzers. Corbin, you will leave someone in charge with enough men to man the two howitzers from Fort Union, and then accompany us into the woods with the rest of your men."

"Artillerymen, man your posts. Gentlemen, Good luck," Steele shouted, and when the artillerymen departed, he spoke to the remaining soldiers.

"The overgrown shrubs and trees in the woods are thick and shadowed, so stay mindful because it will be easy to get disoriented and separated from your fellows or lost. Our fighting with the Confederate infantry will come at close quarters. We won't be able to use our regular formations because that would be close to impossible while dodging natural obstacles. Keep count on your ammunition. Be cautious in the clearings, as you will be more visible in the light. Stay alert in the shadows. Be mindful of your fellows' locations as much as possible, and be ready for threatening movement from any quarter. Remember your training. Let's go."

The howitzers were booming as the men entered the woods. Steele knew the damage cannons would do to the opposing troops. Each gunpowder-filled cannonball exploded on impact launching a barrage of musket balls that would decimate everything around it. Some contained incendiary materials that set fire to whatever and whoever had the misfortune to be close to the impact. Human bodies and horses in close proximity were ripped and torn asunder with each cannon round.

As Steele moved deeper into the woods, sporadic gunfire erupted from the soldiers near him, and tree trunks splintered and popped, sometimes near, sometimes so far overhead that the shooter had to have had no concept of his aim. Steele knew that this happened when men became nervous, especially new recruits. *Mind your ammunition*, he thought again. *Settle down*, he said to them in his mind. *We'll be in a fight soon enough.*

He and these eighty men could be facing twice their number of Confederates in these woods. The enemy could be far ahead, or waiting in ambush, or even in the trees overhead. All would be revealed soon enough. And in the blink of an eye, there was movement all around them, and battle-cries filled the air. Rifles fired and shotguns roared, and the rag-tag uniformed Confederates were on them, and wild in their fervor. Steele called out a warning a split second before he was grappling with a man trying to stab him with a bayonet.

Steele grabbed the barrel of the weapon attached to the bayonet, shifted his weight, and dropped to his back, throwing the man over and behind him. He jumped on top of the man before he could gain is feet, jerked the bayonetted rifle away, and hit him hard with the butt of the rifle. He heard footsteps rushing at him and then a man gave a cry as he flew at Steele, both combatants falling to the ground. Steele rolled to his back in time to catch an arm at the wrist as a knife came at his face, stopping it an inch from his eye.

A pistol roared, the sound deafening him, and the man fell limp on top of him. Steele threw him off, his breath heaving with exertion, and looked up to see Corbin standing over him, his side-arm smoking.

Before either man could recover, there was movement to their right, and Steele was on his feet. He and Corbin were each locked in mortal combat with two Confederate soldiers as more ran at them through the trees, weapons firing. Union shots fired in return, and then more close hand to hand struggle.

Shouts and grunts and screams followed, until there were no more attacks from the opposing force. The skirmishes lasted only thirty minutes, but the intensity made the minutes seem like hours.

Steele was able to summon his remaining forces at the edge of a small clearing. The men had fought well, and their losses had been light.

Corbin came up beside him. "The sounds of battle in the canyon are moving past us toward the artillery. They should be moving along with us or ahead of us."

A man stepped up beside them, a corporal, and asked for permission to speak. The soldier was in his mid-thirties, lean and hard-muscled, and Steele thought he had to be one of the Mexican-American War veterans Corbin had mentioned.

"Sir, I was close to the edge of the canyon while we fought, and the infantry below is being overrun on their right flank," he said. "The cavalry failed to charge, and worse than that, they retreated."

Inside, Steele raged. Colonel Whitmire, the leader of the cavalry, hadn't sent word of the change in strategy, and thus he had put the main attack force and their artillery in jeopardy!

"Thank you, Corporal," he said. "If you'd had no opportunity to observe and report this, we could have been cut off. For now, we must get back before they reach the cannons! Inform the men."

"What do you think happened?" Corbin asked when he and Steele were alone.

"It's hard to say," Steele answered as they made their way back through the woods, their eyes watchful of their surroundings as they moved. "Late reports of the opposing force's numbers or tactics can drive decisions that are later determined to be flawed because there was little or no time to verify the reports. There could have been large numbers of deserters either in the infantry in the canyon or in the cavalry itself. Regardless, the lack of communication of their retreat has put our artillery at risk."

"What about the competence and experience of the highest ranking officer in charge?" Corbin asked.

"We need to be mindful of what we say, Lieutenant," Steele said. Then he asked, "Why was Colonel Whitmire here instead Colonel Anderson?"

Corbin glanced at Steele as they walked along, ducking under tree branches and stepping over dead-fall timber and rocks.

Corbin said, "There was a heated argument regarding General Canfield's orders for Fort Union. Colonel Anderson said that he interpreted the orders as all Federal forces should stay at Fort Union and only engage the Confederates if attacked. But the two officers from Denver said that they interpreted the threat to Fort Union by the Confederates was wherever they found them, and took their men down the trail to here. Colonel Anderson refused to come himself, called them glory seekers. I didn't eavesdrop. I was on post at the door, and the discussion got loud. Colonel Whitmire claimed he had seniority, but in truth he had only been a colonel for a few days longer than Colonel Anderson, and his military service was only a few weeks longer. And he's pretty much had a desk job, while Colonel Anderson has had field duty. And then Colonel Whitmire decided to bring my unit along, sort of commandeered us."

"You said two officers, Lieutenant?" Steele asked.

"Yes sir," Corbin said. "The other officer is a cavalry officer, a major, a big fella. His name is Parody."

****

When Steele, Corbin and the other infantry reached Hawkins and the artillery, the battle was shockingly over. Steele turned at the sound of hoof beats as Kendrick rode up to him with the Fort Garland cavalrymen following.

Kendrick dismounted.

"Captain, what happened?" Steele asked.

"Sir, the Union Army is returning to Fort Union and the Confederate Army is retreating to Santa Fe and then on south to Texas. The Confederates were over-running our infantry in the canyon and Colonel Whitmire believed that our cavalry was outnumbered by the opposing force, and though I believe that to be false, he decided not to attack. Their cavalry pursued us, but somehow word was received that their supplies, all of their supplies, had been seized at Johnson Station, and they stopped pursuit."

Kendrick's expression was one of disbelief. "They were victorious, and they just stopped. Without those supplies, they were defeated. They surrendered. We told them to never bear arms against the United States of America again, and they gave their words of honor. They agreed to give us back our soldiers being held prisoner, and we agreed to give them back theirs. Side by side we are recovering our dead and wounded."

Kendrick paused, and then added, "It's done now. The Union has stopped the Confederate advance in New Mexico."

Parody

Pou Nachay was given permission to leave the station to carry fresh water from the open well across the road. Though still considered under guard, he was one of a few able-bodied men at Johnson Station. Water was needed for drinking and cooking, and also for cleaning the soldier's wounds. He left the station house at frequent intervals to refill the buckets.

Alameda and the children helped Jordan change the soldier's wound dressings while the baby slept. Mersey sat next to Vance and dabbed a soft wet cloth against his dry lips. They talked, and he joked, making her smile. The men surrounding them were quiet, listening, or speaking in soft tones. The thunder of cannons had begun again about an hour before, the concussions resounding against the walls of the station, though the cannons had to be miles away. But at the moment, there was silence.

"My daddy warned me that generals 'n horse soldiers were like eggs 'n ham," Vance said, and his eyes crinkled with his smile. "He said that the chicken is surely involved, but the pig, ya gotta understand, is committed."

Mersey smiled and smoothed the damp light brown hair from his forehead and brushed her fingers across his pale, feverish cheek. She reached for his hand and held it.

Vance said, "A lot of the men say the general in charge of our Confederate forces is a heavy drinkin' womanizer. I only seen General Seagram once and I don't think he was drunk. He was inspecting the troops and he seemed to look right through us, sort 'a like we wasn't alive to him, wasn't livin', breathin' men who needed food and coats and blankets and shelter, and wages to send home to them who was dependin' on us, like we was just guns he could point at a target." He considered for a moment, then added. "But he could 'a been drunk."

Mersey saw Pou Nachay slip through the door and set the empty buckets on the floor near the wall. He met her eyes, then came to sit on his heels beside her.

Pou Nachay spoke in a soft, low tone. "Mersey, the guards outside are dead, attacked most likely from the mesa above us by a forward patrol, and the Union Army approaches from the northeast, about one hundred mounted men. They will be here in minutes."

"Can you see who commands them? Is it Major Steele?" she asked.

"This man who leads, I do not know," Pou Nachay said. He glanced at Jordan on the far side of the room. "A major leads the soldiers, but not Major Steele. I do not believe Major Steele would have ordered his patrol to kill the few men who guarded this place unless it was necessary."

Mersey could not miss Pou Nachay's meaning. It might not have been necessary to kill the guards.

"A major then," she said, a hand fisted at her chest. "That is good news. My father outranks him, though maybe not for long. We could still have a chance to protect these wounded."

****

Mersey met the major at the door, all six foot four inches and two hundred forty pounds of him. He was flanked by two captains. She moved to stand between them and the open door to the station house.

"We have wounded here, Major," Mersey said.

"What color are their uniforms?" one of the captains asked smirking.

Mersey stiffened, but didn't answer.

"May we hazard a guess that, by the few Rebels who guarded the mules and horses and supplies here, that these wounded may be of the Rebel variety ma'am?" the major asked.

The major assessed her, smiled a charming smile and gave a tip of his hat. "And by your speech, that your loyalties lie with the North," he said.

"My father is Colonel Graylon Lockwood, Commander of Fort Garland's Union Army, and I am his daughter, Mersey."

"I am Major Parody of the Colorado Volunteer Cavalry of Denver, and I have authority here. I've heard of your father, that he will be asked to resign his commission soon for incompetency. I pity the poor officer who must take his place and serve his time in hell in that frozen wasteland."

The insult dashed Mersey's hope that her father's authority might grant her a much needed concession. Hating the slight pleading that crept into her voice, she said, "Some of these men are gravely wounded, Major, and in need of medical supplies and food. Surely you can help…."

"Their fate is in God's hands not ours, and our supplies are all dedicated to our own soldiers. Surely, you can understand," he said, a cordial quality in his tone, as if he spoke of the weather, not of the wellbeing of wounded soldiers.

"These men pose no threat, Major," Mersey said lifting her chin.

"If the Rebels are still breathing, Miss Lockwood, they pose a threat," the major said, still cordial. "I ask you to step aside and let us pass to assess the threat to our Union forces by those who lie within." Major Parody turned to the captain on his left. "Captain Simons, destroy the wagons and supplies. Burn them to the ground. Then destroy the horses and mules. Use knives and sabers. Save your ammunition."

Mersey gasped and the captain hesitated.

Horrified, Mersey said, "Major, there must be three hundred animals there. It makes no sense to destroy them and the wagons when they could be used to transport wounded from both armies…"

"Now don't worry your pretty little head about this, little girl. Leave that to the men and to God. Women aren't capable of understanding the business of war," he said, his black eyes hard as coal.

He nodded to the captain and the captain turned to do as he had been ordered.

Mersey stepped to block Parody, eyes fierce. "I'll tell you what I do understand, Major. Memories can replay again and again in the mind, editing until we become the heroes, the righteous, making our actions just and our motives pure, but you, sir, are a travesty to the country you serve and to the God you claim to believe in. The history books will reveal your true character and you will be painted as the blackguard that you are."

Parody's eyes narrowed on her and his fists clenched, and for a moment Mersey thought he would strike her.

Pou Nachay, who had been standing near Mersey, must have thought it too. He took a step toward her.

Parody shifted to glare at him and a dozen rifles lifted to Pou Nachay's chest. Mersey caught her breath at the aggressiveness of these soldiers and feared that, by challenging Parody, she had caused even more danger to everyone in this ungodly situation. She rushed to explain.

"This man is a scout. His name is Pou Nachay, and he is the most valued and skilled scout at Fort Garland," she said.

"If he takes another step, his scouting days are over, if you get my meaning," the major stated with a smile, though his eyes were glacial. "Take the scout's rifle along with the others. I don't trust his loyalties, or the color of his skin," he added under his breath.

Then in a loud commanding voice he ordered, "Captain, see that these Rebel soldiers are relieved of their weapons, or anything that could be used as a weapon. Then gather any who can stand or has use of either arm and bring them out before us."

"Yes sir," the captain on his right responded, and signaled to the men waiting behind them.

Mersey was set aside as the Union soldiers flooded into the station. She turned and followed the soldiers into the building. Pou Nachay stayed at her side. She watched the Union soldiers make the wounded stand, checking their arms, hands, and legs for injury.

One soldier jerked Jordan's sling from his shoulder and then punched Jordan's bandaged bloody thigh with his fist to see if Jordan's knees would buckle, but Jordan didn't flinch, and kept his eyes trained on Mersey from the back of the room.

Mersey recognized the fear in his eyes as they held hers, fear not for himself, but for her. Jordan gave a small tight shake of his head, warning her not to interfere. Mersey nodded her understanding, willing herself not provoke the major further, for he was a dangerous man, and a law unto himself.

The Union soldiers handled the Confederates with rough hands, turning them, dumping them from their cots or bed-rolls, searching the few thin blankets the soldiers lay upon. Mersey ran to Vance, who was at the mercy of a soldier searching his clothing and bedding. Mersey reached his side.

"Please," she pleaded to the Union soldier. "Don't move him, don't hurt him."

"Stand aside, ma'am," the soldier said. "He could be dangerous."

Vance touched her arm. "Help me stand, Mersey, help me stand with my brothers," Vance said, bringing her attention back to him.

"Darling, your backbone is too badly injured, you cannot stand," she said, tears forming in her eyes.

The Union soldier callously rolled Vance from where he lay on his back on his bed-roll. A soft groan escaped him as the blood and fluids ruptured from the wound on his abdomen to spill onto the wood floor. The foul smell of infection permeated the room.

"God Almighty," the soldier said, moving away.

A sob escaped Mersey, and then the tears began to fall in earnest as she gently turned Vance and lifted his upper body in her arms and cradled him to her.

"Mersey," he said, looking up at her face. "You're goin' t' dry up and blow away if you don't stop crying all those tears over every little bitty thing." Then he looked up above them, his eyes fixed as if looking at something far away. "See, Mersey, the sun is shining bright, you should be smiling."

With a sigh, his eyes closed and his breath left him, and his tenuous grasp on life slipped away. For several moments, the only sounds in the room were of Mersey's soft heartbroken sobs.

The young soldier next to her tried to say words of comfort. "His suffering is at an end, ma'am," he said.

She nodded. "I know, but his sweetness and beauty are ended, too."

The soldier smiled. "He would be much insulted for you to think him sweet and beautiful, I vow."

Mersey couldn't help smiling back at the soldier.

The soldier said, "Try to think of him just lying lazy and barefoot under a big shade tree by a little stream with his hat covering his face, with his fishing pole and his old dog lying next to him, and bees buzzin' in the flowers beside him. That would be a perfect place for Vance to rest."

She asked, "Do you know his family?"

"No, ma'am," he said. "But we were both in the Arizona Rangers, and when I get home again, I'll find them and make sure that they know Vance died of battle wounds because he served with honor and courage, and that he didn't die alone, that he died in the arms of a friend."

Mersey's tears streamed down her face again as she reached out and took the soldier's hand. "Thank you," she said.

"Yes ma'am," he said.

Then the screaming began, the screaming of terrified and mortally wounded animals. Salayah awoke with a startle and began to scream, too.

Mersey laid the lifeless body of Corporal Vance Hicks down gently, and then rose to go to Alameda and the children. Alameda was trying to console the infant by rocking her in her arms. When that didn't help, she tried to nurse her, but the baby's distress was too great. Mersey glanced at Pou Nachay and his dark eyes met hers, but he didn't move. Then she joined Alameda and the children, and Cochetopa and Antera huddled into her side, silent tears streaming down their frightened faces.

"Cover your ears," Mersey told them, and they held their hands tight against their ears. Alameda held the baby close to her body, covering the baby's ears between her body and her hand, and tried again to get her to nurse.

Alameda's voice broke on a sob. "My milk won't come down."

Mersey placed her hands over Alameda's ears then, and so she had no protection against the sickening sounds outside the station. Fighting nausea, closing her eyes, she tried to think of anything else, anything that could mask the reality of what was happening that she couldn't prevent or undo.

She didn't see Jordan signal to one of his men, or see the man retrieve his harmonica, but she heard when the haunting melody of Shenandoah began, and continued, slow and sweet.

Even the Union soldiers were not immune to the appalling chaos around them, and they did not stop him. The sounds of the butchering surpassed the sound of the harmonica, and, as one, the men began to hum and sing with the melody.

'Oh Shenandoah, 'tis far I wander,
Away you rollin' river,
Oh Shenandoah, 'tis far I wander,
Away, I'm bound away,
'cross the wide Missouri.'

Mersey's mind reached for the melody, focused on it. The men's voices blended in verse after verse, though the song and the sounds it sought to cover would forever be etched in her memory.

When it seemed the slaughter would go on forever, a titanic boom and the earth-shaking concussion of cannon fire rattled the foundation of the station house, the sound so close that Mersey thought they should feel its heat. The air clouded with dust and crumbled bits of sod from the ceiling, and the smell of smoke and gunpowder permeated the walls.

Within minutes, the sounds of the animals dying grew low, and then blessedly ceased. It was over then. Mersey almost collapsed in relief, never before imagining that the *boom* of a cannon could be a welcome sound.

When she looked up, the Union soldiers were acting uneasy, and the Confederate soldiers were looking expectant. Mersey hadn't thought about the source of the cannon, just that it seemed very close, and had seemed to signify an end to the killing.

A voice outside the stationhouse commanded, "You in the station, come out now," and Jordan jerked his head up.

"Get moving," one of the Union soldiers shouted to the Confederates, and they began to make their way to the exit and through the door, not sure of what awaited them. An entire battle could have been fought outside and they never would have heard it over the slaughter of the animals.

"Stay here," Pou Nachay said to Alameda and the children. "I will be back."

Pou Nachay and the soldier guarding him were the last to leave the room. Mersey slipped out behind them. To her amazement, it was not the Confederate Army who stood beside the smoking cannon facing Parody, but the Union Army, led by Major John Steele. Mersey felt tears of relief begin to fall, but she wiped them, and then willed them, away.

Parody roared at Steele. "How dare you fire that cannon! Who are you and what is the meaning of this intrusion, Major?"

Steele faced Parody undaunted. "I instructed the artilleryman to fire an empty round. I was having a little trouble getting your attention, Major, with all the butchering going on."

Parody spoke in a tone both condescending and arrogant.

"I am Major Parody of the Colorado Volunteer Cavalry and directly out of Fort Union. I have the authority here from General Canfield to do what is in the Union's best interests."

"I trust that you have this authorization in writing, the one that gives you the right to slaughter healthy animals that could serve the Union, Major....Parody is it?" Steele said, his voice cool, his eyes glinting as he patted his gloved hand on the cannon's smoking barrel.

Parody shifted his weight. He, in fact, had no such order, in writing or otherwise. On the contrary, his orders were to stay at Fort Union with his troops and engage the enemy if threatened. He had expanded the Confederate threat to befit his own interests, hoping for a military coup and advancement.

Parody straightened his shoulders and smiled. "The authority I have goes from my lips to God's ears, Major. You still didn't tell me who you are."

"Didn't I? How remiss of me," Steele said, emphasizing his gentleman's southern drawl. "I am Maj'ah' John Steele of Fort Gah'land."

Parody stiffened, his eyes narrowed, and his lip curled at the sound of John's accent. He smirked, deciding to use a tactic that had worked for Whitmire to overrule Anderson at Fort Union, and certain of his advantage over this younger man.

"So, as we appear to be of *equal* rank, and I will remind you that I got here first, let me ask you, sir, to determine seniority and therefore command of this company, when did you receive your commission as Major?"

Steele answered, "July 23rd, 1861, two days after the Battle of Bull Run."

A few murmurs followed his statement as Steele looked around him. His surveillance encompassed the company of soldiers standing behind Parody, shifting their weight, exchanging looks, holding their rifles at the ready. Then he looked at the burned wagons and at the corrals with dozens of slaughtered animals, and where over two hundred others stood with frightened eyes amid the carnage.

He felt the stillness of his own men at his back.

He turned and saw Pou Nachay standing under Union guard beside the Confederate soldiers. He searched the faces of the Confederates, who stood proud, though wounded, amid their guard, and were no doubt confused by what was happening. His eyes widened as they lingered on a tall figure, head dipped down, hat pulled low, standing near the station, almost protectively near Mersey.

Then his eyes met Mersey's.

Mersey was sure her expression must have shown how intensely happy and relieved she was to see him, because she thought there seemed to be something tender and reassuring in the gray depths of his eyes as she tried, but failed to give him a smile.

Then John began walking forward toward Parody.

"You know him," Jordan said for her ears only. "Why did you keep it from me? There could be no mistake who I am to him." His tone sounded more curious than accusing.

Mersey looked up at him. "I….I wasn't, I couldn't be sure what was best for him, or for you. I wanted to keep you both safe," she said. "So I stayed silent."

Jordan nodded.

"How, when did you know?" she asked. "You are not surprised that he is here, are you."

"That he is here, well, that part I wasn't sure, but I knew from the moment I met you, Mersey, that you knew John. When someone mistakes us for one another, and that person realizes it, the expression is always as yours was. The young Indian family had to know John as well because they treated me with familiarity, and Pou Nachay, who I believe does not trust easily, trusted me."

He held her gaze. "And I know how you feel about him. When I touched your hand only minutes after we met to help you with Vance's bandage, you accepted my touch as though a welcome comfort, not as an unexpected touch from a stranger."

Before Mersey could think of a response, their attention was drawn back to the situation happening before them.

Mersey stared at John, at his tall commanding figure, with his feet braced apart, his shoulders back, his eyes intent, a warrior's eyes, locked on Parody. He had fought his southern brethren at Bull Run, and then he had asked to be stationed in the West. He had to have feared that he could face, or unknowingly kill, his own brother in battle, and he couldn't abide that, no matter his commitment to the Union.

She understood, would have made the same decision were she him, but we cannot escape our destinies, it would seem. John didn't yet know what nightmare he had, through his actions, impeded, but his next words revealed that he was sorting it out.

"What are your intentions regarding these wounded?" John asked Parody, his voice steady and devoid of challenge.

"Well, now, Major Steele," Parody replied. "These men attacked the Union and killed Federal soldiers. They will be dealt with as traitors, right here and right now, as God is my witness." He studied Steele for a moment. "You firing that cannon so close to our own noble forces, could be interpreted as an attempt to interfere with official business, or an act of treason."

John ignored Parody's threat.

"The Confederate Army of New Mexico has surrendered." John paused at the rumble of voices. "My orders are to let these men return to Texas and to commandeer these animals."

Rage darkened Parody's face as he seemed to take insult with the statement and the accent in which it was delivered.

"I have received no such orders, Major Steele. I am in charge here," Parody said.

"We have yet to determine seniority, Major Parody. I believe that Colonel Whitmire is on his way back to Fort Union. But I suggest that we send word to him to settle this matter."

As they waited for Parody to reply, all of the soldiers present seemed to be holding their collective breath at the volatile situation emerging before them.

Parody was rethinking his strategy. His men had been with him long enough to know that his promotion to major had been recent, in fact just prior to their march south from Denver to Fort Union. They would know him as a liar if he declared otherwise, and that reputation would not serve him well. His eyes narrowed as he looked beyond Steele at the mountain howitzers and a force equal to his own, but felt that he still had a chance to bully his way into holding the winning hand. He broadened his stance, and crossed his arms over his chest.

Parody said, "Your compassion for these Rebel wounded will get you killed, Major. I will promise you that. It would take hours if not a day to get word from Colonel Whitmire. God helps those who help themselves. We will have to settle this matter the old fashioned way, the way of gentlemen."

His meaning became clear as he began to unbuckle his belt, remove his coat, and roll up his sleeves.

"Just you and me, Major, bare fists, man to man, winner take all," Parody said.

John didn't hesitate. "Your men will honor the victory?" he asked.

Parody called out, "Captain Simons?"

Simons stepped forward. "Understood, sir,"

"And yours, Major?" Parody sneered.

Kendrick stepped forward to John's side.

"Captain Kendrick here, sir, understood, sir," he stated, and to John he said, "We're with you, sir, and good luck."

John undid his gun belt and removed his coat. Sandy appeared beside him to accept his belongings.

"Major," Sandy said. "I seen this man fight once in Denver in a brawl. He nearly killed a man with those giant paws a' his. He claims to be a preacher, but there ain't anythin' God-fearin' 'bout 'im. He's got three inches on ya, an' longer reach, an' fifty pounds more a' pure thrust."

John cut his eyes to the grizzled horseman. "Thanks for stating the obvious. Any advice, Sandy?"

"He swings wide with his left, so if ya can land a quick right jab 'afore the left hits ya, it might help," Sandy shrugged, like he had his doubts. "He'll aim fer yer eyes or yer throat first, dirty fightin', tryin' ta end this quick, an' scare yer men inta followin' orders without question. If ya got any qualms or a sense a' honor that keeps ya from hittin' a man when he's down, put it away fer a spell. If he goes down, get on 'im, keep 'im down, an' finish the fight. He'll do no less fer you."

John nodded. "Anything else?" he asked, rolling up his shirt sleeves.

Sandy grinned. "Don't get hit," he said.

Sandy stepped back as John and Parody squared off, each taking the other's measure.

Parody's confidence dipped a notch as he looked at what he had thought would be an easy victory, a small obstacle, no worse effort than swatting a pesky insect. But as John took a fighting stance, Parody noted the thickness of his opponent's neck and the heavy bulk of his shoulders and chest. John's arms were rounded and bunched with muscles, and his thighs were roped with them. But it was the cold flint of John's eyes that gave Parody pause, and a sense of unease trickled down his spine.

Parody shook off the apprehension and firmed his jaw. No matter, he told himself as they began to circle, closing in with each step. He knew how to fight to end this quick, and this young rooster probably still had scruples, probably hadn't had enough fights that he had learned to brawl. This man was nothing compared to him. His size advantage alone would make this easy. Parody smiled.

When everyone's attention focused on the two combatants intent on each other, Jordan slipped closer to Mersey. Her terror for John and all that he was fighting for must have shown on her face.

"Don't fret so, Mersey," Jordan said. "I sacrificed my pretty face and my ribs too many times to count just to teach John everything he knows."

But when John barely blocked the first vicious punch aimed for his throat, Mersey's eyes filled with tears, blurring her vision of the two men battling to decide the fate of many. She wiped her tears and fought the powerful urge to look away. John deserved better from her than cowardice and tears.

John blocked Parody's right arm, knocking it away, and delivered a right uppercut to the jaw that snapped Parody's head back, causing him to stagger. John followed, staying in close, pounding Parody's face with his fists until the bigger man growled, lunged, and grabbed him in a bear hug, lifting him up, and then slamming them both to the ground.

John protected his head and ribs from the battering that followed by ducking his chin, and putting his fists and elbows in front of his face and chest, but he grunted with every landing of Parody's fist until he could twist from under Parody, kick himself clear, and get to his knees.

Parody turned his head to follow and John's fist connected with the side of the man's head, smashing his ear, driving him to the ground. Parody roared his pain, and when John swung again, Parody shifted his body and caught John's right wrist in his large hand.

John felt Parody's hand clamp over his wrist in a bone-breaking grip, searing his arm and hand with pain, stealing the strength from his arm. He clenched his teeth, swung two fast hard slams into Parody's jaw his left, and jerked his right wrist free. He twisted and spun as Parody shoved back at him, pushing him away, and both men scrambled to their feet.

They squared off again, and in spite of the near-freezing temperature, they were both sweating, their breaths coming out harsh in intermittent puffs of white mist.

The men observing moved forward, getting closer to the fight, wanting to witness what could be the contest of a lifetime, not wanting to miss a single brutal hit. Soldiers started to speak encouragement to the fighter of their company, ducking and rocking themselves, swinging their fists as they watched, as if they joined in the fight.

John watched Parody's dark eyes and saw the white hot rage simmering there. This man would kill him, if he could. Parody took a step toward John and swung his left fist in a wide arc. John stepped in close again and hit Parody in the nose, hard, with two quick jabs of his right. Parody's nose crunched and spurted blood, but he still landed the left, splitting John's upper and lower lips, and he was sure, loosening a few teeth.

Parody stepped back, wiped the blood from his nose and mouth, and watched Steele. This pup shouldn't still be breathing, let alone standing. He would have to kill Steele to defeat him, that part was becoming clear. So be it.

When John swung his right fist, Parody lunged at him, grabbing him again, and lifting him, intending to crush him, to break his back.

John pounded Parody's head and shoulders with his fists, but the man just ducked his chin, locked his wrists, and clamped down.

John groaned as pain seared his ribs. He had made a mistake. He hadn't kept his elbows tight against his body when he swung his fists, and Parody had slipped in under his arms, catching him around his chest in a smothering, rib-crushing hold.

In seconds, John's lower body was starting to feel numb, and he was gasping, hardly able to take in a breath. His lungs started to burn. He felt a desperation to breathe the likes of which he had never experienced before. He was being suffocated. Then, as impossible as it would seem, the bear of a man that was Parody flexed, tightening his hold even more.

Pain exploded in John's head as his vision began to blur. He could see his own blood running down his chin from the cuts on his mouth, and could see his breath coming out in ever-diminishing, shallow puffs of fog, the same fog that was entering his brain, and he felt himself being set adrift in translucent rolling waves on a misty sea.

****

Mersey stood close to Jordan, having lost sight of John in the throng of men around them, and she could feel Jordan tense and strain, sharing his brother's struggle, willing him to keep moving, keep fighting, keep defending. Listening to Jordan, he could have been a journalist giving a continuous commentary of the fight as it played out, including, *Oh, that had to hurt, shake it off John, watch the right, get up John, get up, atta boy John, oh no, get away from him!*

Then Mersey felt the sudden stillness of the men, and an unnatural quiet settled over them, and she looked up at Jordan's grim expression, at his pale face and set jaw, and she knew something bad was happening in the fight.

And it was happening to John.

All of the men had given a pledge that they wouldn't interfere, and would accept the victor's right of command.

But she hadn't given hers.

She began to weave her way toward the inner circle of men, and as she jostled against some of the troopers, she slipped a pistol from an unclipped holster, from the Captain named Simons. When he glanced at her, Mersey began to run forward before he could try to stop her.

Her breath caught when she saw John crushed in Parody's punishing grip, his skin dusky, his breathing shallow, and his efforts to break the hold, ineffective. Parody would kill him if he wasn't stopped. She knew it without a doubt.

Mersey cocked the pistol, drew in a calming breath, took careful aim, and then three things happened in such rapid succession within an eternity of seconds as to happen nearly simultaneously.

From behind her Jordan yelled, "Use that hard head of yours, Johnny Boy!"

****

A deep voice, familiar and urgent, broke through the agonizing haze of John's thoughts and he startled, drawing in a gasping breath, and then his thoughts cleared, just enough, as a pistol shot fired, zinging into the ground between Parody's braced feet. Parody snapped his head up with the sound and shifted his balance as the spatter of rocks and debris hit against his boots and legs. With the last of his strength, John brought the crown of his forehead down hard against Parody's skull, hard enough to dim his own lights, but Parody let go, stumbled, and dropped to the ground, freeing John in the process.

Parody sat dazed, holding his head between his hands, but then he began shaking it as if to clear it, and moving with purpose from side to side as if to get up. Sandy's words came back to John then. *If he goes down, keep him down, finish the fight.* John knew if

Parody caught him again, there would be no breaking free.

With clumsy movements and shaking limbs John managed to straddle Parody, and with his flagging strength, he started pounding. He was so starved of air that it felt surreal. He felt outside himself, numb, almost as if he were watching someone else's fists connect with Parody's face and body, but he kept pounding until the man lay still and unconscious beneath him.

John struggled to his feet, bracing his hands on his legs to stand upright, weaving unsteadily as he stood in the center of the men in the stunned silence that surrounded him, savoring the cold air as he dragged it in and heaved it out of his bruised chest.

Mersey stood unmoving as a cheer went up from the soldiers standing around her. Captain Simons stepped up to retrieve the smoking pistol she still held in her now trembling hand.

"I'll just take that back now, ma'am. That was a nice shot," he said, "And timely."

She glanced up at him but didn't speak because John was walking toward her, battered, bruised, cut, and bloody. His eyes dropped to the smoking pistol. She dropped the gun into Simons' hand and ran to John, threw herself into his arms and then quickly withdrew when he winced. She looked up at him, tears streaming down her face. He reached out and smoothed her tears away.

"John, are you alright? I couldn't watch you be hurt," she said.

Parody's men lifted him and carried him into the station. Sandy brought John his coat and gun belt.

"The men are waitin' fer yer orders, sir," Sandy said.

John looked at the men. "Captains, front and center," he commanded, still out of breath.

Three men came before him, two men quiet and dutiful, and one man, Captain Kendrick, beamed.

"Prepare reports…of men and supplies…to return to Fort Union. Bring your reports to me…in one hour. That is all, Gentlemen," John said holding Mersey at his side, and leaning on her a little for support. Then he turned to face his brother.

"Captain," John said, looking at the bandage on his brother's thigh. "Let's get the wounded back inside. We're freezing our backsides off out here."

Reunion

"You were good with those howitzers," Jordan said with a sad smile. "You knew right where to hit us to shut us down."

John looked down at his bruised, folded hands, and said nothing.

"You saved Ruby," Jordan said. "The mare was with the other livestock in the corral. She would have been killed if it hadn't been for you."

When John still said nothing, Jordan said. "She'll be a good match for your Black. I want you to take her with you. She may not survive," he gestured around him, "All this, if you don't take her."

John nodded, then looked at his brother.

"I would have died in that fight if you hadn't been here, Jordan. I was dying." John's jaw tightened. "If you hadn't called to me when you did....your voice reached me when nothing else could. Thank you."

"Mersey added a little piece of luck for you, too. You aren't forgetting about her?"

John smiled. "Never," he said, remembering the smoking pistol in her hand. After a pause he added, "Why are you here, Jordan, with the Texas Mounted Rifles?"

Jordan shrugged. "After you left, well, it didn't seem right to stick around all the broken hearts, and I....didn't much relish the idea of meeting you on a battlefield. Father knew the general leading the Texas Volunteers, so I signed up. It should have been safe," he said grinning. "It should have been a good plan. It should have been impossible for us to meet this way."

John grinned back. "I thought the same thing about coming out West. What broken hearts? Do you mean Eudora? I thought you were as interested in her as I was. I thought you would step in?"

"I made the attempt, though my heart wasn't in it, but she said that every time she looked at my face, she was reminded of a traitor, so she married Lyle Yancy," Jordan said.

"The doddering old lawyer married twice before? Why in heaven's name did she do that?" John asked.

"You mean besides the fact that he's rich and has one foot in the grave and the other on a banana peel?" Both men chuckled. "He is one of President Davis' legal advisors. She loves being the *adored* hostess, with her name and photograph on the society page every day."

John snorted. "I can imagine," suddenly aware that he couldn't recall her face. It had been replaced by one with lavender eyes.

"I have to admit that I never understood what you two saw in each other. She's such a flighty little thing without a serious thought in her head, and you, John, are no fun, a straitlaced, older-than-his-years, no-nonsense scholar, no offense," Jordan said.

John said, "She seemed incomparable at the time."

"But not anymore?" Jordan asked.

"No, not anymore."

After a moment's hesitation, John asked, "How is our family?"

"All of them are well, the last I've heard anyway," Jordan said, knowing that their father had forbid anyone to answer John's letters. "Jessica gave birth to our fourth generation in Virginia, a healthy little boy, though not our namesake. Her husband Bradley is a Virginia Confederate Congressional Representative.

John nodded and asked, "What of Jarred?"

"Father forbade him to enlist and he's only fifteen, so he had to obey. Father told him that he had a son on both sides of the fight, and he didn't want to tip the scales. He wanted the *right* of the thing to decide the outcome," Jordan said.

John's eyes held a faraway look. "Sounds like father."

"They haven't stopped loving you, John. And they have to learn to respect your decisions. You are more like our father than anyone else I know. You proved that again today," Jordan said.

John stood and moved to the window. "What I proved today was that I can kick a bully's ass with a lot of help from my friends, and nothing more."

Jordan stood as well. "It was much more than that, John, and you know it. It's not a huge leap to think that the pesky wounded Confederate soldiers would shortly have followed the same unpleasant fate as the guards and horses and mules. You saved us all from a shallow communal grave, brother."

When John said nothing, Jordan said, "It's curious, wouldn't you say, John, that neither of us anticipated that we would both choose a distant path to keep from shooting at and maybe killing each other in this war, and then when our paths did intersect, we ended up saving each other instead."

At John's guarded look, Jordan asked, "What happens now, Major Steele?"

"As long as everyone gives their word of honor not to bear arms against the Union ever again, my orders are to let you and the Texas Mounted, now un-mounted, Volunteers, retreat back to Texas, but without provisions," John said, his eyes full of regret.

"No!" came a gasp from behind him.

John turned to see Mersey approaching them.

"John, these men are wounded, freezing, nearly starving. Surely no one can expect them to survive a retreat without provisions. I'll contact my father. Surely he can intercede on behalf of these men who have served their cause honorably, surely...."

John placed his hands on Mersey's shoulders.

"We can't help them, Mersey," he said. "No matter what else, these soldiers took up arms against the government. Parody was right about one thing. These men threatened the Union with their actions and killed Federal soldiers. There will be no concession other than no pursuit. They can wait here for relief, but the rest is out of our hands."

"It's not out of mine," she said, her chin lifted in defiance, and she hurried away.

"She's magnificent, John," Jordan said. "I smile every time I remember that pistol shot, and the way she didn't back down from Parody, well, it makes me proud and humble at the same time. You should have seen her with the wounded, especially...." He looked away. "You're a lucky man to be loved by such a woman. I do so envy you her love."

John's eyes followed Mersey as she walked away from him. "She's everything good in my life. I hope that I'm the lucky man you think I am, because I'm in love with her."

****

Mersey sought Pou Nachay and found him sitting with Alameda. The children were all sleeping.

"Pou Nachay, I need for all of us, Alameda, the children, and me, to get to Santa Fe as quickly as possible. Can you help me?" she asked.

"I will speak with Major Steele. I will need his permission to take you," he said.

****

The wagon was loaded with their belongings and a soldier was hitching the mules. Mersey stood huddled in her cloak, shoulders hunched against the cold, staring past the slaughtered animals in the corral, past the burnt supply wagons, past the smoke from the battlefield. Her eyes were focused on the snowcapped mountain landscape, wondering with all this majestic beauty around them, how it could have come to this.

"Mersey," John said from behind her.

She turned to face him. The pain in his eyes was there for her to see. He was hurting too for being forced to abandon his brother and his countrymen, leaving their lives at risk from complications of their wounds and facing a lack of provisions for an arduous journey. He had told her once that soldiers couldn't chose which orders they would follow.

All at once her resentment of his following orders without question drained out of her, leaving her as vulnerable as she had ever felt before in her life, and empty, too empty even for tears.

"Thank you for giving Pou Nachay permission to take us to Santa Fe," she said.

He nodded.

Pou Nachay approached her then.

"Major," he said to John, acknowledging him, and then to Mersey he said. "Alameda and the children are ready, Mersey."

"Thank you," she said, and Pou Nachay moved back toward the wagon.

"Goodbye then," she said to John.

He nodded again, his gray eyes intense on hers, and then she turned to walk away.

He whispered her name.

And she heard him.

And she stopped, then looked back at him.

He opened his arms, and she ran into them. She clung to him.

"I love you, John," she said against his chest

She felt the tenseness ease out of him.

"I sent Sandy and Hawkins to hunt game. Some of the meat will be left behind by accident," he said stroking her hair.

She looked up at him. "Thank you."

"An hour ago, Pou Nachay and Cochetopa walked into the station with eight plump turkey carcasses, plucked and ready for the cooking pot," he said.

"I'll bet Cochetopa was grinning like he owned the world," she said with a laugh.

He nodded and chuckled and held her in the circle of his arms.

"I love you, too, Mersey, with all my heart," he said, and then he kissed her goodbye.

Santa Fe

Mersey double-checked the address on the card. The house stood in the center of a dormant grassy lawn that was would be spectacular in the spring and summer months. It was a sprawling white adobe ranch house with a wide veranda and two chimneys emitting smoke, and the warmth beckoned her. The windows glowed with welcoming light.

"This is the house," she said to Pou Nachay. "It belongs to Louisa Canfield."

As she climbed down from the wagon, the front door of the house opened and Louisa stepped onto the veranda.

"Mersey Lockwood," she said. "What a wonderful surprise!" Louisa walked to her and folded Mersey into an affectionate embrace.

Pou Nachay helped Alameda and the children from the wagon. Louisa kept her arm around Mersey and walked toward them.

"You all look exhausted," Louisa said as Salayah began to cry. "Come inside, all of you, and you can tell me everything over dinner. Then we'll get you settled comfortably for the night."

****

Mersey was surprised to see the young woman she met on the stagecoach, the mail-order bride, Dinah Douglas, in Louisa's living room. Introductions were made, greetings exchanged and Dinah joined them along with two small children at dinner.

"I arrived at my fiancé's ranch to find him dying," Dinah said. "He had been gored by a bull and had no chance of survival." Dinah paused for a heartbeat and then continued. "He begged me for the sake of these children to marry him and become their mother. He wanted them taken care of without interference from others. The ranch, you see, is very large."

Dinah put her arms around the dark-haired little boy and little girl and smiled at them.

"I'm Dinah Corazon now, and these little loves are Leon and Vivian. Leon is five, aren't you, sweetie, and my darling Vivian is three," she said.

The children looked up at their pretty young mother with love in their eyes, and Mersey was again impressed by the maturity Dinah possessed. She could be no older than seventeen.

Mersey gave her condolences and Dinah accepted them with sincerity, but Mersey couldn't help but notice the frequent glances Dinah directed toward Pou Nachay, who sat next to little Leon.

Dinah spoke to him toward the end of the meal. "Mr. Pou Nachay, do you have knowledge of cattle?" she asked.

Pou Nachay turned to her.

"When I lived with my People, we raised longhorn cattle. The buffalo herds are not so many as before. And I am called Pou Nachay. There is no mister."

"Then you have dealt with cattle thieves, Pou Nachay?" she asked, leaning a little toward him.

He nodded. "My People don't use fences, so we kept our cattle close to home, and yes, we had problems with cattle thieves."

Alameda, who was sitting across from Dinah, spoke then. "Our family lost no cattle to thieves when Pou Nachay lived with us," she said.

Then Antera joined in the conversation about Pou Nachay. "Uncle stood against thirty Apache warriors and didn't even blink an eye."

"How very brave," Dinah said smiling at Pou Nachay, meeting his eyes for a long moment until Vivian began to wiggle on her chair. Dinah took Vivian onto her lap to help her eat. She looked at Pou Nachay again.

"Are you good with a rifle, Pou Nachay?"

"With a rifle, Uncle can shoot a rabbit in the eye at a hundred yards," Cochetopa said.

"And he has perfect aim with a bow and arrow and with a throwing knife," Alameda added, and Pou Nachay gave her a *what are you up to* look.

He held up his hand. "Enough from you, I can answer for myself," he said looking at his family with fond forbearance.

He turned to Dinah then. "I have been trained to be good with weapons and I practice so that I will stay good with weapons."

Dinah looked at Pou Nachay with admiration and he looked pleased that she was looking at him that way, but he added, "About the thirty Apache, I was afraid to blink." His lips lifted in a wry smile.

It seemed to Mersey that Pou Nachay had spoken more words to Dinah than she had ever heard him say at one time in the past. As for Alameda's behavior, Mersey remembered now that after introductions today, she had overheard Dinah ask Alameda if her brother was married. And even more interesting, when Dinah excused herself to get the children ready for bed, Pou Nachay's eyes followed the pretty young woman as she left the room.

Louisa took Mersey's hands in hers and asked, "Tell me, child, what brings you to Santa Fe?"

Mersey gave an account of all that had happened and spoke of her concern for the men of the Confederate army who would be marching hundreds of miles south to Texas through the remaining winter without provisions.

Louisa responded saying, "When my husband left for Fort Craig, I stayed here in Santa Fe. My husband thought that the Confederate strategy would be to lay siege to Fort Craig and so they closed the gates and prepared for one. The Confederates took over Santa Fe instead, and though they knew that I was here and who I am, they were courteous toward me."

Louisa thought for a moment. "This outcome is indeed sad. But I will admit that I am not surprised. General Seagram has been an inattentive leader it seems, and his strategy and timing have proved ill-conceived. It leads one to believe that he had no concept of *striking while the iron is hot*, to the Union's advantage, though the Federal soldiers made their share of blunders as well."

She winked at Mersey. "Don't tell my husband I said that. Seagram's poor planning and lack of foresight left his men starving and freezing and dying from sickness. Though he promised the soldiers gold, I've no doubt, from the Colorado mines, these men endured beyond all that greed could have motivated. If not for the dedication of his officers and soldiers, the Texas Mounted Rifles, the Arizona Rangers, the lancer companies, the San Elizario Company of spies, and the Brigands, he would have been defeated from the beginning."

Louisa was quiet for a moment, lost in thought, and then she brightened. "Get some rest now and leave this to me. I will contact the Ladies of the Regiment from Fort Craig and we will see to the care of these men."

That night a spring storm settled over Santa Fe, covering the land with heavy snow and ice, preventing Mersey and the others from leaving for Fort Union, and forcing them to take some much needed rest. Mersey worked with Louisa and the Ladies of the Regiment of Fort Craig, providing information and detail as they planned to meet the needs of the battered Confederate soldiers who had begun to arrive in Santa Fe.

Provisions to get the wounded to the Confederate field hospital in Socorro some thirty miles south of Albuquerque were implemented so quickly that Mersey believed Louisa to be in contact with legions of angels, but that was what the Ladies of the Regiment were. Temporary shelters with food and warm clothing and bedding were established in Santa Fe, and then further south in Albuquerque as the soldiers continued their journey to Texas.

The children, all five of them, thrived in Louisa's household. Cochetopa and Antera were very attentive with the smaller children, and the smaller children were fascinated with Salayah, almost as fascinated as Dinah seemed to be with Pou Nachay. Pou Nachay stayed busy taking care of the animals and outside tasks for the household.

The afternoon following their arrival in Santa Fe, Dinah and Alameda stood in the kitchen making hot chocolate. The women watched through the window as the children played in the yard in the snow, and as Pou Nachay worked in the far corner of the yard, chopping, splitting and stacking wood for the stoves.

Little Vivian started chasing after Leon with a snowball, her sturdy little legs crunching in the snow with her small steps, but she stumbled and she fell face first into a snow drift. When Vivian started to cry, Dinah moved to grab her shawl by the door, but Alameda stayed her with a touch on her arm and indicated that she should come back to look out the window.

Pou Nachay stopped stacking wood, looked to make sure the blade of the axe was buried into the chopping block, and walked to the child. When he lifted her to her feet, she reached her arms up to him and he picked her up.

"I'm cold, Mr. Powchay," she said hugging his neck, still sniffing back her tears.

He looked at the other children's runny noses and red cheeks. The sun was shining but the wind was bitter cold. Even he had felt the chill when he had been stacking wood, without the exertion of chopping and splitting it to keep him warm.

"Let's all go in and warm up," he said, and all of them headed for the door, the older children running in front of him.

When Pou Nachay entered the kitchen, Dinah went to him to take Vivian from his arms. Her warm hands brushed his cool ones, and without thinking, she reached up and cupped his cheek with her palm.

"You are cold, too. Please stay and have some hot chocolate with us," she said.

Pou Nachay looked surprised at her touch, and for a moment he just stared at her.

"Hot chocolate," he said at last. "I don't know this drink, but I take no liquor."

"I am delighted to hear that, Pou Nachay. This drink is made with sweet, warm milk, and has no spirits added. Please stay. It will warm you," she said, helping him remove the coat from his shoulders.

Now it was Alameda's turn to stare. She had never seen her self-reliant brother accept help as he had just accepted it from Dinah. Alameda hid a smile. Pou Nachay deserved to have someone take care of him for a change.

****

Mersey couldn't sleep. She sat at the kitchen table in the wee hours of the morning sipping a cup of milk. She hadn't lit a lamp. Her eyes had adjusted in the moonlight reflected off the snow that spilled through the windows. The peacefulness and warmth and shelter of the kitchen were so at odds with her fears and imaginings for the wounded soldiers.

All of the planning for the wounded had left her feeling anxious and unsettled. Her impatience for getting the Confederate soldiers what they needed was hard to bear. She hoped aid would be received timely and be enough for all those displaced and abandoned young men, an untold number of them wounded and sick. She knew it was foolish to let worry rob her of sleep, worry about things she could do nothing about, worry about what could happen, what was happening, but worrying mostly about Jordan and those men she had come to know and care for, praying that help had reached them, that they were safe and warm and nourished and recovering from their wounds. And she missed John. She had been right. Being parted from him was causing her heart to ache.

She heard a small sound, a familiar one. Salayah was beginning to fuss. Mersey got up from the table and took a quiet step into the darkened living room expecting to see Alameda, but instead she saw Dinah asleep in the rocker, and Pou Nachay was reaching for the baby she was holding. The firelight from the fireplace illuminated them, their faces inches apart.

Mersey stepped back, not wanting to intrude. She heard Dinah say something in a sleepy voice, and then Pou Nachay's warm baritone in answer, and then the both of them walked to Alameda's room, Pou Nachay carrying Salayah and Dinah leaning on his shoulder.

Mersey placed her hand over her heart. Dinah and Pou Nachay and the baby had looked so natural together.

****

On the seventh day in Santa Fe, the ice and snow had disappeared and the sun shined warm in a clear blue sky, giving their little acre of the world the first promise of spring. Pou Nachay had loaded the wagon and they were ready again to travel.

Mersey embraced Louisa as tears fell from her eyes. "I cannot tell you how grateful I am to you. You were the only person I knew with the capability to help. You have made miracles possible."

"I am so glad that you came to me. Working with you, I felt like I was beside your mother again. She would be very proud of you and your compassion for these surrendered and wounded soldiers," Louisa said. "Please come see me often, and I do so want to meet your young man," she added, eyes twinkling.

"Louisa, may I ask you something? Do you believe that my mother was happy, I mean with her choices in life?"

Louisa looked thoughtful and a little surprised by the question. She took Mersey's hands in hers.

"Yes," she said. "I believe your mother was happy. Oh, there were hardships of course, but you and your father were the loves of her life. I believe that she wouldn't have changed a thing."

Tears gathered in Mersey's eyes as she gave Louisa a quick hug. "Thank you, Louisa."

As they stood together saying their goodbyes, Dinah spoke. "When my husband died, I came to Louisa for help as well. She told me that I needed two things. I needed an honest money-manager, and she introduced me to a banker who would give me this kind of advice."

Dinah paused and stepped closer to Pou Nachay, who was watching her.

"The second thing I needed is to marry a man who knows this land, knows its culture and heritage, a man who would care for me and the children, protect us and what belongs to us, a good and strong man to marry me who I could love and who could love me in return." She placed her hand on Pou Nachay's broad shoulder. "Have I found him, Pou Nachay?"

He held her gaze. "My sister and her family…."

"Are welcome in our home. The house is large. There is more than enough room," Dinah said, and smiled at Alameda. "I would be most grateful for your help and your company."

Pou Nachay said, "I must return to Fort Union to resign my job as scout."

"I will wait for you," she said. "I must warn you though. My late husband's foreman wants me and may make trouble because I won't choose him, and he's a white man."

Cochetopa put his arm around Pou Nachay's waist.

"Uncle always does what must be done," the boy said, and Antera nodded.

Alameda looked at her brother and said, "I know a man who might want to be foreman for you."

Mersey knew that Alameda was thinking of Jennings, and knew as well as Alameda did that many questions needed to be answered before that could even be dreamt of.

Dinah spoke again, stepping even closer to Pou Nachay, looking up into his dark eyes. "I know this would greatly add to the responsibility you already have, and is much to ask of you in such a short acquaintance, but for me I have no doubt that you are the man I want and need. There is so much good in you, so much strength."

Pou Nachay was so still it was as if he had ceased to breathe.

"I don't know in your culture, Pou Nachay, if people believe in love at first sight, but I knew from the first time I saw you that I would love you, and I do love you, Pou Nachay. Do you believe that you could feel the same for me and for my children?"

Pou Nachay met Dinah's hopeful eyes steadily, and as Mersey had seen him do many times in the past, in a heartbeat, he made his decision. He gave a small dip of his head, and gave her his answer.

"I will be your husband," he said. "I will love you and your children, and ours when they are born. I will honor you, protect you, and defend what is ours."

And Mersey could only stare as he smiled a smile that made his handsome face fiercely beautiful.

Dinah released her breath on a sigh, stood on her tiptoes and kissed him then as he wrapped her tenderly in his arms.

****

As they were leaving Santa Fe, Mersey searched the riders and wagons as they passed in opposite directions, half-hoping to catch sight of Jordan, but also hoping that he was already at the field hospital at Socorro. She had given up looking through the sea of wagons and faces when she heard someone call out her name.

Mersey halted the wagon and turned to see Jordan help a man with a crutch sit down on the grass out of the way of travelers, and then walk toward her. He looked leaner, and he hadn't shaved, but he didn't look ill, and for that she was relieved. He reached up and covered her hands with his as she held the reins.

"I was hoping that I would see you," he said. "I wanted to thank you for....well, for this," and he gestured around him at the ambulance wagons.

"What you see around you is Louisa Canfield's magic, not mine. I merely served as the proverbial squeaky wheel," she said, and she smiled at him. "I was hoping to see you too, Jordan, to see that you were cared for. I am glad to see you looking so well."

He laughed and said, "Are you sure you're not part southerner to give so false a compliment with such sincerity?"

Mersey laughed too.

"I've been staying at a shelter near here, but it's time I moved on," he said, a haunted look in his gray eyes.

Mersey immediately felt concern. "What will you do now, Jordan?"

Jordan looked up at her. "Don't worry so, Mersey. My father will wire me the funds I need. I have something that I wish to do, that I need to finish," he said, his eyes turning eastward.

"Please be safe," she said. "And my heart goes with you, Jordan."

He winked at her. "I won't tell John you said that, though I know how *sisterly* you meant it. Take good care of my no-nonsense brother, and give him my fondest regards until we meet again."

He let go of her hands, then turned and jogged back across the road, revealing only the slightest limp on the left leg.

When he faced her again, he grinned and shouted, "I only wish I could be at the wedding…."

Her eyes flew wide. "W-wedding?"

He backed away then, and shouted again, "Unless my brother is a complete dunderhead, but if that is the case, I'll be back for you!" And then he was lost to sight behind lumbering wagons.

May 24, 1862
Fort Union

"Master Sergeant Seth Jennings, this court finds you guilty of insubordination and dereliction of duty in a time of war, leading to actions that jeopardized the safety of a military family member, and resulting in injury to a civilian employee, crimes punishable to the full extent of military law…."

"No, please…."Alameda whispered and her breath caught on a sob.

Mersey put her arm around Alameda's shoulders as they waited for the rest.

The judge cleared his throat and looked at Jennings. Jennings stood at attention, his uniform spotless, his service medals on his chest reflecting sunlight, the sleeves of his dress uniform coat stretched tight over his muscled arms, his boots shined with polish.

Jennings waited for his sentencing with his eyes facing forward, his broad shoulders held back, his hands steady. Mersey glanced at John as he stood beside Jennings, thankful for the support he had shown the master sergeant.

"But in light of the unusual circumstances, and testimony heard on your behalf by the victims themselves, and testimony by Lieutenant Colonel Steele, by Major Kendrick, and by Captain Hawkins for courage under fire," he cleared his throat again and smiled. "Not only will you not be hanged, but your prison sentence will be reduced to time served."

The collective breath that had been held in the room was released on a relieved sigh.

Judge Colonel Anderson's expression turned serious again as he looked at Jennings and continued. "In review of your service record, since your enlistment at age seventeen, you have defended your country against enemies both foreign and domestic. During your twenty years of service, you advanced to the rank of master sergeant, fought with valor in the Mexican-American War, and now the Civil War. You are hereby honorably discharged from the United States Army. However, your record will show that you are barred from any military reenlistment. You are free to go, Mr. Jennings."

Jennings looked momentarily stunned, but he recovered and turned then to Alameda with a question in his bright blue eyes, which she answered with a radiant smile.

Jennings turned to face Colonel Anderson, and stood at attention. "Permission to speak Your Honor."

The colonel raised an eyebrow. "At ease, Mr. Jennings, you are a civilian now. Is there something you wish to ask me?"

Jennings cracked a nervous smile and shifted his feet. "Sir, is it possible that you also serve as the Justice of the Peace?"

Anderson chuckled. "I do indeed. I assume you need my services," he said.

"If you'll just give me a minute, your Honor, to make sure…." He walked to Alameda, his heart in his eyes and extending his hand. "….That Alameda will have me as her husband."

"Yes, Seth," Alameda said, and took his hand in hers. "I will."

June 19, 1862
Fort Garland

In the small sunlit chapel, Kendrick stood beside John, and Rosa stood beside Mersey as Mersey spoke her vows to love and honor John as her husband, as long as they both should live.

Commander Lockwood was the proud officiate and he beamed as he said, "By the power granted to me by the United States Armed Forces, a power that I will soon forfeit upon my much deserved voluntary retirement, I now pronounce you man and wife. Lieutenant Colonel Steele, you may kiss my daughter, uh, that is, your bride."

Steele smiled and lifted Mersey's veil to reveal her beautiful face and the crystal tears falling from her lavender eyes. He pulled her into his arms and tenderly kissed her tears away, then kissed her mouth.

When he lifted his head he said, "Please tell me that you are happy, Mersey. I have seen your tears when you are suffering from hurt or anger or sorrow, even with mirth. Please tell me, sweetheart, that these tears are from happiness."

"My darling John, these tears are from pure happiness to be with you for always as your wife. I love you so much," she said.

She felt his low chuckle and the tenseness of his shoulders relaxed as he gathered her closer.

"I'm so glad to hear that, my precious wife. I love you too, and forever will."

Epilogue
April 2, 1865
Petersburg, Virginia

Charity McMillan moved about the wounded as they lay upon the unsheltered ground, their wounds bandaged, but still much medical attention would be needed to prevent infection and disease from taking their lives away from them, though the Union Army had already tried. General Grant's Army had broken through the Confederate lines at Petersburg after nine long months of siege, and Union troops were even now marching north to Richmond.

Cannon fire was muted by distance, but the setting sun blazed with the color of fire, and the twilight clouds billowed unnaturally as if filled with smoke, for surely the city was burning.

Charity returned to the wagon loaded with barrels of water and refilled her pitcher. Her eyes traveled to the medical tent where a doctor sat with his head down, as if defeated, beside a young soldier's dead body. Charity had heard the boy screaming as he died, so injured, so overcome with pain and confusion that perhaps he hadn't even realized that he was the one screaming.

He had died among strangers and far from home, in unimaginable pain, without last words, without a last exchange of testaments of love or heartfelt regrets, without loved ones gathered to comfort and mourn. Was his name even known, so that someone could write to his family, write a kind lie that this boy had died a good death, that he had slipped away peacefully, surrounded by friends who had loved him and would mourn him, and that his last words had been words of love for his family and his fondness for home.

It is weariness, Charity thought, just weariness. She had been bringing water to the wounded for hours. The young man had died among strangers, true, but one stranger had fought for him, had fought courageously to save his life. Charity had a sudden realization that this doctor, who had been at his work since before she had arrived, though his wounds weren't visible, was wounded as well.

Charity reached for one of the beef sandwiches that an army of women had packed, picked up her water pitcher and walked into the tent. When she reached the doctor, she peered down at the man's lowered head, at his thick, tousled dark hair. He sat with his elbows resting on his knees. His hands, still covered in the young soldier's blood, hung loosely before him. His face was hidden from her, but he looked young, and vital, with broad shoulders and strong arms, capable of enduring the endless hours of physical and mental strain required of him.

Charity knew each doctor could only spend about ten minutes with an injured man. If there were wounds to the torso, the man would not live. And if there were injuries to arms or legs, the most expedient use of time, was to amputate.

The courage of the doctors was unquestioned, for if the injured were taken prisoner, the doctors were taken prisoner to care for them, and they were often shot at by the enemy, though they carried no weapons.

She said, "Doctor, would you like some cool water to drink, or even just to wash your hands?"

It was as if he hadn't heard her, but then after a long moment, he lifted his head, and she looked into his eyes, clear gray eyes, and he had been crying. He had blood splattered on his face, and he had been crying, quietly, privately, and unobserved.

Before coming to help on the battle field, Charity couldn't remember ever having seen a man cry, but now, she had stopped counting the times.

When he didn't move or answer her, she knelt before him. She took a clean cloth from her pocket, wet it with water from the pitcher, and wiped the blood splatter from his face. He closed his eyes when she wiped away his tears. Charity wet the cloth again, then she wet his hands, and washed them.

"Thank you," he said when she finished.

Charity brought a cup from the pocket of her smock and poured water for him, and as he drank, she handed him the sandwich.

He gave it back. "This is for the wounded, I…"

"The wounded are depending on you to keep their wounds from killing them, so you need to maintain your strength," she said.

He nodded, and then he looked at the boy lying lifeless on the table. "We ran out of chloroform," he said. "There were too many wounded."

He felt numb, as if he could no more lift his arms than the men whose limbs were stacked in a bloody heap six feet away, could no more pull a gaping wound closed for stitching, or amputate one more limb, or dig for a musket ball. He felt as exhausted as he had ever been, nearly beyond his endurance. He hadn't felt his tears leave his eyes, but he had watched them fall on his bloody hands. He felt no shame in shedding them for the misery and suffering of those that he had no power to ease.

"He reminded me of my younger brother," the doctor said. "I shouldn't even have tried with a stomach wound." He shook his head. "I pray that my father kept his word, and kept my brother home, that he is not lying out there," he said, and his eyes searched the vast field of fallen men.

But how could his father keep his promise not to let his brother join the army, because the boy would be eighteen now, and could decide for himself, or would be swept into the river of need for young men to come to the aid of their country, and he wondered which army his brother would choose.

Charity handed him the sandwich again, closed his now clean fingers over it, and began talking to him, telling him about her family, about how bringing clean water and broth and bandages, and aiding in transport of the wounded to hospitals made her feel like she was helping, doing her part to serve the Confederacy. She talked to him of simple things, ordinary things, and when she stopped talking, he had eaten the sandwich, eaten it automatically and without conscious thought, as he listened.

"I have watched you over the last several hours," he said. "As you appeared again and again, bringing a drink of water and a kind word to the men, as you now have to me."

His eyes had searched for her in the fields, clung to her in moments of deepest grief for what had to be done, or couldn't be done. His eyes had followed her, bringing him a feeling of calm amidst the chaos as he worked. She was slender and feminine and she had moved with such grace. She wore a sort of apron over her dress, and her hair was covered with a white cotton scarf, and he suddenly, foolishly, inexplicably, wanted very much to know the color of her hair.

He was staring at her he knew, but he couldn't stop looking at her face. She was pretty, so pretty, and her expression was so kind.

"You reminded me of someone," he said. "But now I can see that your eyes are more like emeralds, not amethysts."

She blushed under his intense stare.

"Thank you again. I do feel like I'm getting my strength back," he said.

She stood then, and he stood with her. He was tall, and commanding, and even beard-shadowed and haggard as he was, he was still wonderful-looking, Charity thought.

"I'll let us both get back to our work then," she said. She smiled at him.

He would have smiled too, but the smiles came not so easily as before….this. "May I know your name?"

She looked at the wounded scattered beyond them as far as she could see. "Today, my name is Sorrow," she said, and she left the tent.

Dr. Jordan Steele watched her walk away, and he hoped he would see her again, after the eternity of this war, and history was written, and the people in this country questioned how any of this could be allowed to happen, and vowed that it would never happen again.

****

Thank you for reading *A Distant Path*.

I first became interested in the Civil War history of the West when I visited Fort Garland Museum in Fort Garland, Colorado, just twenty-five miles from our home. It was there that I was introduced to the lesser known battles of Valverde and Glorieta Pass in what was, at that time, the New Mexico Territory, and I became aware that the Union cavalry and infantry soldiers of Fort Garland had participated in those battles.

Standing on that historic ground, my imagination was sparked, and I began to read and do research, and then to write. Some of the characters in this story are based on what my imagination applied to actual characters, my favorite being Louisa (Canfield) Canby, wife of Union General E.R.S. Canby. Louisa was recognized for her efforts in Santa Fe to aid the defeated Confederate soldiers in their return to Texas.

The Battle of Glorieta Pass is known as the Gettysburg of the West because the Confederate Army's northward progress advanced no further, the same turning point as Gettysburg. The battles of Valverde and Glorieta Pass were smaller-scale versions of the horrific battles in the East. The actions of soldiers on both sides of the battles ranged from gallant heroics to mass desertion. Soldiers suffered the same lack of infrastructure to manage the dead and wounded, and too often, to even have their most basic needs met. Battles were won and lost with the same confusing communication. Leadership varied from brilliant to inept.

By some accounts of the Battle of Glorieta Pass, it is believed that more than three hundred Confederate horses and mules were slaughtered at Johnson's Ranch. The Union officer believed to have given the command for the slaughter was also credited with the capture and destruction of the Confederate supplies, changing the Confederate victory into defeat.

This same Union officer became infamous in 1864 for an atrocity against a peaceful camp of Native Americans in an incident where approximately two hundred Cheyenne and Arapaho tribal members, many of them women and children, were killed and mutilated in what is called the Sand Creek Massacre.

****

Like an actor in a play, I tried to 'get into' the character and the setting of the Civil War in the West by watching war documentaries, all kinds, and by reading accounts of the Civil War, as well as the books included under Acknowledgements.

My husband and I visited the National Parks and walked some of the sites, and though it felt terribly sad, it was still hard to imagine all that had occurred.

I remember a time in my nursing career when I had been out of hospital nursing for a number of years, and I was going back into the hospital to teach first semester nursing students.

I felt some apprehension that I had lost some of the skills needed to rejoin nursing at this level, that is, until I saw the patients. The patients were the same.

Procedures may have changed, treatments and medications may have changed as well, but the people with illness, people with injury, they were the same, as was the struggle with pain and suffering that we tried to alleviate. That part I knew well.

If you look at photographs of faces of men and women from the time of the Civil War, other than clothes and hairstyles, the faces are the same as any you might see today, the young men as handsome, the young women as pretty.

I played a bit with the dialogue, trying to capture what different backgrounds might sound like, and thought that they were not totally unlike some variations of speech we use today.

My daughter is a nurse who worked as a civilian at Landstuhl Military Hospital in Germany, where wounded are brought for treatment from Afghanistan and Iraq. She helped care for an untold number of young soldiers who had lost limbs, or eyes, or had sustained brain trauma or other life-changing injuries. She's a strong person.

I have seen the statistic that the Iraq War is the first war to equal the Civil War in the numbers of soldiers with amputations. It's devastating now, it surely was devastating then.

For human beings, war was surely the same.

Titles by Pamela Burns

Sunrise Series:
Chasing Sunrise
The Return to Roah
The Healers
Tapestry of Destiny

High Adventure Series:
High Adventure
Dangerous Games
The Last Witness

So Much More Than Chance

A Distant Path

White Daughter of Thunderbird

Made in the USA
Middletown, DE
08 November 2021